The Parrot and the Pig

ISBN-13:
978-0692164204 (Bryan Hope)

ISBN-10:
0692164200

THE PARROT AND THE PIG

by Bryan Hope

1

"Are you almost finished?"

Tabitha quickly dabbed at the corners of his eyes with a sponge applicator. "Just about."

Pretty Boy hated Tabitha. While applying face creams, she acted as if she was sculpting David, but she was no more a makeup artist than he was a model.

Ever since reaching the bad side of thirty, the time spent getting moisturizers, eyeliner, and face creams layered over his face seemed to extend drastically. He pretended not to notice, and when he couldn't ignore it, he blamed Tabitha. But being that he was the man wearing gobs of makeup and thick mascara, it was hard to be judgmental.

A white cloth backdrop hid behind it display shelves of bongs, pipes, and other drug paraphernalia and curved onto the floor like the train of a wedding dress. Pretty Boy stood on the tail of the backdrop and was immediately illuminated by spotlights reflected in the underside of umbrellas. He didn't even squint reflexively anymore. Through the doorless threshold, floor to ceiling tapestries bearing the carnage-filled album covers of death metal bands and the occasional, amiable face of Bob Marley outlined in smoke stared back at him. The corridors gleamed with the plastic bindings of endless CD cases, aisles that he had perused and virtually memorized since he was a kid. Out there, that was home. In here was something very different.

Mike was crouching behind his camera. He would stretch to the left to take notice of a shadow or wrinkle that he couldn't detect through his viewfinder, then would recede behind the camera again.

Mike was the reason for all of the wooden Buddha statues, the eight-armed Durga figures, the green aventurine Anubis by the entrance, and the incense burning at every corner. He was the proprietor of a small shop at the mall that specialized in religious paraphernalia from around the world. Polly was one of those ladies that claimed to be "spiritual, but not religious," and was fascinated with cultural keepsakes from across the ocean. After spending a large percentage of her revenue at Mike's shop, she conversed with him enough to learn that he had a passion for photography. She paid him handsomely for these short little jobs, and in turn, he undercharged her for her totem poles and pharaohs and such.

"Alright. Hang your right hand on your left shoulder and flex your bicep." Mike hid behind the camera atop a tripod stand and worked studiously. Although he never brought it to Pretty Boy's attention, he knew that – as of lately – he had to work fast before Pretty Boy's sweat would darken the armpits of his shirt.

Tabitha sat in the back facing the wall adjacent to the photoshoot, prodding at her cell phone with both thumbs. She glanced occasionally at Pretty Boy and would issue a smirking grin somewhere between a scoff and a genuine smile, like a giftwrapped pile of dog shit.

Pretty Boy couldn't wait to get done. The shirt was tight around the arms and armpits. The shirts he would wear used to barely touch his abs as they hung off of his defined pectoral muscles, but lately, he felt them constricting his midsection, making him suck in his gut even more than normal. The only thing worse were the jeans. Every time he strained to pull them up over his calves, his thighs, and finally, his waist, he would worry that he would need assistance in getting them back off. Everything about the scenario screamed discomfort. Just a few more minutes and he could appease his friend and make a quick three hundred bucks.

"Put your hands behind your head like you're relaxing, but… you know…. flex."

Two small circles of dampness presented themselves under his arms, and Mike knew he had to work quickly. He hated unnecessary photoshopping. He had Pretty Boy change into a second outfit.

Pretty Boy sighed in relief as he looked at a pair of black slacks draped over a folding chair in the back office. He pulled them on and felt a very welcomed breath of cool air slither up the ankle toward his crotch, cooling the thin layer of sweat that encapsulated his body. The fabric of a white shirt with black tribal patterns extending from both shoulders down to the shirttail stretched as Pretty Boy pulled it tight to fasten the buttons. He thought nostalgically about the days when baggy skater pants and tee-shirts were all the rage. He marched back into the makeshift photoshoot waxing confident.

"Looking great. Now put your hands in your pockets and give me a little laugh."

Pretty Boy accommodated. Every moment made him thankful that his bandmates couldn't see him here, even if they all saw the finished products. The makeup, the lights, the materialism, the disingenuous nature of it all, these were all the things that he and his band stood against, yet none of them, he knew, were above it so much as to refuse a quick buck. And so he endured the fake smiles and stupid poses and tried to forget those moments during the shoots, much like a part-time prostitute struggling with the atrocities that came with making rent.

"Put your hands back in your pockets, but draw one side of your shirttail back with your hand to show your stomach."

As his midriff was exposed, he noticed Mike's brow slightly furrow as he paused before snapping one quick photo and said, "Cool. Now cross your arms across your chest."

Pretty Boy tried to let the moment go, but he couldn't help but wonder. Had he gained a couple of pounds? Was it the fact that the seductive little patch of hair beneath his naval had widened with age? Was he *really* getting old? Already?

He noticed Polly darting through the clothing aisles with a solitary garment draped over her forearm. It was difficult to tell, but he presumed it was a wifebeater.

Since he was old enough to make the walk to the store, Polly had been like family to him. Pretty Boy never knew his mother, and yet Polly didn't replace her. Polly was more like that cousin that drinks too much and awkwardly kisses your neck to say goodbye, the sister that isn't invited to family get-togethers but still shows up every other year with a drug dealer boyfriend and a bottle of Wild Turkey, or the crazy aunt that shows way too much cleavage and uses high school lingo well into her sixties. Pretty Boy had a very warm place in his heart for Polly.

"Great. Great. Let's do the last outfit, huh?"

Polly finally came back from rushing up and down the clothing aisles and whispered in Mike's ear. She drew her head back from his as the two connected eyes and nodded gravely.

"I think I misplaced the last shirt I was gonna have you wear," she told Pretty Boy. "That should be good for this one. The third one's always backup, anyway. Great job, Dale."

The next week when Pretty Boy was brashly turning the pages of the local newspaper, he found himself staring right back into his own eyes, arms curled behind his head, stretching the skin of his torso upward to flatten his belly, a black tee-shirt that read "Buried in Bile" stretched tightly around his arms and chest, sweat stains completely erased, as he smiled tightly, ambiguously playful and diabolic at the same time. Next to that photo was another man, one whom he had never met before, wearing the white wifebeater with tribal designs printed on one side that Polly was carrying through the store, lifting the shirt tail to reveal his hairless naval.

2

"Would you rather," Rex announced, the three words always greatly accentuated to clarify the name of the game, "be able to fart fireballs, OR shoot poison darts out of your dick?"

"Hmmm," Timmy replied, deep in thought. Timmy was the only one that answered these types of questions with serious consideration. Because of this, Rex was always quick to grab Timmy in the mornings and solidify him as Rex's permanent fire watch. "Farting fireballs would do more damage, but shooting *anything* out of your dick is infinitely sexier. Would either of them hurt... you know, coming out?"

"No."

"Then I'd have to go with the dick darts. Sounds hot." They shared a chuckle. Rex lowered his welding hood and struck the rod against the steel. Timmy averted his eyes, staring blankly into the metal jungle in which they worked, wearing a fluorescent green vest over his blue, flame-retardant coveralls, one hand resting atop a large, red fire extinguisher.

Rex had an unusually large amount of welding to do in that area, so he stayed perched in his little nook surrounded by fire blankets like a tree fort in the I-beam racks. Ten feet below, Timmy's knees were rocking beneath his body like he was standing thigh-deep in the ocean.

Rex finished his work and swiveled his welding hood up atop his thick, brown dredlocks that had finally gotten long enough to graze the tops of his shoulders. He then began taking down the clips that were holding up the fire blankets. One by one, he lowered them down to Timmy. Rex descended the ladder after unloading the blankets, clips, rods, and welding leads to his fire watch.

"Alright, I know it's your turn, but I've got a good one," Rex announced enthusiastically. "Would you rather bang Michelle, or the monkey from Outbreak?"

"I don't feel so good," Timmy answered. The sweat was soaking through his coveralls – not to mention the clothes he wore beneath them.

"C'mon, answer the question!" Rex belted playfully. "Then we'll go get some water. And maybe we could even find you a tampon."

Timmy's eyes went skyward as the rest of him dropped to the ground like a giant action figure whose batteries had just died.

"Two hands… One atop the other… Push with the heel of your right hand… A little faster… Remember, think of the song 'Stayin' Alive.' That should be your tempo."

A butch blonde with broad shoulders was coaching one of Rex's coworkers how to resuscitate a limbless dummy while Rex watched from the back row of folding chairs. Ever since Timmy's heat stroke, they were all required to have CPR training.

Timmy was fine and already back to work. He didn't blame Rex. More importantly, no one at his company put Rex at fault, either. But Rex wasn't concerned with all that.

Had Timmy died, he might have been affected by the episode on a grander scale. He might have felt guilty about not reacting to Timmy's symptoms. He might have questioned the six minutes it took him to find a safety representative to tend to his friend's needs. But right now, Rex was just trying to think of a metal song that had the same tempo so he didn't have to play The BeeGees in his head any longer.

Around the same time, a stubborn cow was being lead down the chute at the local slaughterhouse on the north side of town, minutes away from the oil refinery where Timmy had fainted a week prior.

Randy Fuentes was training a new hire on the processes involved in the cow-killing business. Randy's wild and brutish methods for corralling the cattle had earned him the nickname "Rowdy," a name that he donned proudly in front of greenhorn newbies. He had his trainee put on rubber boots, rubber gloves, a light blue water-resistant gown that went down to his ankles, a white disposable dust mask, safety goggles, and a yellow hardhat. Rowdy wore none of these. He wanted to show that he was above even safety regulations. He wanted to make his trainee feel inferior. And he wanted to enjoy the one part of his day where he didn't have to suffocate under all of the personal protective equipment.

The two of them were walking alongside the narrow chute where a dark brown cow was reluctantly awaiting death. While Rowdy liked to abandon his electric cattle prod and rope the cows legs and head and drag it or push the 1,600-pound animal from behind like a linebacker, it was a battle that he didn't always win, and he didn't want to lose face in front of the newbie. The chute was designed with an elevated walkway beside – where Rowdy and his trainee were standing – so that the animal could be forced toward the yoke with a partition between the animal and the worker. This partition, Rowdy believed, was what separated the men from the boys. Rowdy hopped the railing behind the animal and shoved the two-pronged end of the hot shot into the cow's hindquarters, sending 9,000 volts into the steer's ass. The cow darted forward, ramming its head into the steel railing just beside the yoke, then attempted to reverse out once more. Rowdy sent another jolt to the steer's midsection, but not before the ass of the cow nudged into Rowdy's shoulder. The fear mixed with electric shock evacuated the animal's bowels, a fist-sized mound clinging to the sleeve of Rowdy's button-down, flannel work shirt. The steer plunged its head through the gate and the yoke clamped down on its neck while Eddie shot the animal in the head with a captive-bolt gun. The mammoth body on the other side dropped heavily. The shit on Rowdy's sleeve oozed downward before falling to the warehouse floor.

Cal was the drummer in Rex and Pretty Boy's band. He was always the quiet one. They all found it ironic how shy and timorous he was in contrast to the brutal way he pounded the drums. He would speak hardly above a whisper and would rarely interject as the band determined the progression of a new song, but once he clicked his drumsticks together four times, his head would bang and his feet would bounce on his double bass pedals as his arms vanished in the quickness in which they swept across his toms and snare. He was the youngest member of the band at twenty-five and had the luxury of a bill-free lifestyle living at his parents' house. But now that his drum heads were all dented, his high-hat cymbal was cracked, and he had a desperate yearning for a set of roto toms ever since hearing the latest Buried in Bile album, he needed a job. He was to be hired on with Rex's employer, but after the heat stroke incident and the mandatory CPR training of all employees, the company had put a freeze on hiring new employees, and so Cal found himself following a deranged, animal-torturing psychopath through a slaughterhouse.

Cal saw the cow shit that was still smeared down the outside of Rowdy's tricep, but refused to say anything, partially because of his quiet disposition, partially because he was unsure if this was a mundane occurrence, and mostly because he didn't like Rowdy and didn't care to assist him even so far as informing him that he was covered in shit.

"You'll probably start out in here, seein' as Felipe hurt his back and can't carry nothin' anymore," Rowdy continued as he escorted Cal through another room in this hellish labyrinth of a workplace. From the street, the warehouse looked like its own subdivision. The smell of death carried on for nearly a mile downwind.

Cal looked around at the giant, skinless carcasses hanging from meathooks all around him. The room reminded him of countless movie scenes. He thought of Rocky Balboa sending uppercuts to the colossal hunks of meat. He thought of comedies where this was the rock bottom job for the protagonist just before making it big. But most of all, he thought of Leatherface, the villain from Texas Chainsaw Massacre, becoming desensitized to death and learning to kill after years working at a place as such. He wondered if *he* would forego some mental and behavioral transformation working at a slaughterhouse, if he would develop an inability to connect with other humans and a numbness to pain and fear in others. He knew the thought was absurd, but as meat cleavers and carcasses decorated the album covers of all his favorite bands, he immediately felt more *bad ass*.

Rowdy led Cal through a few more corridors of flesh, intermittently glancing back at the new kid, anticipating looks of fear and disgust, but only finding a subdued smirk on the silent face of his newest coworker. As he glared back at Cal and Cal glared at the endless aisles of fresh meat, Rowdy's shoulder grazed against a carcass leaving a spot of cow feces between the sirloin and tenderloin cuts of meat.

"Marry, fuck, kill," Timmy shouted up the racks, "Hillary Clinton, Rosie O'Donnell, a dog with rabies."

"Too easy," Rex retorted while handing down a can of cold-galvanize. "I'm gonna marry Hillary and have her do my bidding for me, I'm gonna kill Rosie with a baseball bat, and I'm *definitely* gonna fuck me a dog!"

Rex was glad to have Timmy back as his fire watch. He was worried that they wouldn't let Timmy go back with him and he'd have to train a new kid the ways of crude and rudimentary dialogue. He was even happier to have Timmy back without a cautionary speech from his foreman or a "Don't Worry About It" speech from Timmy. The two went about their tedious jobs and adolescent conversation as if nothing had happened.

It was Friday and everyone was filled with an anticipation for the weekend that coincided a lack of morale and production across the entire jobsite. For Rex, it was a little bit bigger than that as Saturday brought with it another show. While *true* heavy metal remained underground and didn't appeal to the masses, ever since the band *Dead Still* (the one metal band that got heavy rotation on both local rock stations) announced a tour date in their primarily country music-listening South Texas town, the crowds at Rex's shows began to multiply. Every other Friday, the trash cans around the refinery were filled with the flyers that Rex handed out to all of his coworkers, and every Saturday, no more than two of them would show up to watch him bounce around the stage like a guitar-wielding

PCP addict. But as a good chunk of the refinery population had already purchased tickets to the Dead Still show, their acceptance of heavier music broadened and Rex would find himself elated any random Saturday night seeing a group of electricians from the refinery bashing their way through the mosh pit.

But no matter the swaying public opinion of his music, they all collectively pitied Rex for his undying and childish ambition that was lasting straight into his thirties. They would accept his flyers with wide smiles and promises of attendance, then would privately scoff at his inability to let the dream die. And although Timmy considered himself a close friend of Rex, he shared the popular view that Rex's aspirations were pathetic delusions of a middle-aged child.

Still, he accepted the flyer and agreed to watch his friend make a public mockery of himself, just before clandestinely tossing the flyer in the garbage drum and thinking of the excuse he would tell Rex for his absence come Monday.

Saturday morning, Rex went about his usual pre-show ritual in which he would frequent his favorite breakfast restaurant alone and gorge down abnormally large portions of steak and eggs for fuel before the big night.

He sat in meditational silence as he stared at the plate before him, the T-bone steak vaguely resembling the shape of South America. Rex thought about Brazilian tribal metal bands as he stared at the hunk of meat on his plate. He heard the pounding percussion as he thought about ancient war dances, men painted from head to toe before an angry bonfire, the chanting and screaming, the energy that only these primitive people knew how to harness, and how he would exude that same raw and chaotic power for the show tonight. He looked at the dark spot on his steak that existed right around Paraguay and wondered of its origins. It didn't look like a burn mark. Before questioning the discoloration further, he decided that it was a concern that didn't affect the primitive people of the Amazonian tribes and, therefore, didn't concern him either. He devoured the hash browns, three bacon strips, biscuit, two sunny-side-up eggs, and the steak – cooked fecal matter and all – and washed it down with a black coffee and iced water.

That night, as Rex cranked up on the hand brake of the Vanimal upon arriving at the venue they had been playing at for over a decade now, he felt something foreign and caustic rumbling through his digestive system. As he slurped down foamy beers watching the opener, his belches tasted acidic. The other band members knew that while Rex was the spastic madman on stage, he always remained silent in the moments leading to their set. To them, this was a hobby. It was fun. It was a way to cut loose and – if they were lucky – to get girls. To Rex, it was more than that. It was everything that he was and everything that he ever wanted to be. Those anarchic moments on stage belting out backup vocals from the depth of his stomach, wielding his guitar like a battle axe, and jumping off of the PA and diving out into the crowd were the only times in his life that he felt like the person that he was supposed to be.

Rex's intestines twisted in knots. A bead of sweat rolled down his face alongside his sideburn. He contemplated running to the restroom to shit before their set, but no, it was time. He could wait.

Greg Beattie was the son of the multimillionaire,

Geoff Beattie. After years of working as an investment banker, Geoff learned how to compute mission statements as equations and which equations equaled profit. He had an overwhelming talent for his craft and turned that talent into riches. Once his bank statement read an amount of zeroes that Geoff could comfortably gamble with, he resigned from the company and used his acquired wealth as startup capital for various business ventures. With his ability to discern profitable companies from deadbeats, all of his new business endeavors multiplied his income and his undertakings grew in size and in risk.

One of his more recent projects was an amphitheater – more specifically, the amphitheater that Dead Still was to play at in one month's time. He saw the proposal as low risk as it drew definite revenue with very little expenditures, aside from the large chunk of money it took to build the place. It was outdoors, and therefore required very little building material or complex craftsmanship, aside from the stage and sound booth. The rest of the place was a giant pile of concrete and steel – two things that weren't cheap, but were vastly cheaper than the price of an indoor arena. After the amphitheater was constructed, Geoff only needed to pay off a series of unskilled workers to provide security and tear tickets, along with a handful of sound and lighting specialists. With ticket prices skyrocketing and the unwavering demand for live entertainment, Geoff made a killing.

The amphitheater was the first business that his son, Greg, was intrigued by. Greg had always had an interest in music, particularly the mixing aspect. He loved going to shows and watching the men behind the boards orchestrate the madness that ensued on stage. He had experimented with his own projects. He composed music on his laptop, but knew that the artistic side wasn't the end of the spectrum that suited him. He bought his own board and studio and began recording for local bands, but as the first couple of bands that hired him were his guinea pigs, Greg did a less than mediocre job. The bands that he recorded released their albums online with Greg's name plastered all over their websites as their producer, and the poor recording quality yielded no further customers.

Greg continued working on his craft and became exceptionally more skilled, but still, no further clients approached him. He knew he had the biggest lead in his back pocket, but refused to ask his father for a job at the amphitheater. Although upon hiring, his skills would speak for themselves, it still felt like *cheating*. He had to get there of his own accord and hard work.

Greg was doing his usual weekend shadowing of sound booths at a local rock venue. All of the usual sound technicians knew Greg, only they knew him as Vinny, the alias Greg gave to ensure that his father had nothing to do with his imminent success. As soon as he approached, all of the sound guys sighed in displeasure. Greg's incessant interrogation of their techniques, clients, and bosses was never a welcomed intrusion.

"Listen," said Tony, the head sound technician, "we've got ten minutes before the next set, so if you wanna talk shop, you gotta do some talking with your nose."

Tony let his second-in-command do the pre-show level adjustments as they were all predetermined; he needed only to match the levels to the numbers written on the provided paper. Tony led 'Vinny' to the restroom and locked the door before pouring a pile of white powder on the countertop.

Greg, stuttering in fear, had never partaken in any recreational drug use aside from marijuana. He tried to spout out as much of his pitch before it was his turn.

"I... I mean... If you were to put in a good word for me with your employer, it would be a no-risk investment.

You know how dedicated I am to my profession, and –"

"It ain't a profession if you ain't makin' money, kid." Tony chopped up two fat rails with more precision than he exhibited behind the soundboard and sniffed one up his left nostril. His head tilted back like the powder may have spilled right back out the way it came in if he didn't. "And even *I'm* barely makin' any money in this. You're up."

Greg's quivering hand took the rolled up dollar bill that was extended in his direction and approached the counter. "If you just..."

"I got five minutes. Sniff and pitch, sniff and pitch," Tony said while snapping his fingers, hurrying Greg like the scared puppy he was. The cocaine was already up his nose and into his brain before the essential, first-timer line of questioning ensued. *Will this have any long-term effects? Will I be able to drive home later? Was that too much for a first time?*

Tony was now open for interrogation, but Greg no longer had it in him. As Tony didn't have time to cater to aspiring sound techs struggling with the onset of a huge coke high, he swept the remaining powder into a cellophane baggie and pushed them back out to the concert.

As the bathroom door opened up to the crowd, everything had dramatically intensified. The crowd was louder, the lights were brighter, and it seemed that someone jacked the thermostat up fifteen degrees. Greg was sweating and shivering at the same time. Tony was already back at the sound booth, oblivious to the petrified 'Vinny' who was clawing at his chest and terrified at what was happening beneath the skin.

Right on cue, the next band took the stage with a grindcore opener that mutilated Greg's eardrums, pushing him almost physically out the side door. Greg stumbled through the alley along the outside of the venue, fearing that he might have been experiencing the onset of a cocaine overdose.

Had Greg been more into sports in high school as opposed to music, there is a good chance that he would have been dead already. Unbeknownst to Greg, he had a rare condition called hypertrophic cardiomyopathy in which a part of the heart muscle is thickened. It is a condition that results in hundreds of high school athletes inexplicably dead on the playing field every year, a condition that makes the heart work overtime to pump blood to the body, and a condition that is very negatively affected by the use of stimulants such as cocaine.

Greg fell to the concrete and died.

Leviathan, as they were called, had finished setting up and testing their instruments. The crowd's mounting anticipation resulted in raucous drunken banter. Rex, Sonny, and Pretty Boy faced the back wall motionlessly as the samples they had prepared two nights previous squealed out the speakers. Pipe organs growled low, drawn out notes as an inharmonious sludge of eerie audio movie samples blended together and sounded like tortured souls wailing in agony. As the collective pitch of the samples peaked, Cal struck the high hat with four quick taps before the other three members turned to face the crowd in a villainous scream. Their opener was loud and chaotic, crash cymbals and grind-picked power chords assaulting the audience's eardrums. Rex's head banged as his right hand twitched angrily, picking at his low-end strings. Sonny's left arm pulled back repeatedly like he was violently attempting to start a lawnmower, the fretted arm of his bass guitar making vicious slashes through the air. Pretty Boy's wrists were cuffed with black sweatbands, blue flame tattoos bleeding behind them as he brought the microphone to his lips and roared like a demon.

Rex stepped up on his floor monitor as he was about to make his signature, mid-air, 180-degree, overhead guitar throw, but instead backed off at the last minute, stopped playing altogether, heaved once, and then rained vomit on three different bobbing heads in the front of the audience. The guitar and bass cut out immediately as Rex was puking and Sonny was in disbelief at the spectacle. Cal was oblivious from behind the blindspots created by his overhead cymbals and his long, curly hair that was thrashing in front of him with every headbang, and so the drum line belted on. Pretty Boy's opening death scream faded to a low-pitched, "Whoa! Holy shit!" as the three victims were thoroughly drenched.

Pretty Boy threw an arm around the back of Rex's neck and quickly escorted him offstage as two of the three vomit victims stormed toward them seeking bloody retribution. Sonny and Cal, although completely hardcore about the way they dressed and played, were anything but hard when it came to a brawl and cowered away from both the potential assailants *and* their friend and bandmate in need. Luckily, a security guard rushed the stage and stood in between the sick guitarist and the vomitously assaulted. Pretty Boy threw Rex out the side door and promised to meet him at the Vanimal after ensuring that no one was following him to issue a beating, and went back inside.

Rex stumbled outside, somewhere between pleasantly drunk and violently ill, stomach bile and saliva still hanging from his bottom lip, as he noticed a lifeless body sprawled across the sidewalk. Judging by the clothes and the awkward position of the body, Rex knew it to be someone in trouble and not the normal, Saturday night hobo. Fresh in his mind, the CPR training rushed into his head to the tune of The Beegees, to his dismay, and somehow erased the panic that should have probably been felt in that particular scenario. Even as Rex turned the body face up and checked for a pulse, he grunted out, "You can tell by the way I use my walk that I'm a woman's man, no time to talk." No blood flow could be felt, but the skin was still warm.

Rex put his fingertips in front of the man's gaping mouth and felt no breath. He pinched the victim's nose shut and looked around for any bystanders to catch him lip-locking with another man. He took a deep breath, but instead threw up once more just beside the man's head, small droplets clinging to stray hairs. He spat remnant chunks of steak and swallowed the remaining burning liquid as best he could before again attempting to resuscitate the unlucky bastard. He finally was able to blow a deep, smelly breath into the man's lungs, fearful of another unsuspected and angry blast from his purging stomach. He put his hands together and pushed down on his chest, belting out his own lyrics, "You know I'm bad ass, 'cause this motherfucker is savin' your life! Savin' your life! Ah, ah, ah, ah, savin' your life! Savin' your life!"

As Pretty Boy peeked around the corner from the front parking lot where the Vanimal was awaiting their getaway, he caught one more presumable makeout session before Rex shouted out the second verse, and Greg's heart, once again, started beating.

That night, Rex didn't feel quite like the revered hero as he was puking into a toilet and shitting his pants simultaneously. During a short respite his body granted him from the purge, Rex threw his shitty jeans into the wash, forgetting that his cell phone was still in the front pocket. Before he could realize what he had done, Rex was hugging the toilet again.

This went on for eight straight hours, completely

ridding his body of all fluids and probably bringing him just as close to death as Greg was hours prior.

Early Sunday evening, just as the nausea was beginning to subside, a chubby man in slacks knocked at his door.

One of the local news stations had done a story on the six o'clock news about the son of a hometown entrepreneur and "philanthropist" dying temporarily last night outside a downtown rock venue. They went on to mention that the guitarist of one of the performing bands performed CPR, saving the twenty-three-year-old's life.

After getting Rex's name and information from the club owner, a reporter for the station had been attempting to contact Rex all day, calling a phone that was enduring a spin cycle in a pair of shit-encrusted blue jeans.

Geoff Beattie had gotten Rex's information from the club owner, as well, just after the story aired. He, too, tried calling Rex's phone, but when he didn't answer, Geoff made the trip to his house to thank him personally.

He looked like a basset hound with clipped ears and a smile. His rosy cheeks were smooth and shiny and hung down with age on either side of his chin. The bags under his eyes were substantial, whether his natural state or because he had been crying in a hospital over his son all day. His hair was gray and severely thinning on top. His black polo shirt stretched tight over his beer belly. He hugged Rex as soon as he opened the door.

Rex's immediate reaction was to hide the weed paraphernalia, but he wasn't sure why. The man obviously wasn't a cop, but exuded a quality that commanded fear and respect from others.

He identified himself as Greg's father, a clue that illuminated no lights in Rex's brain. The name Geoff Beattie, however, was quickly recognized, only because of the amphitheater and not his countless other businesses that earned him local celebrity status.

Geoff sat down on Rex's bongwater-stained futon while Rex perched atop his secondhand recliner throne, still shirtless and reeking of the night's illness. Given the setting, Geoff looked like an animated children's cartoon character caught in a porno film. Looking unfazed by the disheveled apartment, Geoff spewed out his gratitude, his sentimentality not at all representative of the cutthroat CEO that Rex had envisioned. Rex watched in awe, not acknowledging the previously unknown fact that he actually saved a life last night, but mesmerized by the powerful man sitting in his living room and weeping in gratefulness.

As soon as Geoff reached the part in his declamation that stated, "If there is anything I can do for you…" Rex wasted no time, interjecting, "Let us open for Dead Still," in speech so fast it seemed he had been holding his breath during the entire conversation. It was the first time that Rex had spoken since Geoff's arrival and it caught him off-guard, but with minimal thought, he agreed.

The next morning, Rex had breakfast at his favorite restaurant. Although the steak and egg breakfast was usually reserved for the pre-show ritual, he needed something hearty to replenish his body that had been all but eviscerated for the past thirty-six hours, and wanted to celebrate after the great news. He looked down to find a slight discoloration in his steak, similar to the spot he had seen the day before yesterday. Without contemplation, he cut up the steak in large pieces, and devoured it.

3

Dale tossed three pink pills into his mouth. It had only been a few days, and already the coarse lumps sliding down his esophagus felt like coming up for air just before drowning.

"You're beautiful," Virgil squawked from the other room. He had been taking care of the macaw for five days now, but its pleasantries were still reassuring, especially since it had been almost ten months since Polly's had called and, for the first time, Dale was feeling the debilitating impact of age.

Polly was a tattooed, pink-haired mother of three and had no relation to the bird. She owned a retail store that specialized in all things heavy metal and uniquely named it after herself. The outside of the store looked like the wholesome family home from a 1970's television program – white siding, a wraparound front porch, cherry red front door – but had been worn with decades of pothead ownership. Waist-high weeds grew through the cracks in the concrete driveway. Each parallel board cried mildew down to the next where the nails were rusting, like the mascara lines of a weeping model. The rear-facing wall was completely covered with graffiti, but beneath the orange spraypaint in the lower right corner, the names 'Dale' and

'Rex' were still etched in the wood from before the initial mural was painted. The inside of the store was a pleasant constant, remaining incorrigible through the decades.

Dale and Rex frequented Polly's long before they were allowed behind the beaded curtains to the smoking paraphernalia section. They would hike the sweltering streets across town, dodging traffic and transients, to arrive sweaty and sunburnt to their hometown Mecca. Most days, they would wander the corridors of rock 'n' roll apparel aimlessly, finger through the thousands of CD's, or talk shop with Polly, but would seldom purchase anything. On those rare occasions when one of them scraped up a few bucks, they would spend hours scrutinizing track listings before settling on a CD. Then they would make the two-hour trek home, both of them gawking at the unfolded lyric sheet as if it was an ancient scroll handed down from the gods. To them, this metaphor was not far from truth. Once home, they would blare the music on Dale's boombox – to his father's dismay – and stare wide-eyed at one another as they complimented the band's usage of arpeggios, harmonies, and other musical jargon with definitions that eluded them.

The day the new Meshuggah album came out, Dale and Rex left the house first thing in the morning, purchased the CD with minimal chit chat with Polly, and rushed back home by noon, aching to headbang in Dale's room to the chaotic symphony, only to find a new friend in the front yard.

It's hair was fine and stuck out in all angles like it had just received a jolt of electricity. Its fur was a light tan – almost white – but its ears darkened toward the tips and its fur blackened around the muzzle. His build was like that of a Labrador, although its tail curled up over its back like a Chow. His forehead crinkled like he was always very worried about something. When the boys arrived, he was taking a milky shit in the grass.

Dale had wanted a dog since he was old enough to verbalize the desire. He quickly learned to pucker his bottom lip, downturn his eyes, and beg pitifully for a puppy, yet his pleading left his father unmoved. And when Dale arrived home, astonished by the addition to the two-man family, Frank offered no hint as to why he had warmed to the idea of having a canine around the house.

"The shit's white because of the shots," was all he said.

Frank named the dog Enkidu after the character in the ancient Sumerian epic poem, Gilgamesh. Frank taught literature of the Western World at the community college and loved throwing out obscure references, a backhanded way of boasting of his scholarly achievements. Despite the esoteric nature of the dog's name, it was the connection between Enkidu and Dale that was foreign to Frank.

Dale and Enkidu would wrestle on the floor for hours. After fatiguing themselves completely, they would lay on the living room floor and watch television, the dog nestled comfortably in Dale's arms. Enkidu would only sleep in Dale's room, coiled up by the threshold, guarding his master's chamber.

Enkidu began accompanying Dale and Rex on their long walks to Polly's. Even Polly warmed up to the dog and began inviting him inside the store as Enkidu was always on the verge of a heat stroke upon arrival. Just as the boys, the dog viewed the store as a home base. He had his corner just as he did at home, along with his own bowl of water – thanks to Polly.

On the days that the boys would make the pilgrimage to Polly's, Dale and Enkidu would come home so exhausted that they rarely made it back to their room and would pass out on the living room floor watching television. Frank would retreat to his room after eyeing his son spooning the dog.

"They did always argue that Enkidu and Gilgamesh were lovers," he'd grumble to himself. No one else seemed to notice how bothersome it was to Frank that the dog he bought for himself only bonded with his son.

Dale and Enkidu both grew up. Dale found girls and marijuana, and so Enkidu found solace in Frank when he wasn't whining by the front door, anxious for his real master to return. But Frank wasn't comforted by the dog's shift in loyalty as his son was frequenting their home less and less. It wasn't fear that Dale was hurt or in jail or any of the other clichéd parental worries. It was just *irksome*. Frank always felt better when there was something close to home to complain about, and when the dog failed to be a substantial complaint, Dale filled that gap perfectly.

"You're beautiful," it squawked again. Words that used to be so monotonous to Dale, but now, ironically, were pleasant and musical now that they were squealed randomly by a screaming bird.

By the time the numbers on his ID allowed him to enter the mysterious room with the glass shelves at Polly's, Dale had become quite handsome. His dark hair grew in thick and wavy. His prominent eyelashes stood out like eyeliner. As his baby fat melted away, his jawline became sharp and angular. His waistline thinned out as his chest and shoulders thickened, like a squeeze toy constricted around the midsection. The tattoo shop across from Polly's inked his forearms in blue flames extending upwards from his wrists.

After a slump in revenue, Polly put out ads in the local newspaper. Instead of seeking professional talent, she had a friend with a high-dollar camera take some pictures of Dale wearing some of the store's undersized tee-shirts and captioned them on her laptop. The modeling gig earned Dale a free glass pipe, superfluous female attention, and the nickname, "Pretty Boy."

Dale would come home at odd hours, change his shirt, put on some deodorant, pet the dog, and go back out to meet another young lady. In the style of his old man, Dale would quickly deem most girls he met intellectually inferior and toss them to the proverbial curb, not before fornication, of course. He was quickly infatuated, doting on a girl's knowledge of Hawthorne or Huxley, then quicker to dismiss the attraction after a mispronounced word, a confused look, or a bad blowjob.

A high school diploma and a superiority complex never got Dale far career-wise. By the time the novelty of buying beer legally had worn off completely, Dale had waited tables at the majority of the restaurants in town and worked on and off at the local bookstore. He and Rex had started a metal band years previous that landed them shows around town twice a month, but they rarely played for more than twenty people and never played for money. Polly's still hired him sporadically for modeling gigs and paid in actual money that you couldn't smoke weed out of, and a few other stores around town had hired him after seeing his advertisements. Financially speaking, Dale wasn't doing horribly. But he was reaching the age where seeing a friend from high school while wearing his nametag and apron had become shameful.

While heavy metal didn't offer the artistic satisfaction of communicating your feelings to a vast audience as the words were indecipherable through the screams, writing lyrics was a platform to convey his intellectual superiority amongst his bandmates, and so Dale inherently became the vocalist. Back when Dale was saving up for a car, Rex was blowing his money on guitars, amps, pedals, cables, strings, straps, and the occasional dime bag and had become a monster on the lead guitar. Sonny and Cal were brothers that they knew from junior high. Conveniently, Cal played the drums, Sonny played the bass guitar, and their parents were gone most of the time, making their house the official Jam House.

Playing in a band was the coolest thing you could do as a teenager, and it gave all four of them superfluous amounts of self-esteem. After their first show, Dale would walk into his high school feeling like a god. He was a celebrity amongst mere students, even if no one knew it but him.

At least three times a week, the band would practice, and every time it was nothing short of *magic*. While heavy metal might not be the most digestible genre of music, its emotion is undeniable. It's in-your-face, chaotic, abrasive, aggressive, and at times, celestial, but more than anything, it's unavoidable. Anyone can skip over a hip-hop or country radio station without the slightest reaction, but two seconds of a good metal song will instill a deeply felt emotional response to the music, even if it is distaste. And when Dale, Rex, Sonny, and Cal would transition from a melodic chorus to a low-toned drop beat sending all of their heads banging with enough velocity to kill a billion brain cells, their eyes would light up and look at one another in astonishment. The music was a beast that not even they could control. They roped it and followed along as it sped through the opening snare grinds and roared through the chest-thumping double bass kicks, they glided alongside it through the intricately harmonious melodies, its wings scaled with sliding octaves and pick harmonics, then dove down low with a pounding fury as the breakdown scorched the earth in its flaming breath. By the time the beast landed and the last note rung out, the jam room was filled with the same euphoria that an underdog army feels after conquering its enemy.

Every other Saturday they would play a show. This meant spending all day dismantling their thousands of dollars of equipment and throwing it into the back of the beat-to-shit, primer gray Ford Econoline, aptly named The Vanimal. Cal and Sonny would ride in the back perched awkwardly atop the sound equipment while Dale would sit shotgun with his feet in a puddle of green antifreeze that was leaking through the dash. Rex would usually drive. The driver-side door didn't latch and was held shut with a red and yellow striped bungee cord. The brakes were shot and Rex had to stand on the brake pedal while cranking up on the hand brake at every red light. Once at the club, the four would guzzle beers while watching the other bands with criticizing glares, itching on every note, praying for a slip. By the time it was their turn to set up, the anticipation had melted off with inebriation and only Cal would remain meticulous in the setup process, sliding his floor tom and bass drum pedals back and forth fractions of an inch, perfecting the arrangement. By the end of their set, every member and every instrument would be dripping in beer, strings would be broken, drumsticks would be cracked, cymbals would be dented, and Dale would be bruised from entering the mosh pit during instrumental sections. Everything back to The Vanimal. Same shitty van, same shitty drive, only now blanketed in the euphoria of another show and a 0.29 blood alcohol level. Sometimes there were after-parties. Sometimes there were groupies. Sometimes they didn't play so well.

With Dale lost in the luxuriously clichéd worlds of sex, drugs, and rock 'n' roll and Frank lost in the TV, Enkidu had become a lazy dog. Enkidu grew up with Dale, but he grew *old* with Frank. He sat by Frank's recliner and waited for a doorbell to ring, a treat to be served, any break from the tedium of the living room. He no longer went on long walks to Polly's. He didn't have a wrestling partner anymore. He was a Christmas elf with no Santa. He was sad and broken, but only Dale saw this. He saw it every time he sauntered in the house that he had moved out of, the house that had become a hotel for him, looking for a change of clothes or a nap, or possibly just an escape from a girl that refused to leave his apartment, and instead would find Enkidu glaring up at him, waiting for the Dale of old to take him outside and throw the ball. Sometimes more than the allure of a new girl or a fresh bong hit, it was that pitiful look from his dog that would drive him away from the house, aching to rid himself of the guilt of leaving the dog behind, trapped in a lifestyle that no longer existed.

"I love you. I love you. You're beautiful."
Although he had always loved dogs, Dale was starting to understand why people owned birds. Dogs were family. They could drive you insane. They could use their soulful eyes against you. They could break your heart. Birds were just pets. Interactive ornamentation. And the intermittent compliments that Dale's father had taught the bird were nice, as well.

Frank called Dale one afternoon. The slumber from which he had just awoken still crusted the corners of his eyes. The hangover burned the back of his tongue. The smell of a strange girl still emanated from his skin.
"It's the dog."
Enkidu's kidneys had failed. She had been peeing blood for weeks, but Frank hadn't told Dale. Their relationship wasn't terrible, but didn't create a cause for concern or excuse when non-crucial information wasn't

shared immediately.

Dale met Frank at the veterinarian's office to have one last meeting with the dog before it was put down. Sitting in the hard-bottomed chairs in the waiting room was painfully awkward. Dale wanted to ask about the symptoms leading to this grim conclusion, but rendered that line of questioning to be fruitless. Frank made the same assumption about asking Dale of his career search and home life. And so the two sat, side by side, offering random *"How've you been's?"* and *"What's new's?"* while waiting to see their dog for the last time.

It was at this moment that Dale realized that it was Frank – not Enkidu – that was repelling him from the house. He was struggling to become a man, to become his *own* man, choosing books and tattoos that defined him as a person. When spouting off his new lyrics to the band or reciting his critiques of Tomas Pynchon to flings, he felt like he was not just a man, but a man to be *followed*. When in the presence of his father, he was always just a boy.

A sexy, young black veterinarian called them back, her enticing eyes briefly mollifying the brutal concoction of sorrow and guilt brewing in his belly. For a moment, Dale actually wondered if this would be awkward for Enkidu when they arrived, like it was some sort of love triangle reunited, the fun-loving, young fling and the stable, old husband, all finally hashing it out over his deathbed. It was a strange and unwelcomed thought that was quickly dispelled upon witnessing his old friend, shivering uncontrollably, unable to lift his head from his pillow.

Dale and Frank rushed to the dog's side. Their hands ran through the dog's thick fur as they both issued an unintelligible stream of not-quite-consoling words. Enkidu's quivers grew stronger, like their reaction solidified the unbearable and undeniable realization that was washing over the dog: This was the end. The dog didn't whimper, but breathed with whispering squeals, singing painfully, so quiet it was almost inaudible. Without realizing it, Frank and Dale's cheeks were wet with tears.

They were ushered out of the room, and the dog was killed.

The two went back to their old ways, but suffered silently. Immediately following Enkidu's death, Dale suddenly noticed all of the ways that he, too, was aging, crawling toward death. His hair was thinning subtly. His pants had gotten tighter. Hangovers lasted days rather than hours. And just as these symptoms of a fleeting youth presented themselves, they consumed him. Dale began fingering his scalp compulsively, his fingertips prodding different spots, testing for irregularities. He started running habitually, struggling to keep the weight of alcoholism away from his flat stomach. While the bathroom scale always read the same number, the image in the mirror seemed to get flabbier and flabbier. On top of that, jogging had now made his knees constantly ache. While all of these signs of aging could have been imagined, the decline in modeling gigs was quite concrete. Playing in the band was becoming something that drained his self-esteem rather than replenished it as they hadn't made it any further than they had in high school. What was once the essence of what made him cool had become the lingering aspiration of a pitiful adult.

Dale started going out every night to pick up girls. Although his efforts produced a smaller percentage of successful outings than they did in years previous, every notch in his belt made him feel a little younger – or, at least, less affected by his age. As long as his list of girls bagged ran longer than his number of years lived, Dale thought, he could never be *that* old. But no matter how many girls he banged or how many miles he ran, he could only see the face of his dog behind everything he did. It wasn't the pain that his old friend endured that haunted him. It wasn't even the goodbye. It was that inescapable fact that the dog *knew,* that dark epiphany of a creeping death, sneaking in and stealing everything that he was, that petrifying fate that we all have to look forward to.

Frank reacted a little differently to losing his dog. He bought a parrot.

He named the bird Virgil, and it was one of the few references that his father made to which Dale actually knew its origins. What connection the bird had to the ancient Roman poet eluded him, however.

Although a new companion to his father, the bird was a despicable, intolerable guest. It had a yellow belly and teal wings. Its face was an intricate design of white and black, and its beak was large, lethal, and anything but welcoming. When Dale came to visit, the house reeked of bird shit. The bird squawked cacophonously. The floor around its cage was riddled with discarded birdseed. Dale couldn't imagine why his father would want to keep a pet as such. How could he go from a pet as loyal and wonderful as Enkidu to this feathered demon? Any species other than canine, to Dale, seemed emotionless, but this was more than that. This was a *nuisance.*

It wasn't long before the squawking became commonplace and looked over. The spilled birdseed was avoided and ignored. And even the smell of bird shit just became part of the ambiance that was Dad's house. And just when everything was settling back into normalcy, Frank broke his ankle.

While he was usually short with explanations and long with trivial anecdotes, Frank gave excessive reasoning for why he tripped in the yard. The garden hose was left out. He wasn't wearing his good shoes. The grass was wet with dew. Dale ignored the superfluous details, the way his father would touch his face as he talked in a slightly higher pitch than normal, all of the tells that gave away the lie. Dale had missed all of the signs of his father's body failing him. He didn't notice how his strides had shortened and slowed. He didn't notice how the slightest cuts would produce a permanent scar on Frank's body. He didn't see the pain behind his eyes when he had to stop throwing the ball for Enkidu and go rest. The truth was that he had slipped in the shower. While the two versions of the story might have seemed ineffectually different to Dale, slipping in the shower was such a categorically *old* thing to do to Frank. Admitting to the folly was succumbing to old age, and more substantially, admitting to an aspect of his life where he could be dubbed *inferior*. It simply wasn't going to happen.

Lucky for him, Dale was unfazed by the story and more caught up in the inconsequential detail that *he* was to look after the bird while Frank's leg healed. He wanted to argue that an ankle couldn't possibly impede one's ability to perform the menial task of keeping a bird alive, but restrained himself after envisioning his father struggling with a bowl of birdseed and two crutches, cursing his son's name. He wouldn't, however, accept the chore free of charge. He knew that with a broken ankle was sure to come some good prescription medication, and he would make a point to pocket a handful of pills from a little orange pill bottle that would more than likely be sitting in Frank's medicine cabinet the next time he used the restroom.

Dale loaded up a birdcage, a bag of bird seed, a pile of old newspaper, a swing, three mangoes, a box of strawberries, a water bottle, a half a dozen pink painkillers, and a giant, annoying parrot named Virgil.

The first three days, Dale ignored the bird as best he could. Virgil only seemed to squawk when Dale was on the phone or watching a good movie. By the third day, the smell became unbearable and he was forced to clean out the cage. The only consolation was the little painkillers that were floating through his veins.

It was the first time Dale had ever handled a bird. He fearfully extended his forearm into the cage and gave Virgil a gentle nudge in his underbelly, waiting for the parrot to bite. Virgil didn't bite, but he didn't climb aboard Dale's blue flamed forearm, either. After being a little more forceful in his movements, Dale got the bird to perch on his arm, and he still did it without drawing blood from neither his arm nor the parrot. Just as he started to embrace the victory and open up to the idea of creating a kinship with the winged companion, the bird dropped a puddle of white and green fecal matter on Dale's arm.

Dale reflexively shook the bird from his arm. The bird flapped its wings frenetically and squawked vehemently as it flew around the room as much as his clipped wings would allow. Stumbling backward from the three-foot wingspan that bounced from wall to wall, Dale knocked over the birdcage, spilling water, bird seed, and shit-smeared newspaper onto the carpet.

Before addressing the situation in any manner, he went to the bathroom and popped two more painkillers.

It was really amazing the effects the pills had on him. Growing up with Rex, he had partaken in recreational drug use of all sorts. He had eaten Xanax all night accompanied with straight whiskey to create a memory-erasing trip that lasted more than two days. He had watched his bedroom walls move like the ocean surface under the effects of psychedelic mushrooms. But this, this was much more subtle. It was a high that could be forgotten or passed over if he hadn't anticipated it. It tickled his legs slightly. It wrapped his brain in a warm, wet paper towel. Small sensations nearly unfelt. His speech wasn't slurred. His eyes weren't bloodshot. He could walk a straight line and recite his alphabet backwards. But all of the uncertainties and fears of everyday life dissolved in the gentle, soothing rush of inhibitors swimming through his bloodstream.

He let the opioids take effect, then alleviated the bird situation.

Dale began visiting his father more often after he broke his ankle, less for concern for his father's well-being and more to seek refuge from the macaw. The parrot was a reminder of his dead dog. His dead dog was a reminder of his mortality. His mortality was the cause of his aging. His aging was the end of his life. With a balding pattern and a beer belly came a decline in his modeling career and, more importantly, a decline in female attention. It was the first time in his young life that he glimpsed the impending end of all things and he tied it all to that shrieking bird.

"I feel bad for Enkidu," Dale confessed to his father. Frank groaned inaudibly, attempting to comment, but retracting it before the sounds could form words.

"I can't stop thinking about him," Dale continued. "I hate to get theological, but if there is a god, no religious doctrine I ever read mentioned anything about an afterlife for dogs. And Enkidu's entire life revolved around me… and you. We're not there, so what could eternal splendor be for him without us? And then I think that dogs can't *fathom* the concept of a god, and therefore, death is just the end, and watching him suffer in that vet's office, he *knew* that death was coming. He knew it was all over. He was terrified. I can't stop imagining what that feels like."

Frank leaned forward in his chair.

"First of all, that dog didn't know anything. He might've felt like the end was coming, but not on a much larger scale than him knowing that the end of a bowl of food is coming when his tongue tastes plastic. You wanna know what the end feels like? It's Sunday evening. It's that gloom of another school week rearing its ugly head. That blue feeling in the pit of your stomach when bedtime approaches on Sunday night. But worse. It is the last Sunday at the end of the best summer vacation ever, and tomorrow morning starts life at a new school with horrible teachers, mean students, the worst everything. That is my life, every day, every minute. That is what getting old feels like."

Dale was taken aback. He had never heard his father speak like this. It was jarring and sudden, but every word struck home so perfectly. He wasn't sure if that was the power that fathers had, or just the power that *his* father had.

"And secondly," Frank added sullenly, "there is no god."

Dale slushed morosely into his car and popped a couple more pills. He drove home feeling like his dying dog, feeling the emptiness and dread all around him as life had finally shown its teeth, the piercing reality of how temporary we all are, how quickly we break, fall, die, and become erased.

He was angry at his father for dismissing all religion with such a definitive and short statement. He had heard his father from time to time ranting about Christians at dinner parties or making jokes that assumed all theology was nonsense, but Dale never really believed that his father completely bought into all that, and more importantly, Frank never told the same jokes to his son. Putting the mental burden of a godless existence on his son was sinful, even if there wasn't a great being in the sky to dub it as such.

Dale entered his house just as the Lortab was washing away his worries. His father, his dog, his expiring life, his transparent god, they were all gently receding to the background and life could resume.

"You're beautiful."

Dale looked back at the bird with a satisfied smirk.

He had hated bird owners for so long, but now he understood that parrots served the same exact purpose as dogs. While canines used their emotional personalities, loyalty, and their dependency on humans to keep them alive in the city, parrots used their physical beauty and their ability to mimic phrases, and both ultimately achieved the goal of making their owner feel a little more secure in a world that had no place for them.

"Thanks, Virgil," Dale replied. "I *am* beautiful."

The macaw squawked three more syllables, but the words didn't make sense to Dale. They weren't words that a bird should have been trained to repeat, nor words that he would've learned just by living in the vicinity of his father. As if to clarify his intent, the bird repeated the phrase three more times, the second word raised dramatically in pitch like a short melody.

"Get NEW job."

4

When Pretty Boy awoke the next morning, the effects of the Lortab had worn off and he was left with the sour taste of his father's speech. Mortality seemed to be consuming Pretty Boy, both the finality of death and the more pertinent signs of aging, and he felt just like his father predicted (only thirty years early), like it was Sunday evening and tomorrow morning bore the worst of conclusions and he just couldn't enjoy the present.

Perhaps the parrot was right. Maybe finding a new job would give him purpose, make him feel more like an adult. He had been drifting in the same lifestyle for so long now that any sort of change was welcomed. He needed a career that he could be proud of, something substantial that could encompass a vast part of whom he was, and if it all worked out, maybe he could travel toward his deathbed with more satisfaction for the choices he had made in life and reach some sort of peace with the fact that *everything* was so painfully short-lived.

He scoured the internet for job listings and suddenly realized how little he had to offer. He had no marketable skills, no college education, and no references aside from a few crappy restaurants and a bookstore. He felt so much more significant than his life on paper.

"Get NEW job! Get NEW job!" Virgil squealed from the adjacent room.

"I'm trying, you dumb dick!" Unleashing his angst on a bird, unfortunately, didn't mollify the disillusionment of how valueless he was.

After scrolling through endless job openings with minimum requirements far exceeding anything that he had to offer, Pretty Boy threw on a pair of long pants and went to work at the bookstore.

Life went on just as it had before, but where Pretty Boy was once content with all aspects of his life, he now saw them as a waterslide filled with sand and thumbtacks leading straight to his grave.

He began getting head rushes every time he stood. Where he once enjoyed the sensation and viewed it as a free drug trip, he now questioned its existence and linked it to his aging body. And worse than that, he was constantly constipated. He'd spend an hour on the toilet and work out nothing larger than a rabbit's foot, feeling worse than he did before he used the restroom. While this problem might not have seemed the most catastrophic of ailments, Pretty Boy had an uncle and grandfather who both died of colon cancer.

Every day, Pretty Boy would look up doctors specializing in such, then dismiss the idea of investigating further. He didn't want to know what demons lurked in the recesses of his body, but was it better to know and confront, or to ignore and agonize? While the scales seemed equally balanced, Pretty Boy always sided with the latter as it was the option that required no work on his part. He would discontinue his search for doctors and resume his search for jobs, an endeavor that was no more lucrative than the previous.

There is a pivotal point in the life of every potential addict, and it comes when the initial supply runs out and he has to make a choice to either chalk the experience up to a short holiday, or to replenish the supply. Pretty Boy was at this intersection.

Pretty Boy followed the normal protocol in which his initial instinct was one of logic, then began engendering a line of reasoning to support the idea of going further with the experiment. After feeling the hold that the painkillers could have on him, he knew that taking it further was more than dangerous. But he began to come up with reasons why he *needed* to take it to the next level.

He thought about job hunts and interviews. The Lortab made him a much more amiable person, and how could that be construed as negative? He thought that the effects of the painkillers, if anything, would *help* him find a new job.

He thought about his father's speech and the debilitating effect it had on him. He felt that he was owed a little tweaking of the mind to deal with the shit that was being crammed into his head.

He spent two hours sitting on the toilet, straining to produce anything to ease the pain in his gut. When he finally stood, his buttocks were numb and the toilet was empty. He thought about Uncle Darryl and how he looked toward the end after the cancer got a hold of him. He lost so much weight he looked skeletal. He could barely get out of bed. His breath was strained and raspy with pain. It was this image that pushed Pretty Boy to go to a clinic to ask about the symptoms of colon cancer and what he could do to avoid it – or possibly, detect it. Simultaneously, he could exaggerate the pain he was in and use it to score some more sweet, sweet relief in the form of little, pink pills.

Everyone needs an escape. It's why men fill their

garages with neon bar signs and ping pong tables. It's why women join book clubs. It's why every teenager has that *one* friend whose house everyone goes to after school every Friday. Everyone needs that one sanctuary where the bills, the exam scores, the relationship problems, and the thoughts that eat away at sanity like an acid burn aren't allowed inside. For Pretty Boy, that place was Polly's.

He had gotten his fill of Lortab from the doctor, but rendered it too late in the day to waste any part of his supply. He could feel the lingering effects of the drug more than eight hours after ingesting them, and wasting a high from his sacred supply on sleep was akin to barbecuing an American Bald Eagle and throwing away the leftovers. And being that he wasn't high, the residual effects of losing his dog, his father, and his ability to look in the other direction from his impending death were highly prevalent.

Pretty Boy arrived at Polly's and was greeted by an old Native American in a feathered headdress smoking peyote. The pipe was long and thin. It could have been mistaken for a weapon if the man's demeanor wasn't so sullen and languid. He was carved out of one, solid piece of driftwood and stood up to Pretty Boy's chest. His face was wrinkled like a peach pit. Lines sunk in the skin in places where one wouldn't think the face would crease. At first glance, the wrinkles looked merely like the flawed texture of the wood, but upon closer inspection, it could be seen that each line was intricately and deliberately notched into the surface. His head was downturned and his eyes were vacant yet knowing, like the look of the last man who could see while the rest of the world had gone blind.

He was a new addition to the asymmetrical ambiance of Polly's, one that Pretty Boy had yet to meet. And to explain his appearance in the establishment, Mike was leaning over the counter, sweet-talking Polly in the best way a gay man knew how, probably to get more money out of her for the wooden chief by the doorway.

He was slightly chubby, mostly in his face, but he wore it like a fine suit – which he was also wearing. The suit was a shade of blue just one tone lighter than would be acceptable at a business meeting. The same applied for the shortened length of the trousers, the thinness of the tie, and the amount of foundation he wore beneath his eyes.

Polly was taken by Mike. She knew he was homosexual, but pursued him just the same. It wasn't an active pursuit that had any emotional toll on her, but merely a consistent line of flirting that could hopefully lead to a late-night, drunken mistake. She smiled and twirled her solitary, blue strand of hair behind her oversized, dreamcatcher earring. She rolled the golden Om pendant on her necklace between her thumb and index finger. She played with the gum inside her mouth, letting it make a cameo appearance between her lips. Pretty Boy would watch these encounters and wonder if she was oblivious or just careless of the fact that most normal gay men were completely turned off by gum-chewing, whimsical belief systems, and obvious signs of mid-life crisis – not to mention, vaginas. He had to admire her confidence, even if it was an ignorant one.

When he emerged from behind the Native American fellow, Polly appeared shocked. Mike looked back over his shoulder, smiled slyly, then turned his attention back to Polly.

"Dale!" she exclaimed in a tone between excited and afraid. "It's been a while. Where's Rex?"

Pretty Boy shrugged his shoulders. "Dunno."

He went about his normal routine of perusing the CD aisles, although he knew there would be nothing that he hadn't seen, heard, and studied for years. He would look at the posters, some of which were already hanging on his walls. He rarely bought anything. It just felt good to be lost

in that world of music. He was surrounded by heavy metal.
Power chords, pig squeals, pick harmonics, double-bass
kicks and down-tuned, seven-string grind riffs created a
world where *everyone* – not just him – was angry. When he
was younger, he felt almost like a different species from
everyone else, an endangered one at that, and then came to
Polly's and stumbled upon this whole world that existed
only of his own kind. And now, as an adult struggling with
aging and death instead of girls and geometry, he still felt
that lingering sensation. It wasn't just *home,* but a home that
he *found* rather than one that he was born into, and those,
sometimes, were the most profound.

He walked by the checkout stand on his way to the
paraphernalia section when something caught his eye.

Atop the counter was a stack of thin newspapers,
articles that the store would produce every once in a while
in no set frequency. The cover was a picture of five men
standing in front of tall flames, the five band members of
Dead Still. Above the picture, in bold capital letters, were
the words, 'DEAD EXCITED FOR DEAD STILL,' and
beneath it, 'Story by: Tabitha McDowell.'

Pretty Boy looked at Polly, holding the paper in her
direction.

"Are you serious?"

"What?" Polly continued to stock clothes, clutching
the tee-shirts like lifelines.

"You let *Tabitha* interview Dead Still?"

"Why not? She's a journalist."

"She *pretends* to be a journalist."

"She's studying at Del Mar."

"Big fucking whoop!"

"Did *you* want to write the story?"

"No."

"Then why are you mad?"

"Because she's a cunt!"

Polly finally shifted her attention from the clothing in her hand and looked Pretty Boy in the eyes for the first time in their conversation. "Dale! Shh!"

"It's okay," Tabitha said aloofly as she casually strolled out of the back room, eyes locked on the phone she was thumbing at. "It's natural for an aging model to take his aggression out on others."

Pretty Boy glared at her, fuming, grinding his thumbs against his knuckles.

"Tabitha," Polly muttered angrily.

"What?"

She breathed in spurts, trying to make something come out, as her eyes shifted between Tabitha, Dale, and Mike. "Nothing."

Polly went back to hanging apparel. Tabitha sauntered out the front door before Pretty Boy could make any sort of rebuttal. Everything went back to normal, but everything, most certainly, was not normal.

"What do you think of this one?"

Polly displayed a white tee-shirt with a black skull on it in Pretty Boy's direction. He shrugged.

Mike was left still standing at the counter, looking impatient, as Polly continued to stock the inventory. She seemed busy and distracted, two things that she never was, especially in the presence of Mike.

And then the catalyzing agent for her peculiar behavior came walking out from the back room, looking like a tattooed and pierced James Dean, puffing on a cigarette inside the store, careless and confident, wearing one of the shirts that Polly had just got done hanging on the rack, stretched so tight across his abdomen that the indentions between his six-pack abs were highly visible. Pretty Boy had never met him, but only seen him in a picture next to his in last month's newspaper.

He froze.

He wanted to hit him, but he had no grounds to do so. He wanted to scold Polly, but given the audience, it would only humiliate him further. He was caught directly between Polly and his replacement. An encounter was inevitable. His only two options were to introduce himself, or slink away into the corner. Neither was very enticing.

Polly had to turn sideways to creep around Pretty Boy on her way to the counter. She kept her eyes down as she popped open the cash register and extracted two wads of money bound by rubber bands: the larger one for Mike, and the smaller one for Pretty Boy's new nemesis.

She handed over both payments. The replacement offered thanks in the form of blowing a cloud of cigarette smoke diagonally upward over Polly's head, winked, and brushed by Pretty Boy on his way out the door. Mike stayed behind. Polly and Mike went back to their conversation, but Polly was obviously distracted.

Pretty Boy hadn't moved since the replacement emerged from his makeshift dressing room, one that used to belong solely to Pretty Boy. His eyes were wide. He was careful not to make eye contact with Polly or Mike, but was taking note of both of their dispositions in his peripheral vision. He tried to act like he was nonchalant about the entire ordeal, walking his fingertips back down the CD spines, but quickly abandoned that effort and walked out the door without a word to Polly.

He drove back home feeling like he had just walked in on his spouse with another man, then allowed them to finish, and then allowed his wife to pay the man for his services, all while he watched on silently, submissively.

Everyone needs his sanctuary, his little place away from the world, and Pretty Boy felt like his had just burned to the ground.

5

Cal and Sonny's mother and father – Maria and Sergio, respectively – had both been brought up in Hispanic families. Sergio had the principles of hard work and a patriarchal household firmly ingrained in him. Maria, raised by her mother and abuelita, was taught the mystic side of her heritage. Before they met, Sergio was building fences while Maria was using broomsticks and eggshells to cure chronic nightmares and common colds. While both Maria and Sergio were taught the Hispanic ideals of a tightly knit family accentuated by boisterous gatherings packed with loud music and enough food to stock a doomsday bunker, Maria was raised by spiritual and theological elements and Sergio had two work boots pressed firmly to the ground.

As a wedding present, Maria's father bequeathed half of his ranch to his daughter and son-in-law. A small cabin sat on a hundred acres of sweltering Texas greenery swarming with mosquitoes, wild hogs, rabbits, cicadas, and the occasional scampering doe.

Sergio loved the ranch and spent all of his leisure time mowing the fields, mending the fences, setting the hog traps, stocking the deer feeders, and spraying the musk thistle. He prided himself on keeping the place pristine, and although Maria's father passed away shortly after they inherited the ranch, he was quite content with Sergio's upkeep of the property that was to be his legacy.

Sergio and Maria grew apart over the years. Maria had become loosely involved with the Wiccan religion, worshipping nature and using ritual magic to achieve her inner peace. When Sergio would come home from a long day of work at the machine shop, Maria would tell him of her new discoveries for casting spells. When Sergio seemed distraught by this line of dialogue, she would suggest that she could instill happiness in him using hyacinth and catnip. Sergio quickly learned to stop asking how her day was. Maria became more interested in her two sons' lives, and Sergio became silent.

When Cal and Sonny took an interest in music, Maria used her husband's credit card to purchase instruments and set them up in their respective rooms. Sergio was less than pleased to come home to the discord of wall-rattling drums. When he confronted Maria about the purchase, she offered him some rosemary and thyme to help him sleep. After that, Sergio began staying at the ranch more often than not and making the hour-long commute to work every day.

Over the years, Cal and Sonny complimented each other musically and began playing together every day. They moved the drum set into Sonny's room and both beds into Cal's. Before long, they were like twins finishing one another's sentences, only instead of words, they used bass line transitions and drum fills.

Maria loved watching them play, even if she did have to plug her ears with her fingertips to withstand the decibels. She became their friend rather than their mother, talking to them about girls at school and new R-rated movies that they should watch together. Sergio would come home every once in a while to find the house in a state of disarray, the chandeliers swinging with the vibrations from the crashing cymbals and roaring bass amplifier.

But Sergio was planning for the big move to completely relocate to the ranch house and sell the other, and so Maria accompanied him more frequently on his trips. At the ranch house, she would point out where she wanted a plug or appliance or other amenity, and Sergio would work on accommodating her while Maria would prance out into the woods. What she did all day while Sergio worked was an enigma, but he presumed it had something to do with turning toads into fairies or performing mystical hysterectomies.

Meanwhile, as Sonny and Cal basked in a parent-free lifestyle, the house reached levels of uncleanliness that should have alerted the Environmental Protection Agency. Beer cans covered every inch of flat surface. The linoleum floors were topped with an eighth-inch thick film that clung to the soles of their shoes. The smells of spoiled milk and dirty socks could be detected from the street. Pretty Boy seemed to be the only one disgusted by the atrocity of the home and would take out the garbage or throw out week old dinner left on the stove when he came over for a practice session. They were infinitesimal efforts to bring the place to anything that could be considered inhabitable, but he thought that just maybe someone would follow his examples.

On the rare occasions that Sergio and Maria would show up during one of these jam sessions, Pretty Boy would be mortified for being seen in the biohazardous wasteland that had become of their home. He could see the wrath and disbelief behind Sergio's eyes upon witnessing the squalor, even if Maria was blithely oblivious. Their visits were always brief.

Sergio was at a stalemate. He needed to sell his house, but first he would have to get it in some condition that could be shown to the public. He barely had the time to work on the ranch house and he knew that he couldn't rely on anyone else in his family to fix the place up. He would like to throw the boys out, but they didn't earn enough to live on their own, and he knew that Maria wouldn't have it. Arguing with her was pointless and got him nowhere. He didn't believe in divorce, although it was such a beautiful fantasy. He had to work with what the Lord gave him, and he felt like he was standing in a pit slowly filling with wet cement and all he needed to do was step out, but his family held him stationary.

He had been silently compliant for so long, and something was surely about to erupt.

Rex called a band meeting, unknowingly two hours after Sonny and Cal's impromptu family meeting.

Two years ago, when the oil industry was booming, Rex's company was put in charge of manning the new construction projects at the refinery. This meant heavy overtime with no foreseeable end. Rex would have turned down the work had it not been for the fact that Cal had recently tripped while carrying his floor tom and broken his arm. Since the injury meant the band would have to go on a brief hiatus, Rex welcomed the abundance of work and the lack of free time. Being unable to jam was torturous for Rex and he needed the distraction, and working eighty-four hours a week meant huge paychecks and no time to spend the money. By the time the refinery projects were nearing completion and the overtime was dying out, Rex's bank account had gone from triple-digits to quintuple-digits. Tired of noise complaints from neighbors at his apartment complex, Rex used the money to put a down payment on a house.

It was a ramshackle dump built in the 1950's on the

corner of a street known for drugs and drive-bys. The shoddy construction suggested that it was full of asbestos and the neighborhood suggested that the backyard was full of corpses. It was the only street near the university that wasn't full of yuppies and fraternity houses. Rex bought it under the assumption that he was going to be swimming in college tail. Although it had been eighteen months and a college girl had yet to enter the domicile, the house had loads of personality, and it quite suited Rex.

As usual, Pretty Boy was the first to arrive. He barged in without knocking, went to the refrigerator, and found himself a beer while Rex was in the restroom.

Rex emerged shirtless, yet his tattoos were numerous enough to resemble clothing. From his jawline to his waistline, he was covered in random images of grim reapers, skulls, words and phrases (both comical and cryptic), cartoon characters playing instruments, and in once case, a sea lion with a machine gun. They didn't blend together like they would on an arm sleeve, but appeared as random thoughts, like doodles and reminders to himself when he couldn't find a pen.

Pretty Boy sat on the futon where Geoff Beattie had sat last night. Rex sat on his recliner. No greetings were issued. The two called each other every time anything happened in either one of their lives – so much as having a hot waitress at a taco shop – and seeing one another didn't seem like anything that elicited an introduction. Rex asked about Pretty Boy's dad. Pretty Boy asked for a bong hit. They ignored the subject of the show.

"The old man's wigging out," Pretty Boy admitted, using light language to conceal the fact that his insides were hollowed and it felt like his head had been run through a blender. Rex offered squinted eyes and a nudge of the chin to prod for an explanation.

"He's getting all Poe on me." Pretty Boy looked to

Rex to check for recognition. "The injury finally made him aware that he's getting old. Now he's all gloomy, thinking he's gonna die and there is no god, like he's just slowly being erased, I guess, and it's freaking me out, too. Oh, and he got a parrot. A parrot that *I* gotta watch now."

"A parrot?" Rex's head perked up, shifting from awkwardly sympathetic to oddly intrigued.

"Yeah. I think we're both still bummed about Enkidu. Now he's got me thinking about god and religion and death and aging... Like I don't know what I'm doing... What the hell are we doing, man? I mean, I'm feeling too old to be what I *am*."

"...Like a big-ass parrot? Like the ones you see on TV... or in Hawaii?"

Sonny and Cal walked in – also without knocking – and cut the conversation short. Pretty Boy was aching to get it out, even if Rex wasn't the best of listeners.

"Great show the other night," Sonny laughed with a hint of contempt.

"Fuck you, man. I saved a dude's life and then I saved the fucking band!"

This statement drew the band's intrigue, and they all sat and listened intently as Rex told of his meeting with Mr. Beattie with an enthusiasm that they just couldn't match. He told of their spot in the lineup for the Dead Still show with wide eyes and excited shouts that weren't expecting to be met with silence. Pretty Boy was reservedly delighted by the news. Cal and Sonny were not.

"Listen," Sonny said with his eyes on the stained carpet. "Me and Cal are out."

"What the fuck do you mean, *you're out?*" an infuriated Rex replied.

"I just got promoted at work. I'm moving into the office."

"What the *fuck* does that have to do with anything?!"

"Really?" Pretty Boy asked Sonny. "Do you think you could get me a job?"

"What?!" Rex exclaimed. "Am I the only one that heard what he just said?"

"Not sure," Sonny somberly replied to Pretty Boy. "Maybe."

"Is anyone listening to me? Can someone tell me why a bullshit promotion is ending our band?"

"It's more than that," said Cal. He always had everyone's attention as his interjections were so very rare. "Dad is kicking us out. Now that I've got a job and Sonny is making more money, he thinks we can afford a place of our own. We've got nowhere to jam."

Rex visibly deflated. Pretty Boy was obviously still hanging on the prospect of a new job.

"Alright," Rex finally responded. "We can get through this. When do you have to be out?"

"One month," said Sonny.

"Alright!" Rex said optimistically. "That's when the Dead Still show is. Can we still jam there until then?"

"Maybe. I could ask."

"So are we still a band?" Rex knew he sounded like a desperate ex-girlfriend, but he didn't care.

"I don't know, man," said Sonny. "I feel like I need to grow up, like I *am* growing up, and this band thing is starting to feel kind of... *childish*."

"Why the hell is everyone trying so hard to get *old?*" asked Rex. "Since when was that what we were all striving for? Yeah, this band is a *young* and crazy thing, but isn't that the point? We're all still bad ass, and I feel like you guys are forgetting that."

"Yeah, but –"

"Listen," Rex cut Sonny short. "I've got an idea. I think we need to do something to bind us back together as a band, and something to prove that we're still *young*." He went to the kitchen and grabbed a sheet of paper before ripping it haphazardly into quarters and handing a piece to each member. His gaze lingered on Pretty Boy's as he gave him a pen before continuing, letting him know that this was for him more than anyone and that his previous speech didn't go unnoticed. "Let's all think of one thing that we have always wanted to do, something wild and unexpected, something that we might even be embarrassed to mention, and write it on your paper. Every week until the show, we'll read one of them and do it. No judgment from anyone. It can be the weirdest shit anyone of us has ever heard, but no one is allowed to criticize, and no one is allowed to bow out. We all do it together. What d'you say?"

All four of them eyed one another, scrutinizing each other's reactions, all of them guardedly intrigued.

Pretty Boy, as usual, led the example and silently began scribbling on his piece of paper before folding it in half and passing his pen to Sonny. It was these kinds of ideas that made Pretty Boy love Rex eternally. While they may not have been identical in their thoughts and ideals, Rex's raucous tendencies combined with Pretty Boy's more elitist and artistically-fueled behaviors created a perfect symbiotic relationship.

Each band member – Rex included – scribbled down a few words and threw the papers into a brown paper bag on the coffee table. Rex – never one to get discouraged – wasn't thrilled by the band's reaction to his astonishing news, but was hopeful as he had bound them back together, at least as far as the show, and he knew that the concert would bring them to new levels that they wouldn't be able to back away from.

And so, Sonny, Cal, and Pretty Boy left the apartment still a band. Pretty Boy would have liked to linger behind and resume his conversation with Rex, but he knew that Rex was now even more distracted than before. Besides, he had the voice of the parrot ringing in his head and a new job to find. It wasn't until he left Rex's apartment that he began to fear the three, horribly shameful words he wrote on that sliver of paper.

Rex walked down to the university. On days of celebration or mourning, he would often make the trek to the school and eat lunch in the concourse area of the University Center, eyeing all the lovely, young girls. Although this had never proven prosperous, he knew that one day he would meet a nice girl who had just left her parents' house to set off for college, drunk on the newfound freedom and ready to unleash years of pent-up sexual desires upon a moderately handsome metalhead with the bad boy appeal.

Unfortunately, as the new semester was still a week away, the concourse was relatively empty and all of the restaurants were closed. Still, he walked the campus grounds, if anything for a little sun and therapeutic exercise, and combed the area for pretty girls.

The university had an aesthetic appeal to it. It was advertised as "The Island University," as it existed on a small peninsula connected by an isthmus just large enough for a road. To accentuate the feeling of island life and to mask the stress of mid-terms and student loans, the entire campus was landscaped with palm trees and flowering plants. The student center and sports buildings were painted with loud shades of blue and green. Walking from building to building, one could almost forget that the starting salary of nearly any job offered to the recipient of a bachelor's degree would take decades to pay off the student loans. Lucky for Rex, he had no financial investment in the institution and could admire the scenery without the worries of grades and tuition payments.

Boys in skinny jeans and lime green sunglasses rolled by on longboards. A couple did yoga in the grassy area adjacent to the Center for Science and Technology. Young people were different, nowadays, and he understood how Pretty Boy was suddenly feeling the weight of his age. These feelings – although understood – were entirely unfelt by Rex. People were all different. Times changed and Rex was fully aware of these changes, they just didn't concern him. While Pretty Boy would let the habits of strangers ruin his day, Rex was known for getting in all-out brawls, then befriending the opponents of the fight within minutes. So when Rex saw a new generation that bore no resemblance to his own, rather than seeing himself being distanced from the group he identified himself with, he only saw it as a new group of friends that were more than likely just dying to hear his music.

Other than the girl doing yoga with her presumable boyfriend, the only females that Rex came across were two fitness freaks with dynamite bodies. They were interrupting their jog to gush over a puppy strung by a leash to a neckless meathead. It got Rex thinking about Pretty Boy's parrot. *Pets.* That had to be a surefire approach to attracting female attention. *All* girls loved animals, it didn't matter the species. Show any girl an animal and you've got her locked in your proximity for at least a couple of minutes, plenty of time to flash some tattoos and flaunt blonde dredlocks to let them know that they just met the bad boy of all of their fantasies. Despite his involuntary celibacy, Rex always felt like he was just one step short of becoming a professional playboy, and once he found the missing ingredient, he'd have to beat them off with a stick.

After reaching the library, he strolled back the way he came, once again walking through the University Center, all thoughts of finding girls thoroughly dissolved and replaced with finding a pet. Before leaving the building, he perused the bulletin board to see if anyone had posted anything about the Dead Still show, or for any new up-and-coming metal bands that could become their competition. He found neither of these things, but what he did find was a little more enticing.

URGENT! Taiwanese exchange student needs a place to live for next semester· Call Yoyo if you are looking for a roommate

Rex jotted down the number, fantasies of an Oriental porn star lounging around his house in a bathrobe briefly erasing any thoughts of pets, aging, or even the brief breakup of his band.

Rex organized his thoughts on the arrangement, trying to figure a decent price for rent – cheap enough to be irrefusable, yet substantial enough to earn some income, income that could possibly be used to rent a storage unit as an alternative jam space. But more than the business aspect, Rex was preparing a charming greeting and playful quips that would fit in with the conversation to lay the foundation for some sort of in-home courtship. Unfortunately, the call went to voicemail, and so Rex reverted to the idea that all the charm he needed could be found in a pet.

Just as Rex left campus, Pretty Boy was coincidentally arriving at the university. He had thrown on his only dress shirt, his only tie, and his only pair of slacks and had taken to the streets armed with a bundle of resumes with lengthy lists of past jobs that required no skills and references that bore no merit. He was aiming for that non-existent job market of prestigious jobs that were available to self-proclaimed geniuses with no experience. He had dropped off resumes at four different banks, a marketing firm, and now was heading to the university. After human resources directors at two different banks had asked him what position he was applying for and his response was a solemn, "Anything," he was now expecting call-backs for janitorial positions. Since then, he had begun answering the question with, "Any job that I can turn into a career."

The university, he knew, was a long shot as it could be presumed that they would give nearly all jobs to students and alumni. Even if there were jobs to be had, Pretty Boy discovered – just as Rex had no more than an hour previous – that the university was all but abandoned as faculty and students alike were out binge drinking in celebration of another semester completed and in mourning of a short break leading to the Spring semester. There was no one there to interview him.

Pretty Boy did what he always did in times of despair: He drove to the shoreline and watched the ocean.

There was something calming about the infiniteness of the water. He liked to watch right where it met the land and imagine how long that had been the place where the two came together. He imagined dinosaurs roaming the coastline, colossal feet splashing through the crashing waves. He saw the next seventy million years in fast forward, culminating with him sitting in his car and watching the subtle dips and rises in the ocean surface. It made all of his problems seem insignificant, but today, it had a different effect.

After his father's speech and the sudden impact of middle-age, the coastline that had existed for eons now made *him* feel insignificant, rather than his worries. He saw the dinosaurs basking in the cool water one moment, then getting wiped out by a meteor the next. Everything was so fragilely temporary.

His eyes moved from where the ocean met the land to where the ocean met the horizon. And suddenly, a memory sprang to life.

After becoming infatuated with the works and life of Ernest Hemingway, his father became an avid fisherman. Reading of the fishing tournaments that Hemingway shared with Fidel Castro, Frank thought that maybe there was something beautiful about the hobby. And so he sold his second car and bought a boat. He took Dale with him on these outings and together, the two learned the fundamentals of fishing. Dale, at the time, was old enough to hold a fishing pole but just shy of being old enough to hold a joint, and therefore, was still interested in going on outings with the old man. Frank would actually refer to his son as Fidel when they were at sea. He gave a child's explanation of the nickname, but Dale was just happy to have that sort of familiarity with his dad. In retrospect, it was probably not the most endearing of nicknames for a father to bestow upon his son, and it could also be logically assumed that Frank was Hemingway, a man who got lost in a bottle and his own depression and eventually killed himself. But at the time, it was just another inside joke that stayed out at sea with a father and son who were finding that they really enjoyed one another's company.

The two of them learned how to use live bait to attract larger fish. They learned how to gaff black tip sharks and bring them aboard without losing any fingers. And close to their last outing, Frank even gave Dale a beer. It was a wonderful time in his life, almost like an entirely different life than the one he was leading. And like all things, it was short-lived.

This hobby lasted about four months. One

weekend's trip was cancelled due to weather, and the following weekend Dale spent with Rex walking to Polly's. Rex's parents were going through another violent alcohol binge and Rex needed to get out of the house. But Dale didn't tell this part to his father. He said that Rex had just purchased his first electric guitar and the two were exploring the different noises they could produce and such, which wasn't a lie, except they were playing the guitar at Polly's. Frank, always the pessimist, saw it as the end to that era and found a new group of friends who enjoyed hunting rather than fishing. Within a couple of weeks, Frank sold the boat and used the money to buy rifles and ammunition just before Dale could ask to go on another father-son outing. The two never mentioned it, but both felt equally guilty and angry about how quickly that bond was broken, Dale blaming his father for replacing him with new friends and selling the boat, Frank blaming his son for abandoning him after they had had such amazing times out on the water, and both of them, somehow, blaming themselves.

While the memory produced feelings of aching nostalgia and again, the temporary nature of all good things, Pretty Boy remembered that he had *one* marketable skill.

He drove to the marina to find a job as a deckhand.

Meanwhile, Rex was visually scanning chameleons and bearded dragons at the pet store near his house, trying to determine what species would be irresistibly cute to any female, yet still masculine enough to be *metal*. Although he was drawn to the idea of a reptile, scales and cricket-eating weren't things that would elicit a lot of insipid baby-talk from college chicks. Dogs were cool but clichéd, and Rex made a point to make every aspect of his life strangely distinguished.

He passed by the fish, the hamsters, the guinea pigs,

the parrots, and even the tarantulas before he found it.

The pig was two months old. It had a white stripe that wrapped around its midsection and a white spot on its nose, but everywhere else, the animal was black. It looked up at Rex with curious eyes, and with its wet and scrunched snout, it gave a small snort of approval.

Rex could see its potential for cuteness. He could imagine girls gushing over the little bundle of bacon. And he could also remember horror movies where victims were bound to walls while a sounder of swine would eat them alive from the ankles up. It was unique, it was cute, and it was metal. Rex paid the hundred and fifty bucks and took the pig home. He named it Brutus.

7

Pretty Boy clenched an aluminum beer can in one hand and a microphone in the other. He did what all singers did at practice sessions during instrumental sections and bobbed his head while eyeing all other members of the band as if he was the orchestrator, sporadically sipping his beer, and breathing deeply as he awaited his introduction to the song.

The room was littered with beer cans and paper bags filled with the remnants of last week's fast food dinners. The carpet was so stained that its original color wasn't discernable. Cal was barefoot, as usual, slamming the balls of his feet down on his bass pedals. Sonny's hair that was usually tied back in a ponytail (ever since his promotion) was now frizzy and unkempt as he had just woken up. Rex was shirtless and even with the disgusting olfactory overload that the room contained, his body odor didn't go unnoticed. His gaze was intently focused, eyes burning into his fretboard even as his head banged vehemently.

A repeating chromatic riff on the high E string ending with a note that kicked up a full step and bent up another half step provided an elegantly haunting melody that was the cue for Pretty Boy's vocal introduction to the song. With a raspy, melodious growl, he sang:

Your eyes give me such sweet reprieve
Your perfume smells like flesh, and I never want to leave

And then, as the melody dropped to a pounding drop beat:

But just like Jon Savage said to Crowne:
This place is going down
And when the pied piper comes around
Your children'll leave the town

The song was called "Wasteland," and was Pretty Boy's futile attempt at waxing poetic about his distaste for his hometown and humanity, in general. The music's brutal tone escalated throughout the three and a half minutes that the song encompassed and ended abruptly, like a freight train bashing into a steel wall.

Rex seemed to be the only member completely absorbed by the music as the other three were all enveloped by their recent career changes. Sonny was working in the office, Cal was working in the slaughterhouse, and after a short and informal interview, Pretty Boy had gotten the job with an offshore fishing company.

"Let's try the new one," Rex said ardently. His enthusiasm always seemed to peak when the others' began to plummet. "You got lyrics yet, Pretty Boy?"

"Still workin' on them," he lied. "I don't want to put them out there until I've got them down pat."

As the rest of the band played a rhythmic tune comprised of jumpy triplets, Pretty Boy shouted along with the music in growling gibberish. This was the greatest part about being a heavy metal vocalist: when you didn't know the words, you could always fake it and no one would be able to tell.

Pretty Boy had worked on the song insofar as brainstorming how to begin, although he had yet to come up with the first line. Given his recent internal conflicts with aging and mortality, he wanted to write a song with a similar theme. The problem was that he had to make the lyrics cryptic enough to throw the rest of the band off of the scent of *old,* because no matter what he was feeling on the inside, being old and being metal *never* coincided.

When the song came to an end, Pretty Boy announced that he needed to go home and get some rest before his first day on the new job. The rest of the band – Rex excluded – seemed relieved that Pretty Boy made the announcement that they were all aching for. Although they were only five songs in, Rex offered no resistance as he knew it would only distance the rest of them from the band, and instead, greeted their new endeavors with a supportive curiosity.

"So, you're going to be working on a boat, going offshore and shit?"

"Yeah."

"And you've got a parrot now? Is there anything you want to tell us? Are you becoming a pirate?"

"Yeah, now all I need to do is get you to teach me how to stop showering." They all shared a laugh.

Pretty Boy went on his way. Luckily, Cal and Sonny didn't have to act busy or distracted to hint at Rex's cue to leave as Rex needed to get home to tend to his hungry piglet.

Pretty Boy had to be at the dock by 5:00 A.M., a time that usually caught him awake from the night before. But the exciting prospect of a new job commixed with the lovely morning high of three Lortab put a skip in his step as he slid out the door, whistling the tune of the band's new song.

While most metal songs didn't have a vocal melody, but moreso, a vocal *rhythm* (as screams didn't provide pitch), Pretty Boy knew that this particular song needed a vocal rhythm that matched the rest of the song. Up until this morning, he thought that the song would be about a robot losing his bolts and cogs and what not, slowly falling apart, but now he was writing a love song. As he drove down to the docks, he was singing his experimental new lyrics.

> *Lori, Lori, you never seem to bore me*
> *You pick me up when I'm feeling sad and horny*
> *I hate to say it 'cause it's sounding sort of corny*
> *But when I kiss your lips I know that you adore me*

Although the song was no longer about struggling with a mid-life crisis, Pretty Boy still had to remain elusive with his words. While the entirety of the band habitually used marijuana and alcohol and dabbled with other drugs, writing a love song about Lortab was still a cause for concern that could have potentially resulted in a band intervention, something that none of them needed at this point. It was strange, Pretty Boy thought, how all drug users, from heroin addicts to cigarette smokers, drew a thick line between morally ethical and unethical drugs. And whether it be because of its addictive qualities, the way in which it modified behaviors, or its overall public perception, he knew that Lortab addiction would not be deemed as permissible.

During his interview, he had embellished his qualifications a little, making himself the "guide" of his father-son fishing trips with his "associate," and failed to mention the fifteen-year hiatus from fishing that he was coming off of. The interviewer was a man named Captain

Eddie. Captain Eddie was exactly what Pretty Boy had come to expect from a fishing dock manager and owner. He worked in an office that reeked of fish guts and never wore close-toed shoes or long pants. He hadn't been seen without a baseball cap in years. His hairy forearms stuck out of pastel colored fishing shirts, the ones with the ventilation flap that runs across the back. He always had scruffy facial hair – never enough to be considered a beard, but also, somehow, never so little to be considered clean-shaven. What was less of a cliché was his love of literature. Pretty Boy claimed that his – not his father's – passion for fishing had stemmed from his love of Ernest Hemingway. Immediately, the conversation switched gears as Captain Eddie had a similar beginning and a love for Hemingway. Although Pretty Boy had never read a Hemingway novel in its entirety, he knew the titles, and claimed to have read <u>The Sun Also Rises</u>, <u>A Farewell to Arms</u>, and – what he said to be his personal favorite – <u>For Whom the Bell Tolls</u>. Under the effects of the Lortab, Pretty Boy was quite sociable and amiable, and was quickly liked by Captain Eddie, who asked no further questions pertaining to his fishing background, to Pretty Boy's relief.

Crossing the Harbor Bridge into Portland, Texas, Pretty Boy's thoughts should have been racing, trying to remember the best spot to gaff a shark and how to gut a kingfish. He should have been wondering why he even took this job, as it showed no more potential for a career than working at the bookstore. But instead, he was singing an ode to a drug and anticipating his life as a pirate.

Captain Eddie greeted Pretty Boy as he arrived at Marlin Marina, but fortunately, had long relinquished his duties as captain, and would not be accompanying Pretty Boy on his first day on the job.

On the boat still tethered to the dock, Manny and Tre were smoking cigarettes and languidly mopping the deck.

Both were younger than Pretty Boy by at least eight years. They seemed to have a rough-edged amicability that endeared Pretty Boy, but weren't very inviting. They were attentive to his first-day confusion, telling him where to mop and what to bring aboard, but seemed too caught up in their own conversation to include him. Perhaps they were so set in their ways that any change was unwelcomed.

Forty-five minutes prior to departure, Pretty Boy was instructed to load up the concession cart and stock it with various corn chips, cereal bars, soft drinks, and sunscreens. It wasn't until this point that he was made aware that he was there not to reel in fish, but to dish out snacks. He was told that this was the starting position for all new hires and he could move up quickly, but today, while Manny and Tre enjoyed continuing their boisterous dialogue and gaffing black tip sharks, Pretty Boy would be locked in seclusion, offering smiles and Fritos to rich, white people. A diehard optimist under the influence of the Lortab, he viewed this only as time to work on lyrics and enjoy the endless horizon of beautiful, blue water.

The customers arrived and boarded the vessel. As predicted, they were all pasty white, overweight, and donning previously unworn, name brand fishing attire. Manny and Tre seemed delighted as this was the easiest to please demographic of their clientele. They all seemed like extremely wealthy homebodies with very little fishing experience. They all enjoyed an off-color joke from a true-to-life middle-class boat boy and would surely marvel at catching a single trout or sighting a dolphin.

It was an hour-long ride out to the first fishing hole, during which time they would all be below deck sitting on chairs and cots just in front of Pretty Boy's concession stand. With nothing else to distract them, they proceeded to stuff their faces with anything Pretty Boy had to offer. They would all approach him with condescending smiles, making brief chitchat about the weather or the fish dinner they would be eating tonight. Pretty Boy was quick to act the long-time employee and avid fisherman, saying things like, "The currents are perfect to bring in the grouper," or, "We've been slaughtering the amberjacks lately." All seemed enthusiastic about his claims and responded with hefty tips. As long as he could get more Lortab to keep him this sociable, Pretty Boy thought, he could enjoy this job and make decent money.

The seas were choppy and he had trouble standing still, taking quick steps in the direction that the boat would shift. The painkillers didn't help his sense of balance. While all of them walked slightly different, arms outstretched like tightrope walkers, ready to grab onto a chair or wall for stability, Pretty Boy was quite obviously the most unstable. This image of a wobbling soda salesman wasn't the same as the lifelong fisherman that he had claimed to be. He became self-conscious of his inability to acclimate to the rocking boat. He tried to keep his feet planted to appear unfazed by the unforgiving waves, but this only threw his balance further off, now randomly sprinting three quick steps to keep from falling. On one instance, he stumbled into his own cart, knocking the display rack of chips to the floor and drawing the attention of all the clients. He kept his smile, but it now only seemed to be masking his embarrassment.

The boat finally slowed as it approached the first fishing hole. Pretty Boy couldn't have been more relieved when they dropped anchor. His stomach, contrary to his legs, was more aggravated by the subtle rocks of the stationary boat than by crashing full speed through choppy seas. He tried to remember if he had ever gotten seasick on any of his outings with his father. The sludge in his stomach felt unfamiliar. Surely, sea legs were something that didn't go away no matter how long they went unused, like the ability to catch a baseball or write in cursive. But before the first line was cast, Pretty Boy found himself sprinting to the railing of the ship and puking overboard. An obese woman who was in the closest proximity dropped her fishing pole in the water and fell on her butt in attempt to avoid any collateral damage.

At the bow of the boat, Tre yelled, "Ladies and gentlemen! It appears the corn chips have been contaminated!" followed by a collective guffaw from the fishing group. This was where Tre shined. Manny was the fishing expert while Tre was the color man. Tre could make a customer laugh after getting his hand bitten off by a boarded shark. Pretty Boy wasn't offended by the joke made at his expense, but nonetheless, didn't enjoy being the one with the missing hand.

He continued to heave louder and louder, visibly startling the patrons of the ship. Tre continued making light of the situation.

"This is actually good news," Tre announced. "He's been trying to get pregnant for some time now. I think this is just morning sickness." Once again, a bunch of fat white collars and their spouses chuckled heartily.

The woman who fell was still fishing just beside where Pretty Boy was throwing up, glancing worriedly in his direction. Not to be outdone by Tre, Pretty Boy smiled at her between regurgitations, saliva still dripping from his lips, and said, "That'll teach me to drink on the job." The joke fell flat and was received more as a confession. The woman looked at him disdainfully and went back to her fishing, now less concerned by his pitiful state.

The fishing trip lasted six hours. Pretty Boy spent five of them vomiting. As his loud upheavals became the static noise to the trip and he lost everyone's attention, he began to wonder if he would get paid for this.

It wasn't until they were making their way back to dry land that he remembered that he sold Dramamine at his concession stand. He opened up the lipstick-shaped tube and popped six pills, unsure of whether or not taking it this far into a bout of seasickness would do anything to alleviate the nausea – not to mention if he could even keep the pills in his stomach long enough to dissolve.

When they reached the docks, Manny and Tre offered him their first signs of concern. In front of their customers, showing any worry would only destroy the light-hearted atmosphere. Now out of the customers' view, they placed consoling hands on his back as he vomited yet again. Rather than telling him everything is alright or asking him what he needs, Tre only said, "Maybe this isn't the best job for you."

Had Pretty Boy been in better condition, he probably would have hit him. Instead, he vomited once more and stumbled toward the parking lot to drive home in shame. Manny yelled behind him, "And I hate to say it, but you're gonna have to pay for the pole you made that lady drop in the water!"

He drove home silently. He muted the radio and listened to his breath, fuming with anger and nausea. When he arrived home, Pretty Boy slammed the door shut and started crying. It was the first time he had wept in years, and he did it grandly. He whimpered like a toddler with a broken leg. He fell to the floor in the fetal position and turned red-faced. It wasn't the shame. It wasn't the job that he had just presumably lost. Once again, he felt devastatingly *old*. He remembered going to carnivals with his friends and riding every ride multiple times while others got sick and bowed out. He remembered the looks on Manny and Tre's faces as he boarded the ship in the morning. It wasn't the look of potential friends, but of youngsters disillusioned by their new, older coworker. He suddenly felt like he was back in high school, only as a thirty-one-year-old man, trying to find a lunch table to sit at.

As his sobs died out, Pretty Boy stood and felt like he was still on the ship. He clutched the wall for support. The walls were swaying. The mirror on the wall was crawling around like an insect by its thousands of legs that lined the frame. Small waves were rolling through the carpet. Virgil squawked from the adjacent room, "Get NEW job! Get NEW job!" He stumbled through the funhouse that his living room had become and approached the bird angrily.

"I did, you feathered moron! I got a new job and it sucked shit! I made a complete ass out of myself, thanks to you!"

The bird turned to him slowly, looking directly in his eyes, and said with a slight British accent, "No, you misunderstood me. I didn't say, 'Get new *job*,' I said, 'Get new *God*.'"

After a week of working at the slaughterhouse, Cal was ready to become a vegetarian. Most days, he worked on a platform wielding a huge band saw known as a beef splitter. The beef splitter was suspended by a retractable metal hoist so that the worker – in this case, Cal – could maneuver the heavy equipment with the least amount of physical exertion. By the time the cows reached Cal's station, they were already dead, de-hoofed, beheaded, and skinned, hanging from meat hooks on moveable chain hoists. It was Cal's job to split the carcass symmetrically, starting between the rear legs and finishing at the open neck hole. This was the extent of Cal's new job description. Carcass after carcass. Crotch to neck, crotch to neck.

But it wasn't the grotesque nature of the job or sympathy for the animals that he was being paid to rip apart that was turning him off to meat, but the smell. It didn't come in waves, like most smells, but like an uppercut that could render a grown man unconscious. And just when Cal would feel that he was growing immune to the odors, he would split open another carcass and all kinds of horrible scents would come pouring out.

While he only had to see Rowdy for brief moments throughout the day, his presence was also not the greatest perk to the job. Once or twice a day, Rowdy would wander the entire premises, just to scold an underling and flaunt his power, his regal presence like the inbred emperor of an island comprised of eviscerated cows and fecal matter.

Cal would have quit. He didn't need the job so much as he needed *a* job, and he could surely find one more alluring than this one. But every time he split through bone with his giant, rotating saw, every time he watched an organ split open sending a pocket of blood splashing to the concrete floor, he felt awesome, like the basis for a metal song or horror movie. He felt powerful.

Staring at the inner anatomy of such huge beasts, he got a glimpse of a world hidden from the general public. Everyone had their own specialty at their job, an aspect of the world we live in where one could consider himself knowledgeable, something that gave him anecdotes to bring up in conversation, and now Cal was no different. Everyday, he was involved in a process that concerned 97% of Americans, but less than 1% actually saw. It wasn't the most fashionable profession, but it was, indeed, a profession.

Cal rarely spoke to any of his coworkers. Wielding an enormous bandsaw, his coworkers weren't even allowed in a close proximity. He ate his sack lunch in solitude, going over drumbeats in his head. The only time spent in close confines with his colleagues was when they would line up before and after lunch, and at the beginning and end of the workday, either to put on all of their safety gear or to take it off and wash the blood from their persons before eating a sandwich or going home to hug their children.

During these times, the quiet, timorous Cal wouldn't shy away from random conversation as the thrill of tearing apart flesh and bone doubled his confidence level. But lately, he made a point to be the last one in line, allowing himself time to peruse the chemicals and tools that were lying around the washing station that he could possibly take home for personal use.

At 5:00, when the last person was disrobed of their bloody garments and thoroughly sanitized, whistling on his way to his vehicle, Cal looked through the cabinets beneath the sink to find about a dozen different chemicals and cleaners in white plastic containers. He grabbed the first two that he saw, held them precariously beneath the wings of his jacket, and went home.

Sonny worked at Gregory Metals, a plant with the primary function of extracting aluminum oxide from bauxite ore. The aluminum oxide, or alumina, would then be used to produce the aluminum that exists in every household. Alumina plants were notorious for being loud and dirty, and Gregory Metals was no different. Everything inside the plant was covered in red-stained dirt – as was everything a half a mile downwind – and made the entire jobsite resemble a hellish version of the Martian surface. Loud motors and sweltering heat intensified this horrific ambiance.

For years, Sonny worked as a foreman overseeing all new construction in one of the four digester units, aptly named Digester Unit #4, more commonly known simply as DU4. Sonny had worked his way up to foreman status solely by seniority. The filthy and deafeningly loud atmosphere made for extremely high rates of job turnover, and within a few short years, Sonny was the only member of his crew that knew the mental and geographical landscape of the job, and so he was promoted. But Sonny was the type of guy that needs power like a person with bulimia needs food poisoning, and was quickly transformed by the new job title. After countless incidents involving

Sonny scolding his crewmembers, belittling them, threatening them, and in one case, throwing a man's lunchbox over the perimeter fence, the higher-ups in the office were forced to relieve Sonny of his duties. With their pockets run down to loose change after a few costly lawsuits regarding unfair treatment of employees, they couldn't just fire their longest standing employee in that unit. Instead, they moved him to the office with very little financial incentive, knowing that the sense of entitlement was enough for Sonny. They gave him the title of Quality Control and instructed him to receive progress reports from each of the four foremen, but was adamantly instructed not to intervene in any way, but rather to make notes of how things were running and where changes should be made in a fashion that could be presented to the next up in line. The job was basically a made-up position and a loss of money on the company's part, but it was a much less significant loss than the potential lawsuit that Sonny could ultimately make, even if he wasn't treated unjustly.

During his rounds to collect information from the foremen of the different units, Sonny had been pocketing handfuls of powdered aluminum and bringing them home. Once this became habit, he instructed his brother to bring home any chemicals he could find laying around his jobsite.

When Cal arrived home with his two containers of mystery liquid, he and his brother read the labels and looked them up online.

"So this one is phosphoric acid. There's not much we can do with it," Sonny announced. "But *this* one is ammonia, which by itself, just smells really strong. But if you bring home some other chemicals to mix it with, we could probably make something."

"It looks like they just have a whole bunch of this stuff. All of the labels looked the same."

"Is this *all* they had in the cabinets?"

"Yup. Just like ten of these bottles and a bunch of steel wool."

"*Steel wool? Are you serious?* Bring home as much of that stuff as you can."

9

Rex loved any sort of change. While his band, his house, and his career all remained constant for years, it made the small variations in life seem so huge to him. And right now, he had a new pet, he had a new roommate set to arrive in a few days, he had a monumental new gig coming up, and tomorrow was to be the day the band opened the first paper stating one of their life aspirations. Rex was elated.

Yoyo had called him yesterday and formally accepted his invitation to room together. He had yet to see her, but his imagination was running wild. His past roommates had all been filthy, late with rent, dinner-stealing, freeloading, bathroom-hogging annoyances. More substantially, they were all *male*. Yoyo's arrival had been more anticipated and fantasized about than most human babies.

Almost as exciting was tomorrow's adventure with the band. They had called it The Fantasy Checklist and decided to go in alphabetical order, making Cal's paper the first to be read and executed. Rex knew that this would bind them back together, but more than that, the idea was fascinating in its endless possibilities. Tomorrow night, they could be doing anything. They might be getting facial piercings or firing a pistol at a shooting range. They might be trying a crazy, new drug or stealing a car. For all he knew, they could be committing a *murder*. And Rex was down for anything. He didn't know how the rest of the band felt, but he couldn't wait.

Rex was coming home from the jam session in the Vanimal, still cranking up on the hand brake at red lights and praying not to plow into the car in front of him. He often worried about the Vanimal not surviving long enough to haul their equipment to the Dead Still show. Everyday, he would tell himself that he would talk to Timmy, who claimed to have vast auto-mechanical knowledge, to see if he could bring the Vanimal back up to something that could possibly pass a vehicle inspection, but the thought was always drowned out amidst games of Would You Rather and Marry, Fuck, Kill.

As he turned right onto his street, the driver-side door inched open as the momentum stretched the bungee cord that was loosely securing it shut. Rex was infinitely excited to see Brutus. They had spent the previous day crawling around the carpet, Brutus exploring his new territory and Rex mimicking the pig's movements. Brutus scampered like a puppy and even scratched himself with his hind leg just like a canine. Contrary to Rex's preconceived notion, Brutus' tail wasn't curly. It was straight and hairless, the width and length of a pencil, and it wagged happily. He was easily excited and hopped around playfully. He even slept in bed with Rex. Brutus was a noisy breather when he slept and readjusted his position around the bed throughout the night, keeping Rex awake. Still, his presence was very welcome and Rex enjoyed being briefly woken every hour as a reminder of his new pet.

As Rex sped down his street, he was anticipating how Brutus would greet him. It was the first time that Rex had left Brutus since he bought him yesterday, and therefore, it was to be Rex's first homecoming. Although he had never owned a pet before, he was very involved in raising Enkidu, and he knew the joys of having a happy, furry face awaiting your arrival every day.

Only Rex wasn't greeted by a panting smile and a wagging tail, but by a big, wet pile of pig shit.

Brutus was sitting up behind the pile of feces, staring at Rex intently, proudly, *humanly*, as if to openly state that this act of defecation was meant to incite war. Brutus, apparently, wasn't fond of time alone.

Rex was quickly taught that pet pigs were very different from dogs in two distinct ways. For one, pigs were not loyal and obedient, but more like a roommate. Brutus felt like he was equal with Rex. If anything, *he* was the master. A dog cowered away when spanked and learned from this negative reinforcement. Brutus, however, seemed deeply offended after Rex gave him a stern slap across the face. The pig eyed Rex with a humanlike sense of disbelief, then stormed around the house squealing hysterically, clearing tables and knocking over chairs. For the rest of the day, Brutus refused to be in the same room as Rex.

The second difference was that pig shit smelled infinitely worse than dog shit. As Brutus was disheveling Rex's bedroom, feeling out the best spot to lay down and take a nap, Rex was employing every household cleaner in his kitchen cabinet trying to rid the carpet of the smell of shit. He would walk outside in the driveway to cleanse his nostrils of the scent, then would return to his house to find that in terms of smell, he would now be permanently residing in a barnyard.

By the second day, Rex and Brutus had cemented the terms of their relationship in that they were both continuously battling for the status of alpha male. Rex would coax Brutus into his good graces with soothing tones and the two would spend a half hour watching television together in a peaceful silence. Brutus would inevitably break the serenity by chewing on the couch or clearing the coffee table with his inquisitive, soggy snout. Rex would reprimand Brutus with angry shouts or a slap to the behind, and Brutus would respond by breaking everything else in sight and retreating to a different corner of the house. Rex felt like he was living with a psychotically moody girlfriend, only without the sex.

That night, Rex brought Brutus up in bed with him again as a peace offering. Brutus used his snout to forcefully nudge Rex toward the side of the bed every ten minutes. When Rex's left leg was hanging off the side of the bed, he realized the pig's intentions. Refusing to surrender the bed, he put Brutus on the floor to sleep alone, an action that sent Brutus into a frenzy. The pig squealed piercingly loudly as it ran half circles around the bed, reversing direction when it hit the wall, and sideswiped the bed frame. Rex tried shouting at the pig, which only escalated the situation. Still screaming, Brutus began chewing on the wooden bedpost. His gnawing mouth opening and closing made the squeals sound like a wailing siren. Rex finally threw him in the backyard. The pig continued to squeal, but Rex was able to mute the sound with his head sandwiched between two pillows.

Somewhere around 3:00 AM, Rex awoke to the sound of more squealing. He groaned exhaustedly and got out of bed, ready to turn the new pet into a bacon breakfast. But before he exited his bedroom, among the squeals he heard the sound of footsteps on the linoleum floor of his kitchen, the rubber soles peeling like velcro from the layer of unmopped filth with every step.

Growing up in South Texas where every moron had a fully automatic rifle, Rex – always the odd man out – wasn't a gun fanatic. He did, however, own a machete and slept three feet away from where it resided on his dresser.

Wearing nothing but boxer shorts and a hundred tattoos, he quickly grabbed the machete and tiptoed out into the hallway. Before he made it to the kitchen, a man walked confidently through the entryway, stopping mid-stride as the two locked eyes.

He was dark skinned, yet the sun-scarred condition of his skin made his race indeterminable. His attire suggested that he wasn't homeless, or even poor, but also not greatly concerned with his appearance. Both his shirt and pants were wrinkled and greatly oversized, but also bore the logos of high dollar name brands. He wore a purple baseball cap backwards and small gray patches in his beard. The most peculiar thing about the man was his overall disposition. He wasn't walking like a man breaking into a house, but more like a man on his way to a business meeting. While the two of them were staring each other down, his expression suggested that it was Rex, not himself, that owed an explanation to his presence in the home.

Rex was thrown off by the man's demeanor, but finally spoke. "Listen, if you're here to take the TV, I don't give a shit. But if you're looking to hurt me, I ain't going down without a long, bloody fight." He breathed heavily, summoning adrenaline.

The intruder looked optimistically confused.

"So... I can take the TV?"

Now Rex was confused.

"Um... Yeah. What the fuck ever."

Without giving a second thought, the intruder continued his confident stride into the living room toward the wall where the flatscreen television was hanging.

"Wait a second. This doesn't feel right. I don't think I want you to take the TV."

"But you said you don't give a shit."

"Yeah, but now I feel shitty about myself, just letting you take my stuff. Just get the fuck out of here."

"Nah, I think I'll take the TV."

"But what if I stab you?"

"First of all, you don't stab with a machete."

"You know what I mean. What if I… you know… whack you with it?"

"I don't think you will."

"Come on, man! This is bullshit!"

"Exactly. You won't do it."

"Alright, how about I give you fifty bucks and you leave the TV?"

"Nah, I think I want the TV. But look at it this way: I ain't here to hurt you and you get to keep your fifty bucks."

"I could call the cops."

"I'll be gone before they get here. With your TV."

"I could easily kill you while you're carrying the TV."

"We've already gone over this. You won't do it."

"Maybe not, but I could easily fight you while you're holding a TV."

"But then I'd drop it and break it, so either way you're out a TV. Now would you give me a hand? I've got a bad back."

Rex felt outsmarted and backed into a corner. He always said that he could never kill a person over material possessions, but he felt emasculated. Although he had participated in a few barroom brawls, he was never the violent type, and fighting with a criminal who was breaking into his house in the middle of the night elicited so many horrible scenarios. The man could have a weapon. He could have friends outside. He could have a disease. And if he successfully defeated the criminal, there was nothing to stop a man as such to come back to seek retribution. He tried to feel better about the situation by thinking the man really did have serious back problems that kept him from steady work and this could be construed as an act of charity. As the two loaded up the TV in the back of the intruder's

SUV to the soundtrack of haunting pig squeals, Rex really wished he would have bought a pit bull. Once inside, he opened the back door, pointing the machete in the pig's direction, and shouted, "This is your fault!" before slamming the door shut and going back to bed.

He awoke the next morning to find that he no longer had grass. The entire backyard looked like a graveyard that had just been robbed of all of its residents. Once again, Brutus sat proudly upright, gazing at Rex with a diabolical sense of satisfaction.

Rex was almost as awestricken as he was angry. The pig had to be up all night to do that level of damage. Unknowing of how to reprimand the animal, he allowed the pig inside. Brutus seemed satisfied with his vengeance and the two spent most of the day sitting on opposite sides of the couch. Rex would stare at the animal, trying to make sense of what it was thinking. It's instinct to establish dominance was quite obvious, but at that exact moment, *what was it thinking?* As if in answer to this unspoken question, Brutus glanced back at Rex like a prison warden staring through the bars at a livid inmate, knowing that he held all of the leverage, then looked back at the wall where the TV used to reside.

Pretty Boy arrived that afternoon. After lying down for four hours, his stomach had finally settled, his room had stopped swaying like the boat, and his parrot was no longer talking like a British poet. He had thought about bringing the bird in hopes that it would talk to Rex as well to prove his sanity, but he eventually chalked the occurrence up to hallucinations caused by a strange mixture of Lortab and seasickness.

Rex hadn't seen Brutus for an hour and a half as the

two weren't on speaking terms at the moment. Rex was sitting on his couch missing his TV, when just as soon as the door opened, Brutus came darting across the carpet in front of him and toward the door, squealing with the shrilly voice of a thousand terrified, little girls. Pretty Boy had one foot across the threshold when Brutus bit him. The bite didn't hurt through his jeans, but the spectacle of a screaming piglet sprinting to gnaw at his leg made him think that his drug trip wasn't quite over.

"Brutus!" Rex shouted. "Get back here!"

Brutus looked at Rex and gave him an angry snort as if to say, 'We'll talk about this later.' It only took Pretty Boy a few moments to accept the occurrence as reality and not a hallucination. A crazed pig attacking him actually didn't seem like such an odd occurrence at Rex's house. Rex and Pretty Boy sat on the couch while Brutus retreated to a corner to observe the intruder's interaction with Rex. Sitting like a docile canine, the pig locked eyes with Rex and wouldn't let go. His scrunched up pig face had a daunting expression. Superficially, he looked so cute and innocent, yet something dark and manipulative lurked deeper in his eyes, like a toddler pointing a pistol at Rex's head.

"Brutus?" asked Pretty Boy. "What, like *Et tu, Brute?*"

"Huh?"

"You know, from Julius Caesar?"

"I don't know what the fuck you're talkin' about, man. He's Brutus because he's fucking *brutal*. He could be the mascot for our band."

"And how is it living with a filthy swine?"

Rex sighed in defeat. "Brutal."

"I was talking to the pig."

Rex told him about the new Asian roommate and expressed his excitement for The Fantasy Checklist, but his enthusiasm was suppressed by the shame of assisting an intruder in robbing him. He didn't tell his best friend about that part of his evening.

Pretty Boy told of his first day at the docks. He told of the seasickness, of the fat woman dropping her pole in the water (that he would now have to replace), of how he embarrassed himself thoroughly. He didn't mention how old he felt and his weeping session afterward. He was never ashamed in front of Rex, but he knew that Rex was the only one in the band that wasn't suffering from age and talk of it brought him down. Rex, although not as happy-go-lucky as he may have appeared to most, was most definitely unconcerned with things like age, mortality, and losing one's sex appeal. Convincing Rex that they were getting old was akin to converting a pious Catholic to Atheism: It was pointless and cruel, no matter your beliefs.

How tragic the day's events were for both Pretty Boy and Rex was obvious, as was Rex's disappointment in his new pet. The two sank pitifully into the couch, Brutus showing the only signs of contentment before scampering off back to the bedroom. By the time Sonny and Cal showed up, the whole house reeked of defeat – not to mention the lingering odor of pig shit. Still, Rex sprang to life at their arrival.

"You guys ready for this?"

Sonny and Pretty Boy looked equally indifferent, casting fake smiles with raised eyebrows around the room. Cal looked worried.

Without further introduction, Rex produced the brown paper bag and fingered through its contents, searching for the folded corner of paper that read CAL on the outside. With the facial expression of a toddler opening a gift, he opened the paper and read it to himself. His smile slowly dissolved. He glared up at Cal.

"Really?"

"What? It's something I've always wanted to do."

"What is it?" asked Pretty Boy.

Rex tossed the paper into the air above the coffee table. It spiraled down like a falling aircraft. He puffed a weighted breath of air. "It says, 'take a painting class.'"

"That's cool," said Pretty Boy, trying to assuage the tension. "I've always liked art. And so have you, Rex."

"What, because I said I like that picture with the clocks? How is this something for a fucking *metal* band to do together? I mean, if one of our fans saw us all taking an art class together, we'd lose all credibility."

"C'mon, man," said Sonny. "We don't have any fans."

"God damn it! Of course, we have fans! We might not after our little Ladies' Night Out, though."

"Holy shit!" exclaimed Sonny. "Is that a fucking pig?!" Brutus was peeking his head out from behind the hallway wall.

"Don't change the subject!"

"Seriously, you *do* realize there is a pig in your house, right?"

"*Of course,* I do. You think I wouldn't notice a pig running around my living room?"

"It *is* pretty dirty in here."

"*You're* one to talk!" Rex cut himself short. He pinched his eyes shut and shook his head in agitation. "Damn it! You're derailing the conversation. Quit changing the subject."

"And what were we talking about?"

"What color panties you're wearing to the painting class we're apparently going to."

"You don't know," said Pretty Boy. "It might be fun."

Rex pounded the coffee table. The sound visibly startled all of them. Rex caught their shocked and disapproving glares, and he dialed his voice down to calm his abrasive disposition. "Fun? Yeah, maybe. I guess it just wasn't what I had in mind."

"Well, we'll get to yours, too."

"Yes, we *damn well* will. And it's going to be fucking awesome. So where do we take a one-time painting class, anyway? The YWCA?"

"There's this place," Cal's face lit up briefly, then sank back down timorously, "where you drink while they teach you to paint a picture. And they've got one tonight. I reserved us four spots already."

"See?" said Pretty Boy. "We get to drink. This might be pretty awesome, actually."

"Yeah," Rex sighed sorrowfully. *"Awesome."*

"Don't sound so dejected." Pretty Boy's attention shifted up as his eyes squinted and his brow furrowed in confusion. "What happened to your TV?"

Each of the four walls was a different color – lime green, sky blue, black (behind the instructor's canvas), and white. The black wall was left bare to limit distractions from the main focal point, while the three other walls were littered with vibrantly colored, mediocre artwork. Above the mounted paintings on the green wall were black, wooden letters that spelled the name of the establishment – Bubbly Brushes – in one of those fun fonts where the letters curled into spirals at the tips. Extending perpendicularly from the black wall were four long tables draped in black plastic tablecloths with six canvases perched atop each – three facing one side of the table and three facing the other. A metal foldout chair sat beneath each canvas. The setup was to prevent the canvases from blocking anyone's view of the instructor and meant that all of the students would have to crane their necks to one side during the tutorial.

The place was packed by the time Rex and Pretty Boy arrived, and every customer's attention was drawn to their appearance. Pretty Boy entered first, wearing a sleeveless tee-shirt with the words "Fuck My Life" written in white across the chest. His pale calves extended from ratty, gray cargo shorts riddled with holes. Rex wore a plain white wifebeater to reveal his numerous tattoos that extended all the way down to his black leather wrist cuffs. A long, silver chain sagged from his front belt loop down to the side of his knee, then back up to the wallet in the back pocket of his faded black slacks. His eyes were bloodshot and with him came a cloud of alcohol fumes, cigarette smoke, and stale sweat that was detectable from the far side of the room. The two seats in the back corner were the only ones left vacant. Cal and Sonny had arrived fifteen minutes earlier and sat at the next table over from the remaining empty seats so that Rex and Pretty Boy would be facing their backs during the lesson. Sipping a can of beer and carrying another five by the one empty plastic ring on the six pack, Rex sauntered over to his seat while Pretty Boy – who carried his beer in a small, Styrofoam ice chest – paid the class fee. Both of them refused the khaki aprons that the rest of the class was wearing. Given their apparel, this line of reasoning wasn't questioned.

"Thanks for saving us a seat," Rex grumbled sarcastically.

"There weren't any spots for four by the time we got here," replied Sonny. "And try to look just a little bit excited about being here."

Before Rex could reply, Pretty Boy made his way to his seat and interjected, "I think it's gonna be awesome! I've never painted anything before."

Rex turned to Pretty Boy. "You do realize we're the only dudes at this place, right?"

"So the odds look pretty good, huh?" The middle-aged, emaciated widow who had the ill fortune to sit next to Pretty Boy glared worriedly in their direction, careful not to allow her gaze to linger for too long.

A portly, middle-aged woman made her way to the easel that stood just in front of the bare, black wall. Her hair was somewhere between light brown and dark red, but was lined with frizzy, white hairs that seemed to hang lighter than the rest, making their way to the more noticeable surface. She seemed to carry most of her weight in her arms; her elbows were merely V-shaped folds in the fat between her triceps and forearms.

"Alright. Let's get started." A few ladies in the middle two rows raised wine glasses and whooped enthusiastically. "My name is Veronica and I'll be your instructor for the evening. And tonight we're going to paint a Tuscan landscape."

Rex groaned in disappointment from his corner, loud enough to draw half of the room's attention.

"Is there a problem, sir?" asked Veronica. Rex looked shocked, as if he didn't realize how loud he was. He was definitely trying to make his distaste apparent to his bandmates, but while staying just under the radar of the rest of the class. He was failing miserably.

"Um… not really…" he struggled for an answer. "I just didn't realize we were using *acrylic* paint. I'm more of a latex kind of guy."

"I'm sorry, sir. Latex paint is just usually used for painting *houses*, not pictures."

Sonny turned around to face Rex. "I think he's talking about a different kind of latex," he chuckled under his breath. The skinny widow stared intently at her blank canvas, her face dead with horror. Her body couldn't have been more fearfully still if she was sitting next to a family of hungry grizzly bears.

And so the class commenced. *Paint a swooping, brown*

line here. Mix equal parts green and yellow. Add a dab of white to the tip of your brush. Veronica's instructions were happily interrupted by the playful banter of the elated women in the center of the classroom. Less welcomed interruptions were the cracking open of aluminum beer cans and audible groans and belches from Rex.

After issuing a more complex set of instructions, Veronica would meander up and down the aisles to assist anyone in need. When she would reach the corner where Rex and Pretty Boy were painting, Rex would turn his canvas slightly in the direction of the wall.

"What's the problem?"

"I'm an experienced painter."

"That's right. *Mr. Latex.* So why can't I see your painting?"

"I had a different inspiration," Rex said through pungent, beer breath, "so I'm painting something different. I'm just here to accompany *this* chick, anyway." He raised his forearm and extended his thumb in Pretty Boy's direction. Just on the other side of him, the widow gasped in shock.

Veronica paid him no mind and went back to the rest of the class.

Pretty Boy glanced over at Rex's 'artwork.'

"Are you *serious?*"

"What? I'm summoning the spirit of Georgia O'Keefe."

Pretty Boy looked away shamefully. "At least she made 'em *look* like flowers."

Veronica made her way to the next aisle where Sonny and Cal were painting.

"You're doing an amazing job," she said to Cal. He looked up at her with eyes so wide it looked like his head was about to erupt. It was unclear if he was proud of his artwork or just amazed that a woman was speaking to him.

Pretty Boy and Rex both watched on as Cal did all he could to suppress all the emotion that was about spew out of him in the form of vomit or sperm. Or both. "I love your use of color on the skyline."

"Do you like what I did with the trees?" asked Sonny, drawing her attention away from his brother. Now it was Pretty Boy whose groans were distracting the class.

Rex leaned forward and said to Cal, "Man, you *are* good at this. You could even teach *me* a few things."

Pretty Boy looked at his best friend, always in awe of the way that Rex could surprise him, then back at his grotesque painting, but his admiration refused to falter. He looked back at Cal and winked. "Way to go, pal."

As paintings neared completion, the predominant smell of acrylic paint shifted to the odors of red wine and perfume as the women would sporadically reapply in the bathroom after their buzzes kicked up their perspiration levels. The entire room seemed to shift up a few degrees. The mounting, collective intoxication of the assemblage acted as camouflage for the band's caustic presence in the room as the banter got louder and louder. Hairdryers dried the canvases and aprons came off. Several of the women who feared and loathed the boys when they arrived would have gone home with them by that time.

Although Rex was still quite perturbed by the entire evening, a soft spot opened up in him after seeing Cal's eyes light up when complimented by Veronica – an occurrence that repeated itself throughout the evening. When everyone was standing and the four of them gathered by Sonny and Cal's seats, he looked to Cal and said, "I gotta hand it to you, this wasn't a *complete* waste of time. And you're one hell of a painter," and then to Sonny through an inebriated chuckle, "but *you* suck somethin' awful."

As per custom, every student was instructed to take his or her painting to the front corner of the room for a group photo. Rex held his painting close to his torso, painted end inward. The four of them stood in the back row. As Rex turned his painting around to face the photographer, he held it low behind the girl in front of him. Every canvas contained variations of the same picture: brown and green hills divided into the grid of farmland, a tan stretch of road lined with three Italian cypress trees leading up to a small white cottage with a coffee-colored roof. When Veronica counted to three before snapping the picture, Rex held up his canvas proudly, which was painted almost entirely in the same tan as the roads on the other paintings, divided down the middle by an elongated pink ellipsis resembling an exclamation point, the vaginal opening connected to the small, brown sphincter beneath by a gleaming white trail of semen.

"Cheese!" shouted Rex.

10

Pretty Boy grabbed his keys from the wooden stand next to the front door. The stand was a new acquisition. His apartment had become increasingly more spotless as the Lortab never allowed him satisfaction in idleness. By this point, he had stopped inviting his bandmates over, knowing that they would either wreck the place or inquire as to why he had suddenly become Martha Stewart.

He got in his car and drove to the dock, anxious to give the job another shot. This was very unlike Pretty Boy. His personality was very conflicted in the fact that he was simultaneously judgmental of others and overly critical of himself. He would beat himself up for days over a social folly, yet would also belittle others for their own shortcomings. But these abrasive qualities were laid to rest under the effects of the painkillers. He loved interacting with others, struggling to show his self-worth. He even enjoyed listening and getting to know strangers, whereas without the aid of Lortab, his initial reaction to all strangers was aversion. The more he noticed these tweaks in his personality, the more he questioned the immorality associated with opioid addiction.

He greeted Captain Eddie with a smile and a handful of cash to make up for the fishing pole. Eddie looked confused and Pretty Boy explained.

"Aw, man!" he replied with a smile. "It was an accident. Don't worry about it."

Pretty Boy understood the games that Tre and Manny were playing, but once again, the drugs in his system didn't allow him to react vengefully. He greeted his fellow deckhands with smiles and handshakes, all cordialities entirely genuine. They referred to him as 'Pukey,' and he wore the nickname with pride.

He was much more relaxed, this time, and the customers responded accordingly. His tip jar filled quickly as guests lingered by his concession stand to chitchat. His body moved with the motion of the vessel and no longer sent him staggering with every wave. When they reached the fishing hole, he walked the railing and talked up the customers. When a fish was brought on board, he would quickly identify it – sometimes even before Manny. He couldn't believe that he actually retained the fishing knowledge he gained with his father so many years ago. Some of the fish he had never caught before, but recalled from various shows and movies, little pieces of information that were lodged deep in his brain, miraculously located.

He helped a petite, trophy wife reel in a kingfish, after which she made a point to openly flirt with him. Conflicting with his usual protocol, Pretty Boy paid little mind to the cute blonde in the pink visor, and instead redirected all of her concerns to her husband. The man was obviously aware of his wife's overly gregarious personality and habitually hovered around the concession stand, dropping five's and ten's in Pretty Boy's tip jar in gratitude for not encouraging his wife's behavior.

It wasn't until the fishing was done and they began their hour-long commute back to dry land that his stomach started getting queasy. He immediately popped open a vial of Dramamine and poured half of its contents down his gullet. Luckily, the nausea plateaued right there and never got to any point that would solidify his new nickname with Tre and Manny.

By the time they made it back to shore, Pretty Boy's tip jar was overflowing. Even Manny and Tre seemed to want to include him in their previously closed conversations, especially after he adhered to their rule of splitting the tips equally among the three deckhands. He knew that this was probably bullshit as he saw them pocketing tips over the past two outings, but he thought it would prove more beneficial to make friends with his coworkers instead of arguing over eighty bucks. When they invited him for beers at a local bar, Pretty Boy employed a technique he used for attracting girls and left them hanging, wanting more of his company. He drove home singing his song about Lortab.

> *Lori, Lori, why do you adore me*
> *When everything that's good in me comes from your kiss?*
> *I want to be the hero of your sad story*
> *And forever have your taste stuck to my lips*

Coming home felt ultimately serene as he still wasn't accustomed to walking into an immaculate apartment. He felt like he had so much more space, like the feeling of lying alone in a king size bed for the first time. It was quite symbolic of the way he felt on the whole. The Lortab song repeated in his head. He whistled as he set his keys down on the entryway table and walked over to Virgil's cage.

"Man, I had a great day today."

Virgil looked at him and cocked his head over to one side.

"Oh yeah?" he replied nonchalantly. Pretty Boy's eyes widened and his eyebrows hunched together by the bridge of his nose.

"Virgil?"

"Yes?"

"Are you talking to me?"

"It would certainly appear so, wouldn't it?"

"Am I going crazy?"

"I don't think so. Am I?"

Now Pretty Boy's head cocked over to one side.

"I... Probably not."

"So. What all has happened since the last time we talked. Have you found a new god yet?"

Eyelids still peeled back revealing his white sclera on all sides of the irises, Pretty Boy shook his head quickly, incredulously, fearfully.

"Your father doesn't believe in God, but I'm sure you know that. Such a shame. And you? What religion are you?"

"My... my mother raised me Catholic, but she died when I was nine, and we stopped going to church."

"Catholic. Just as I suspected. That's why you need to find a new god."

"Is there something wrong with Catholicism?"

"No, no, no. There is nothing at all wrong with Catholicism. The problem is that it was what was *given* to you. It doesn't mean anything. It's been there since you were born. If you find God on your own, in your own way, it will be much more profound."

"Couldn't I find the same religion again, but find it my own way? Why does it have to be an entirely different religion?" Pretty Boy couldn't believe that he was so quickly succumbing to the idea of partaking in a theological discussion with a bird.

"It's just like your music. It's powerful because it's so *different*. Sometimes you need to see something from an entirely different angle to really comprehend it. And besides, all religions are the same. It is all *faith*. In fact, most religions are based on the same story. Christianity, Judaism,

Islam – they all have the same basic players, just different takes on the plotline."

Pretty Boy chuckled. *"Players? Plotline? You don't sound like you believe any of this."*

"Oh, but I do. I just believe it in a way that you're not accustomed to. It's just like a great book or movie. The most moving story you have ever read may have been fiction, but the *emotion* was entirely real. God does not lie in the details. It is about the feeling. Just like how a great song can bring you to tears even if you don't know the lyrics. Sometimes ideas are lost when you dissect them too much. No one believes the same thing anyway. All Catholics claim to live by the same set of rules, but they all interpret them in accordance with their own sense of morality. Rules were never really meant to be so stringently intertwined with religion. That was just to keep those who were incapable of understanding basic morality from infringing on others. If the rules were really that important, then more people should be following them, don't you think? But how many Catholics do you know that take the Lord's name in vain or engage in premarital sex? You see, the rules don't really matter to anyone, anymore. And maybe that's wrong or maybe it's right. Still, I think the important thing is the *faith*."

"So what religion do you think would be good for me?"

"What do you think?"

"I don't know. Maybe I could be a Buddhist... or a Muslim."

"Oooh. I've always loved the Islamic faith."

"Why is that?"

"Because it's so widely misinterpreted."

"How do you know it's misinterpreted? How do you know that that isn't the way it was supposed to be perceived?"

"Because it's so widely *interpreted*. No other religion has such vastly different takes on the same doctrine. Whereas different takes on the Jewish faith may abide by different dietary restrictions, different takes on the Islamic faith means the difference between *jihad* and *murder*. And it's always fascinated me that it is primarily the only religion where the jihad – the external jihad, the one that you think of when you hear the word – sustained the test of time."

"What do you mean?"

"Wars have been fought over God since the dawn of time. We can look at a terrorist act committed in the name of religion and easily dismiss it as ignorant and atrocious – and it *is*, don't get me wrong. But if you whole-heartedly believe in an omnipotent being whose entire existence is predicated on gaining followers and making all sentient beings aware of His existence, reverent to His wisdom, and adherent to His laws, wouldn't it make you want to stand up with force to everything that challenges your faith? It's definitely not *right*, but it is, most certainly, *understandable*. And what gets me is that this sort of complete – albeit insane – devotion primarily only exists in this one religion, nowadays… which is probably a good thing. Confusing, nonetheless."

"So how does all of this make me becoming a Muslim a *good* idea?"

"Because you are smart enough and grounded enough to have better interpretations of the religion and to spread it by example. All it takes is a tiny ripple to make a tidal wave. Perhaps you could bring peace and understanding to those who struggle with this – both sides."

"And what happens when my 'followers' find out that my faith was a result of a talking bird?"

"I've always said that religious doctrines could work loads better if they left a lot out."

Pretty Boy looked down to the carpet, chewing on the statement, on the entire conversation, yet no longer on the fact that his new mentor was a macaw. He looked back up at Virgil and asked, "One more thing: Why are you British? Shouldn't you be Brazilian or something?"

"Like I said, don't get hung up on the details."

11

The day Yoyo was set to arrive, Rex locked Brutus in the backyard and spent the morning cleaning his house. While he was not a stranger to the likes of a vacuum cleaner, he was quite unfamiliar with the more intricate side of housekeeping. For every task that couldn't be completed with a broom or vacuum, he used Febreeze and paper towels. Accompanied by the haunting soundtrack of vehement pig squeals, he scrubbed out cigarette burns in the carpet with his citrus flavored deodorizer. He wiped down the mirror with it. He even mopped the floor with it. By the time he was finished, the entire house smelled like a dirty massage parlor, like he was desperately trying to mask the odors of more sinister deeds.

He donned a long-sleeve, gray button-up. It was the only dress shirt he owned and was reserved for funerals. But it was also the only long-sleeve shirt he owned that wasn't a sweatshirt, and he felt like he needed to cover his tattoos for the initial meeting. With most girls, Rex flaunted his tattoos, his dredlocks, his entire rebel persona, but he felt like there might be a greater intimidation factor with a new roommate. And so, he tied his hair back with a rubber band, he refrained from smoking weed in the house for the day, and he endured the discomfort of wearing a shirt that didn't look like an overused washcloth.

Yoyo arrived in a taxicab in the early evening. She was short, skinny, and pale. Her shorts were ivory in color and an odd combination of short and baggy. She wore a white undershirt that probably would have exposed cleavage if she had any, and over it, a gray, button-down, tight-fit blouse with a V-neck reaching down mid-breast and sleeves that extended just past the elbows. Her hair was long and shiny. Her eyes were bright and round – especially for an Asian woman – and looked like they were popping out of their sockets.

Rex met her in front of the house. He smiled sincerely and extended his hand out in front of him. "Yoyo?"

She looked down at his hand, back at his eyes, then covered her mouth with one hand and giggled childishly while she nodded with the frenetic shakes of a bobble-head doll. She finally took his hand weakly and replied with a thick accent, "Nice to meet you."

Rex took her bags from the trunk of the cab and brought them inside. From behind, he heard the cab driver say in an angry tone, "Are you serious, lady?" By the time he dropped her bags in the entryway and turned back to see what was the matter, the taxi was speeding off, leaving Yoyo motionless and confused.

"What happened?"

She shrugged her shoulders pitifully. "I don't know."

"How much did you tip him?"

"Tip?"

Rex chuckled. "Don't worry. Come on in. You hungry?"

Once again, her head vibrated in confirmation.

Crossing the threshold into the house, Yoyo's childlike intrigue and joviality took a violent downward turn. Her face deadened as she saw the interior of the house. Although Rex had cleaned every exposed surface in the place, it still was less than inviting to a timid, foreign girl. Black posters covered every wall with the names of heavy metal bands beneath pictures of blood-drenched zombies, deranged butchers, and the ever-popular "Metal Up Your Ass" Metallica poster – a porcelain toilet with a giant blade sticking perpendicularly out of the water. The carpets were polka-dotted with burn holes. There were randomly placed holes in the sheetrock where Rex had sunk a fist into the wall in a fit of rage. As Yoyo followed Rex to the backside of the house toward her new room, Brutus pounded against the sliding glass door with a thud followed by more livid squeals. Yoyo shrieked and recoiled almost to the point of falling on her ass.

"Don't worry," Rex snickered. "That's just Brutus."

"It has a *name?*" she responded after catching her breath.

"Well, yeah," Rex said confusedly. "You don't name your pets?"

"We don't have pigs as pets."

"Yeah, I guess most people here don't, either."

Until this morning, Yoyo's room had been the Green Room. Rex spent a good part of the morning moving the bongs, pipes, papers, and baggies into the garage, and once again, dousing the room in Febreeze. Yoyo's room was now adorned with an air mattress, a stained comforter, an end table, two pieces of luggage, and a disillusioned, young Oriental woman.

Rex sensed her disappointment in the living arrangements and made a mental note to add a woman's touch to the place the following day. He thought he could stand to rid of a few of the more vulgar posters and perhaps buy a lamp or a rug to embellish the place. Still, he was quite optimistic about the dinner he had planned.

"I figured you would be hungry when you got here, so I tried to make you feel at home." Yoyo looked guardedly enthusiastic as he escorted her into the dining room. "I ordered Thai food. I'm sure it's probably not as good as the authentic Thai food you're used to, but I like it."

Her smile, once again, faded.

"I am from Taiwan."

"Yeah. I know. That's why I did this. You don't like it?"

"'Thai' means from Thailand."

Rex looked utterly confused.

"They are two different countries."

"Oh!" His eyes lit up in understanding. "I'm sorry. Should I get you some sushi instead?"

"That's Japanese." Her giddy disposition had become painfully deadpan.

"So… Do you still want to eat it?"

She spoke in a tone that showed both courtesy and distaste. "Sure."

The two sat down in an awkward silence, amplifying the sounds of forks and spoons scraping porcelain. Rex had so many lines of conversation planned for moments like these, but he never anticipated things to start in such a morose manner. Brutus squealed from outside. Yoyo's cheeks would tighten reflexively in annoyance when he reached the high notes.

"I was thinking," Rex announced excitedly, "that maybe you could teach me some Taiwanese."

"I don't speak Taiwanese." Her eyes remained on her food. Rex, again, was horribly lost.

"Wait… I thought…"

"We speak Chinese in Taiwan."

"Now that just seems *intentionally* confusing."

"I'm pretty tired. I've been on a plane all day. I think I will go to bed. I will do the dishes in the morning, if that is okay."

"Of course. Can I..." Rex searched for something to say, but came up short, and finally allowed her to retreat to her room. Despite the travesties that her arrival entailed, Rex was thoroughly delighted. Good or bad, things were new. And she did, after all, agree to doing the dishes.

The next morning, Rex awoke to find both of his roommates on the front lawn. Yoyo sat on a wooden dining room chair in the middle of the yard. The end table from her room was positioned in front of her along with a stationery set and a stack of printer paper. Brutus sat diligently beside her.

Yoyo had woken up before dusk, the jetlag still taking a major toll on her sleep cycle. She went to the garage and tore the flap off of a cardboard box. After retrieving her stationery set from her luggage and writing CHINESE CALLIGRAPHY on the cardboard in black marker, she turned herself into an entrepreneur.

When Rex walked out onto the lawn to investigate, Brutus puffed an angry snort in his direction, then looked back to Yoyo.

"So what's all this?"

Yoyo issued a slight bow from her seated position. "Good morning."

"Yeah, yeah. Good morning. So what's all this?"

She giggled. Rex couldn't figure out what the joke was. Ever.

"I'm trying to make some money. I'm selling Chinese calligraphy. Do you want me to write your name?"

"Hell yeah."

She proceeded to scribble quickly, yet precisely, in an indecipherable pattern. Rex was awe-stricken. By the time she finished, four characters with endless slashes going up, down, sideways, and diagonal stretched vertically down the paper. Rex was baffled how a three-letter word could be represented in four characters that not even Leonardo Da Vinci could replicate, even in an hour-long class full of alcoholics and easels.

"There you go. *Loo-eye-kuh-sih.*"

"That's crazy. Which part means Rex?"

"No. We don't have the word 'Rex.' This is how we pronounce it."

"And how do you say it?"

"Loo-eye-kuh-sih."

"Why can't you just say Rex?"

"We can't say Rex in my language."

"Yes, you can. You just said it."

Both of their tones were coated with rising agitation.

"But it's not in our language."

"'Loo-lie-kuh-shy isn't in *our* language, either, but *I* can say it. Hell, I could spell it, too."

"It's not..." As she struggled for words, Brutus nudged her dangling hand with his wet nose. She pulled an apple slice from the pocket of her blouse and fed it to the pig.

"Whoa! How did you do that?"

"Do what?" she asked incredulously. "Feed a pig an apple?"

"No. Get him to *not* steal it from your pocket."

She looked down at the pig in thought, then back at Rex. "I don't know. It's not really a problem. I think that we are friends now."

"You've been here one day, and you've already stolen my pig from me?" Rex smiled at the end of the question to show that he was joking, but sarcasm, it seemed, was completely wasted on the Taiwanese.

Yoyo's head slightly lowered shamefully. "Sorry."

"No, no. I---" But Rex was cut short as an irritatingly noisy, white Honda CRX with an oversized, unnecessary spoiler pulled up in front of the house. Two men emerged, ostensibly college students majoring in date rape. Both wore aqua-colored flip flops and undersized polo shirts. The one in pleated, khaki shorts was skinny and handsome. Blonde hair swooped out from under the backwards, sky blue baseball cap that matched his eyes. The one in jeans had a buzz cut and muscles so large that they almost indefinitely defined him as a person. The blonde boy approached her first.

"Well, hello there, Dollface." His eyes darted from Yoyo to the pig, but didn't comment on the strange sight.

Yoyo covered her mouth and giggled. Rex's attention was diverted from the intruding preppies and back to his new roommate. *Was this her natural response to any conversation?*

"My buddy and I were just on our way to the tattoo parlor. It's amazing really. We were just talking about how the Chinese symbols they have at the tattoo shops are probably all bullshit. And then we saw you. Incredible, right?"

Giggle. Hummingbird nod.

"So we were thinking that *you* could draw up our tattoos to take to the shop. How much do you charge?"

Yoyo's palms flattened on her miniature desk as she tried to revert from giggling schoolgirl to professional businesswoman. "Five dollars each."

"Sounds like a good deal," he said while thumbing out two five's from his wallet. "Can you show me how to write 'strong-minded' in Chinese?"

Rex stood behind her like a bodyguard as she drew up the characters with boggling precision and speed. Suddenly feeling like a third wheel in his own house, he retreated to the open garage where the Vanimal faced out to the street, but not out of earshot.

"I like your pig," said the blonde boy.

"Thank you. I like tattoos. Aren't you afraid it's going to hurt?"

"Nah," he replied coolly. "I've got another one."

Rex took off his shirt to reveal his ink. To justify the action, he popped the hood on the Vanimal as if he was going to do some much needed mechanic work, but he might as well have been staring into a dissected cow abdomen for all he knew about auto-mechanics. After reaching in and touching various parts of the motor as if he was inspecting them, he walked back out to the yard to ensure that Yoyo had seen his tattoos.

"Hey, Yoyo. Have you seen my socket wrench?"

Putting the finishing touches on 'strong-minded,' she looked up at Rex confusedly. "Huh?"

"Never mind." He retreated back to the garage, Yoyo left unfazed by his peacocking.

"Finished. *Strong of mind.* And what do you want?" she asked the meathead.

"I want mine to say 'power.'"

Rex's nose puffed in hilarity from underneath the hood. "Could've guessed that one," he mumbled to himself.

"So I was thinking," said the blonde boy. "That you should come with us to the tattoo shop. You know, to make sure they do it right. It's not far from here."

She looked at him in a fearful infatuation. She couldn't produce any words.

"Don't worry," he continued. "I'll give my phone number to your roommate here so he can make sure we don't run off with you."

This time her nod started off slow, but quickly worked its way back to a vibration.

He exchanged phone numbers with Rex and told him the name of the tattoo parlor they would be at. Rex was speechless. The whole point of getting a female roommate was to isolate her from the competition, and now, only a few hours into her stay, she was already being stolen away.

Just before she climbed into the little, white sports car, Brutus squealed mournfully at her feet. She pulled the remaining apple slices from her pocket and tossed them to the ground beside the pig, but Brutus' attention was locked on Yoyo. She crammed herself behind the folded down passenger seat, and Brutus laid down in the grass dejectedly. Even his pleading was obedient for Yoyo.

With a high-pitched groan, the Honda sped off down the road. Brutus picked himself back up, scarfed down the apple slices, and charged at Rex. Rex took one step back and braced his shins for impact, but instead of biting or butting him with his head, Brutus stopped short and grunted discontentedly, then trotted back into the garage.

Rex followed behind him, scratching his head. He wasn't quite upset, but definitely, very confused.

12

The low ceilings in Frank's house seemed to compress the depression, thicken it to the point where he could barely breathe. Wooden bookshelves covered most walls and touched the eight-foot ceilings. It wasn't clear if surrounding himself with the endless works of his heroes was meant to provide comfort or to impress visitors, but neither proved effective in its purpose. The ceiling fan that circled overhead looked decades old. The candelabra style light bulbs that hung from the fan were held by glass reflectors the size and thickness of jelly jars, but were slightly pointed at the ends resembling tulips. Walking through the living room, most would duck under the fan, although its clearance was almost seven feet. It never bothered Frank, but after being confined to crutches that added an extra inch to his height in the pinnacle of his stride, he began to wonder exactly how close his head was coming to the pointed ends of those glass light fixtures. Although he didn't go anywhere these days, he did have to make frequent trips between his recliner and the bathroom, the low-hanging ceiling fan directly in the path between the two.

When Pretty Boy entered, the first thing he noticed was the floors. The same 7"x 8" hexagonal porcelain tile that had been there since he was a kid squeaked beneath his shoes, but for the first time he could remember, he noticed ample amounts of dirt and hair layering the floor. His feet didn't slide the way they used to, but would stick, shortening his strides.

The flatscreen television that was mounted to the wall still had wires hanging down like entrails, umbilical cords tying it to the antiquated entertainment center that sat on the floor beneath. Inside the TV was a family lip-synching to an old Beastie Boys song, the basic daytime television program that existed only to let you know that you had nothing better to do in the middle of the day either because you were sick, you were lazy, or your life had lost all meaning.

Frank sat lifelessly on his recliner, crutches leaned up against the wall behind him, the end table next to his chair covered in cereal bar wrappers and Styrofoam fast food cups, his eyes staring through that television, through the wall, out into the world, into another world, another plane of existence where everything was different, where something mattered. The bags beneath his eyes slouched more than usual, as did his skin in general.

"What's going on, Frank?"

"Eh," he groaned. "Shit, shit, and more shit."

"How's the leg?"

"Still under layers of plaster."

"Does it hurt?"

"No."

Pretty Boy sat on the other recliner, the only other piece of furniture in the living room as the two other walls were inhabited by more bookshelves. Frank never had much company. The two sat in silence, watching mindless television programs. Pretty Boy wondered what good these visits were. It was ironic that the injury compelled him to come by more often, but the broken leg sent Frank into a depression that denied him any sort of social skills.

"Have you gotten out at all lately?"

"I can't, really."

"Why not?"

Frank puffed in irritation. "They've got me on these abhorrent meds. I can't stand them. Needless to say, the side effects mixed with the hindrance of the crutches leave this old bird pretty grounded."

Frank's personality could never have been defined as jubilant, but this tailspin he was in was quite new and jarring to Pretty Boy.

"What are the meds for?"

"Oh, just preventive maintenance, really. Nothing serious. I think I'm gonna quit taking them, anyway."

"I don't think you should."

"Well, you don't know what I'm going through, do you?"

"What's so bad about them?"

"They wear me out. I'm constantly fatigued, I get dizzy spells… among other things."

"What other things?"

"Dale, if you're just going to come over here to lecture and inquisition me, then I'd just assume watch my programs in solitude." His tone was hovering between playful and sincerely agitated. Pretty Boy used it as an excuse to use the restroom.

The restroom was in the same state as the rest of the house – not bad enough to be called 'filthy' (especially after having come from the homes of Rex and the Jam House), but still not the level of tidiness that he had come to expect from his father. His razor and shaving cream were left on the counter in a puddle riddled with stubble, although Frank hadn't shaved in days. There were three towels – one hanging from the shower curtain rod, one hanging from the towel rack, and one strewn across the floor – all of them wet.

The white towel hanging from the shower curtain rod was accompanied by a pair of brown slacks and a pair of white underwear. The underwear had a yellow circle on the crotch. Suddenly, Pretty Boy understood what Frank had meant when he said 'among other things.' He shuddered at the thought of his father pissing himself, struggling to accept what he had just done, then struggling physically to change and wash himself with a broken ankle and a pair of crutches.

He opened the medicine cabinet to find a small, orange pill bottle with a label that read, PRAZOSIN, and beneath that, TAKE 1 PILL THREE TIMES A DAY. He opened his phone and googled the drug to find that it commonly treated high blood pressure, another characteristically *old* ailment, another shameful aspect of Frank's life that he refused to convey to anyone, even his only son.

Pretty Boy had a four-hour shift that night at the bookstore. He was amazed that he hadn't been fired yet as he had been calling in more than he had been working. He figured the next time he saw an old friend from high school at the store, he would take off his apron and walk out the door, leaving the job behind without so much as a declaration of quitting.

Walking the aisles of the bookstore felt familiar and comforting, probably because he had spent the majority of his life cocooned by bookshelves. It was slow that evening. Although he should have been shelving new buybacks, he spent his time perusing the shelves, noting interesting titles written down the spines of books he deemed thin enough to have a look, and occasionally gawking at his female coworkers. Aside from the long-time manager, he was the oldest employee at the store. He realized that his fear of aging and his need for a career were totally incongruous with each other. Working at temporary jobs was a categorically *young* thing to do; nestling into a career was the opposite. But if he could find himself a job title that wasn't shameful to udder at the ever-diluted question of "What do you do?" he could go on enjoying his youthful hobbies of smoking pot and playing heavy metal under that comfortable blanket without questioning the next step.

On his way out that evening, he went through the religion section of the bookstore and swiped a copy of the Qur'an.

He boarded the boat early the next morning, beating Manny and Tre to work. He mopped the entire deck and stocked his concession stand by the time the others had arrived. While Manny and Tre enjoyed their pre-work ritual of cigarettes and light conversation, Pretty Boy hid in the cabin and began reading. After twenty minutes, he helped load up some of the bait and ice chests to show that he was a team player, then went back to his book below deck under the presumption that he needed to tidy up his station. Ten minutes before the customers arrived, Tre caught him. He eyed the cover of the book, first in confusion, then in shock.

"Are you planning on blowing up the boat today, Pukey?"

"Nah," Pretty Boy laughed. "Just studying a little."

"Studying? For what? Are final exams coming up in terrorist school?"

"No." This time, he didn't laugh.

"Are you a Muslim?"

"No, I don't think so."

"You don't *think so?*"

"Yup."

"So why are you reading the Qur'an?"

"Studying."

"Ugh," Tre groaned as he began to turn away. "This isn't going anywhere."

Pretty Boy put his book down. "I'm studying for two reasons. First of all, right when you saw what I was reading, your mind went straight to the idea of terrorism. Why is that? Sure, most terrorist acts are claimed to be done in the name of Allah. But Muslims exist all over the world, and yet almost all terrorists come from one general part of the world. So perhaps the ideology of terrorists could be more directly related to the upbringings and culture of that specific part of the world, rather than the religion. I don't know, but I'm trying to find the parts of this religious doctrine that could be construed as grounds to commit murder." Pretty Boy heard himself talking, and he sounded like Virgil.

"And secondly, did you know that the Qur'an, the Torah, and the Bible all begin the same way? They all worship the same god. Technically, Allah and the god you worship are the same being. The same story just got communicated and interpreted in three different ways. So how are Christians and Jews so much different than Muslims?"

Tre looked confused and uninterested. "I... I don't know."

"Neither do I. That's what I'm trying to find out."

He saw the revulsion in Tre's eyes, however minor it was, and he wanted to retract everything he just said. He wanted to explain himself better, but the only way to do so would be to tell him that he has to read this book as a homework assignment to appease his prophet-like parrot.

The more he backed away from the situation, the more he tried to see himself from Tre's eyes rather than his own, the more he realized how ridiculous this entire endeavor was. Perhaps this little mid-life crisis he was going through was taking a deeper toll on him than he originally thought. He had seen men a few years older than him divorce their wives and buy motorcycles, dye their hair and start hanging out in college bars. It was unattractive at best, but still infinitely better than the path he was currently walking. He put down the book and went out on deck, trying to alleviate whatever harm he had just caused his reputation with dumb jokes and playful banter.

The outing went well. Once again, he generated a great deal of tips that he – once again – shared with the other deckhands in hope to destroy the memory of his conversation with Tre. He walked in his house with every intention of throwing the book in the trash and seeking other means of overcoming his newfound fear of death and aging, but Virgil quickly derailed that line of thought.

"Well, hello."

"Ah, fuck," Pretty Boy groaned. "Are you serious? Again?"

"Again *what?*"

"You're talking again? You're fucking *British* again?"

"Well, excuse me for being me. *Polly want a cracker. Pretty bird. Polly want a cracker,*" he said, but still in his low-pitched, British accent. "Is this better?"

"I've got to be losing my mind."

"On the contrary, perhaps you are just *gaining* it."

"What the hell does that mean?"

"Well, all great discoveries begin with a paradigm shift. This could certainly be construed as such. Have you begun your search for God yet?"

"I picked up a copy of the Qur'an, if that's what you mean."

"And how is that going for you?"

"Not great. I'm only twenty pages in or so, but it just freaks me out. It seems to be more about what *not* to do and the consequences. It's like, if I'm not a 100%, God-loving,

God-fearing, holy man, I will be thrown in the fire 'made of bodies and stones,' to steal a quote. Well, of course I'm not perfect and holy. Of course, I'm unsure about God. Why else would I be reading the Qur'an? So as of right now, my choices are between living a godless existence like my father, or burning in Hell."

"Didn't I tell you not to get hung up on the details?"

"That's all the book is, up to this point. There is nothing beyond that."

"Of course it is. All Old Testament-era literature exhibits a wrathful and vengeful God. Just keep moving forward."

"And how do I read through thousands of years of religious history to get to some point of clarity without getting hung up on the details?"

"I told you I'm a fan of abridged version. Quit reading that book. Just google it."

Pretty Boy continued reading the Qur'an, despite Virgil's advice, but no longer took it word by word. Learning quickly the styling of how the Book was written, he began to skim the first two or three pages of each chapter. All of them started out the same: "God has sealed the ears and closed the hearts of the disbelievers," "The disbelievers will have great torment," "They will wear iron collars and live in the Fire." Over. And over. And over. Again.

He read these lines, and thought of his father.

He didn't want to think of his father shackled to walls of flame for eternity, but worse than that, he didn't want to think of *himself* enduring such torture. His father was just open about his doubts. Pretty Boy was silent.

As a teenager, Pretty Boy had attempted reading The

Bible, but just as now, got hung up on all of the endless, horrible punishment inflicted on anyone who didn't believe. It wasn't fair. He *wanted* to believe, but it just wouldn't come. That's why he was reading The Bible, after all. He was struggling to find God, but God just wasn't coming to him.

He had had a conversation with a coworker at a previous job on the matter, a coworker that said that he believed because it was logical – logical in the fact that if he believed and he was wrong, he would die all the same had he lived a pious life or otherwise, but if he *didn't* believe and he was wrong, then he would burn in Hell.

"But how can you *choose* to believe?" asked Pretty Boy. "If I told you I'd give you ten billion dollars to believe in unicorns, you could *say* you believed in unicorns and take the money, but could you *actually* believe in unicorns?"

His friend looked confused and didn't answer. Pretty Boy knew his friend would be going home that day to question his faith, and Pretty Boy felt his place in Hell was all the more secured.

As the words of the Book in his lap echoed through his head without meaning as they scanned by his eyes, Pretty Boy thought about how the mind works, how the more he tried to expand it, it was just the greater volume to contain masses of worry, fear, and self-destruction. He wanted to abandon everything he learned and to live more simply, without the thoughts screaming at him night and day. He thought about his coworker who could simply make a choice: God or no god. He thought about Rex, who never worried about anything that existed more than twelve seconds in the future, Rex, his best friend who was so completely different than himself in the way he thought, Rex, who could smile while burning in a cauldron of boiling dog piss as long as he was burning next to a pretty girl. He wanted to turn his head upside down and empty it out like a vacuum cleaner bag and start fresh. If he could just unlearn everything that he had lived for the past three decades, maybe he, too, could choose.

It was worth a shot.

13

Rex's head banged vehemently as he slashed at his strings, low-pitched power chords groaning from the amplifier. As the fast-paced triplets fell to a drop beat, Rex pushed his left hand away from his body, sending the neck of his guitar perpendicular to the ground, and jumped with his knees tucked tight against his chest before straightening his legs and bashing back to the floor in exact sync with the following measure.

Pretty Boy started screaming into the microphone.

Lori, Lori, have you got a secret for me?
What do you think of when you're alone at night?
The way I touch you must be an allegory
Because I'm swallowing the world in a bite

As the song ended, they all collectively looked at Pretty Boy, astounded eyes and delighted smiles all congratulating him on his contribution to the song.

"That was fucking amazing!" cried Rex. "This could be our opener for the Dead Still show. What do you think?" They all nodded in agreement.

Meanwhile, Cal and Sonny's parents were finishing up an awkward weekend at the ranch. Maria had told

Sergio that she didn't think it necessary to kick the boys out of the house, that they weren't ready.

"They're thirty, for Christ's sake!"

The exclamation quickly sent Maria back out into the woods to cleanse herself by connecting with nature. Sergio began hammering sixteen-penny nails to a 4x4 behind the house, the purpose only being to relieve his mounting frustration. He was tired of living in a house, in a life, that was run by his family entirely against his will. His father would have never stood for this. His grandfather would have disowned him for allowing it to come to this. His boys were not men, and his wife didn't respect him.

The drive home was painfully uncomfortable. As per usual, the radio whispered classical music at a low volume, to Sergio's dismay. It had always made him want to fall asleep, but at this moment, he was far too consumed in thought to doze off. He grinded his teeth and clenched the steering wheel with sweaty palms. His mind teetered between the two sides: on one, he could appease his wife and children and once again sacrifice his needs for the wants of his family, and on the other, he could be a man, the patriarch of the family, and finally do just *one* thing to please himself.

Maria studied her husband's distraught face. Silently, she reached for the radio and pressed preset 2, a Tejano station, and slightly raised the volume.

Once again, a small and trivial peace offering temporarily mollified a deeply rooted problem that had persisted through the duration of their marriage.

In between songs, Sonny filled up a beer bong with a cold, bottle of Budweiser. He poured it with precision, careful not to leave too much foam.

"You're really hitting it hard today," commented Pretty Boy.

"It's my first weekend after the promotion. I'm celebrating." With that, Sonny went down to one knee as Rex hoisted up the funnel end of the beer bong. The golden liquid quickly drained from the tube as it shot down Sonny's esophagus. Sonny stood, belched, and took the beer bong from Rex, emptying the excess foam onto the carpet.

"Are you sure this is cool?" asked Pretty Boy.

"Who gives a fuck? We're being kicked out anyway. Fuck my parents."

Sergio and Maria pulled up in the driveway that ran alongside the house. The backyard was unmowed, tall grass doing a mediocre job at hiding the empty beer cans that littered the entire property.

They entered through the sliding glass door that opened into the living room in the back of the house, and were almost rendered unconscious from the smell. It seemed that every food, beverage, and drug the boys ingested over the past three days was only partially consumed, the remainders left to permeate through the house. The floor was thoroughly stained, mostly with beer, but also cigarette burns and pizza sauce. Paper bags from every fast food restaurant in the area covered the coffee table alongside a pornographic magazine, an overstuffed ashtray, and always, always more beer cans. The kitchen counters had three different pans filled with the remnants of three different Hamburger Helper dinners. Dishes were piled high out of both sink compartments and overflowed onto the counter beside the sink. The microwave was left open, revealing its interior, which was splattered with the guts of some over-zapped leftovers. Every step they took through the house added another nauseating scent to the olfactory assault they were being subjected to. Shouts and laughter echoed from the last bedroom down the hall, occasionally interrupted by the crash of a cymbal or some resonating feedback. Every muscle in Sergio's body was twitching. Maria rushed to the refrigerator to find some skullcap or chamomile tea for her husband. He threw the bedroom door open just before the boys went into their next song.

The beer bong was wiggling in the air as Sonny had just tossed it aside. It crashed into the carpet spewing out a few more suds from the tubed end. Rex was puffing on a freshly lit cigarette while adjusting the tuning of his high E string. Pretty Boy's hands that grasped the microphone slowly lowered to his sides as his eyes widened in disbelief. Cal slunk down in his chair, hiding beneath the cymbals. All four of them stood motionlessly, silently, as Sergio fumed in the doorway, his eyes darting from disaster to disaster.

"GET THE FUCK OUT OF MY HOUSE! ALL OF YOU!"

"Dad, this is –"

"I don't want to fucking hear it! Out!"

Maria rushed to her husband's side with a tall glass of an amber liquid. "Here, honey. Drink this."

His head darted between his wife and the catastrophe before him. His face melted between wrath and bewilderment. "Drink…? What? Do you not see this god-awful mess?"

"It will calm you down."

"Enough of this hippy bullshit! You!" his finger pointed sternly at Rex, "put that out! Practice is over! You all need to get the fuck out!"

Pretty Boy's thoughts were racing. Although he was eternally mortified by the state of the Jam House (despite his attempts to clean up after himself, as well as his bandmates), verses he had read that afternoon were repeating through his head. *'If two parties among the believers fall into a quarrel, make peace between them.'*

"Sir," he muttered. "If I may say something, I understand what this place looks like. I understand your frustration. But if we agreed to spend the rest of the day cleaning and getting your house back to the condition it was in before you left, could we settle this argument?"

"Before we left?! Do you think this place was anywhere near anything that didn't resemble a *fucking* garbage dump before we left?! You shitheads have been destroying my home for *years!*"

"Alright, so we will all spend the next few days cleaning and bringing this place to your satisfaction, but you still have to let us jam here. You made an agreement, and as the Book says, 'If ye give your word, do justice thereunto, even though it be against a kinsman.'"

Everyone in the room stared at Pretty Boy incredulously.

"Seriously?" Sergio looked at his wife. "Did this little bastard just throw the Bible at me in my own house?"

Pretty Boy thought about his recent studies, his conversations with Virgil, the drugs coursing through his system, and how all of those things were meant to better himself, to make him do more good. Initially, these were just excuses to take drugs and to alleviate his fear of aging, but this was a test, and he had to exercise those same values to do some actual, external good.

"I'm not trying to act self-righteous. We have been jamming at your house for years now, and we *all* greatly appreciate it. And I have to admit that I've been really embarrassed by the way this house gets treated. I know that I'm not totally blameless here, and what we have done is inexcusable. However, I also know what it's like to be on an entirely separate page from your own father – or own children, I guess, in your case. But if we can help each other get through this mess instead of abandoning it, maybe we can find a way to appreciate one another rather than just tolerate each other's presence."

Everyone in the room held their breath and looked to Sergio for a reaction. His breathing deepened, but slowed. His head dropped in thought. When he finally spoke, his voice was terrifyingly calm.

"That... you can't just... this place is fucking *disgusting*. There is no way you four could ever get this place to my satisfaction."

"Leave that to us, right guys?" Pretty Boy whipped his head around trying to incite some confirmations. "And even if you still don't want us to jam here, you don't want to throw your kids out. That's something that you can't go back on. 'Wives and children be the comfort of our eyes.'"

Rex puffed agitatedly. "Dude, where is all this biblical shit coming from? Knock it off."

"It's not the Bible. It's the Qur'an."

Sergio's head popped up as if a shotgun had just fired in the room. Without forewarning, he advanced with the speed and power of a grizzly bear, and landed a right hook to Pretty Boy's left eye, dropping him to the floor.

"So, you're a *Muslim* pirate now?" Rex asked Pretty Boy with something deeply broken in his voice. The four boys stood on the front lawn, evaluating their next move before going their separate ways. None of them wanted to go home, especially Sonny and Cal. They knew that when they walked back in that house, the lives that they previously led would no longer exist.

"I'm sorry. I was just trying to help."

"What the fuck has gotten into you? I always thought I knew you better than I knew myself, but lately, I don't know what the fuck is going on with you."

Pretty Boy thought for the words to say, but the only thing that came to mind were more Qur'an verses, and he knew that they would certainly fall flat. He wanted to tell Rex about everything in his life: the fear, the anxiety, the depression, the talking bird, but even if he found a way to present them, Rex was not in a consoling mood right now. Really, he just wanted to cry.

"Well, I'm going home," Rex finally said. "I've got to figure out how to save this band. *Again.*" He climbed into the Vanimal and drove off. He wanted to screech the tires and speed off to show his anger, but even if the Vanimal was capable of peeling out, it definitely wasn't capable of stopping afterward.

Sonny and Cal trotted inside like they were walking to the electric chair and listened to their father solidify two facts: 1) They were NOT allowed to jam there anymore, and 2) They were now down to two weeks until they had to be out of the house.

Rex came home to find Yoyo and Brutus playing on the living room carpet, much like he had done with the pig the day of his arrival. Her laptop was on the floor next to them, a Taiwanese talk show displayed on the screen. When the door closed behind him, both Yoyo and Brutus looked up at Rex, neither having the excitement for his homecoming that he envisioned before meeting the two of them.

"So what happened with those two douchebags from the other day? Did they call you back yet?"

"*Douchebags?*"

"Those guys that picked you up so you could watch them get their *awesome* tattoos?"

"Oh," she giggled while playing with Brutus. She

was down on all fours, elbows on the carpet, her face low to the floor while Brutus would stare her down, then run circles around her. She paid little attention to Rex. "They were nice."

"You came home pretty late that night."

"Yes." She still smiled, eyes locked on Brutus. She didn't pick up on any of the implications of Rex's line of questioning.

"So, what did you do?"

"What?"

"What did you do with those guys?"

"I watched them get tattoos."

"And then?"

"They took me home."

Rex started to press on further, but he quickly realized that he was getting nowhere.

"We might have a party here next Saturday," he lied. "Do you have any other *girl*friends from the university that you could invite?"

"A party?"

"Yeah, you know. Beer, music, dancing, that sort of thing?"

"Oh, I don't drink beer."

"Vodka? Whiskey? Tequila?"

"No, I don't drink *alcohol*."

Rex deflated like a balloon. "But you're a *college student*." They both stared at one another, but Yoyo didn't understand that the comment should elicit a reply from her. "Do you smoke weed?"

"*Weed?*"

"Yeah, you know." Rex realized where this was going, and accordingly backtracked. "It's a kind of cigarette."

"No, I don't smoke. And can you try to smoke outside, sometimes? It gets hard to breathe in here."

Rex stood still with his mouth agape, trying to figure out what to say, trying to figure out where everything went so hopelessly wrong.

"I'm pretty tired," Yoyo yawned. "I think we'll go to bed." She and Brutus marched off to her room and closed the door, leaving Rex baffled and lonely, standing awkwardly in the living room, no television to provide some much needed static stimulation to calm his screaming thoughts.

The next morning, he awoke with an unexpected optimism. Beyond all of the recent episodes in his life, the one, undeniable truth that it was all leading to was the Dead Still show, and his band, no doubt, was going to steal the stage. It was just up to Rex to make it happen, and he would do everything to ensure that it did.

He decided that he would use Yoyo's rent money to rent out a storage unit to replace the Jam House. Even if she wasn't the porn queen that he had envisioned and was less than taken by him, her emergence into his life had come at such a pivotal point that he couldn't help but believe that it was destiny. Although Rex was always quite a blithe and carefree individual, it was hard denying the tragedies that were firing at him as if out of a machine gun. And when his easygoing personality didn't quash the heartache, the upcoming Dead Still show usually did the trick. It felt really nice having something monumental and irrefutably positive on the horizon. Everything else was just pebbles being thrown at the side of his freight train, and everything would be perfect once he got it to the station.

He threw on his flame-retardant coveralls. He clipped his hydrogen sulfide gas detector to his shirt collar. He threw his hardhat, his welding hood, his light and dark safety glasses, his safety goggles, his leather gloves, and his mechanic gloves into his gym bag. He laced up his steel toe boots and exited to the garage, opened the garage door manually, and climbed aboard the Vanimal.

5:42 A.M. It was still dark outside. The streets were vacated, save for some other early bird refinery workers. It was the earliest he had ever left for work. At the refinery, he had to enter through a turnstile gate and use his badge to clock in. If he was one minute past 6:30, he would be docked a half hour, which meant that more often than not, Rex would race to work (as much as the Vanimal would allow) to badge in some time between 6:28 and 6:29.

He felt like a superhero, the savior of his band, like James Hetfield the week before the Kill 'Em All album was released. Because of him, Sonny, Cal, and Pretty Boy would soon be skyrocketed to statuses they had never previously known. At the very least, they would all be *local* celebrities in a few weeks' time.

He arrived at the Valero Main parking lot just shy of 6:00, a personal record. The parking lot looked so much different without a hint of a sunrise threatening to peek out over the horizon or a thousand other cars and trucks occupying 98% of the parking spaces. He circled around to the front of the lot. In the distance, he could make out the red, digital numbers of the clock above the turnstile entrance gate that read 5:58. He wondered if he would get thirty minutes overtime if he badged in by 6:00, an idea that had never presented itself to him before. On the other side of him were a few, lingering parking spaces in the front row that had also never presented themselves to him. The thought of not having to endure a quarter-mile jog to badge in before 6:30 was enticing enough to make him think that he might start waking up this early every day. As he spotted a parking space opposite the entrance gate that was just wide enough for him to fit the Vanimal, he cranked up on the hand brake, but nothing happened. He stood up in his seat, all of his weight pushing down on the brake pedal amplified by the force of him pulling up on the hand brake, but still, the van rolled on.

"Shit! Shit! Shit!" he yelped as he released both brakes and tried once more, but it was too late. He had already been turning wide right to make the angle into the parking space on the left, and instinct had him doing everything to *stop* the van, but nothing to *turn* the van, and before he could realize what was happening, he had crashed slowly, but loudly, into the metal turnstile. The engine grinded to a halt and refused to start back up.

As it turns out, 6:05 was about the time that the opening rush of employees coming to badge in began, and a crowd quickly gathered as a livid, mortified Rex and a shitty gray van prevented any of them from entering their workplace. Luckily, a few gentlemen whom he did not know helped him push the van out of the way, but the parking space he was previously aiming for had long been taken. They rolled the van alongside the chain link fence topped with barbed wire that surround the premises. But the turnstile, apparently, had bent in two different spots that didn't allow it to turn anymore, and so the crowd continued to multiply. Indistinguishable banter and laughter roared louder as the crowd grew, and all eyes were on Rex, who was leaning against his van and trying to think of anything to do with himself. He wanted to beat the shit out of his van. He wanted to shatter all of the windows. But more than anything, he wanted to run away.

Derrick pulled up in his brand new, navy blue F-150, the red and white company logo that vaguely resembled the Pepsi insignia stuck to both the driver- and passenger-side doors. He was tall, Hispanic, and had a distasteful sense of entitlement. His eyes looked tired and irritated. As he emerged from the truck, he donned his red hardhat, distinguishing himself from the normal white hardhats and identifying himself as a safety representative. He first turned to the crowd and shouted to them to go to the East Gate to badge in. When a few asked if they would be considered tardy, he simply replied, "I'll address that issue later." He quickly dismissed them and moved to interrogate Rex.

"What the hell happened here?" he asked Rex without a salutation.

"Brakes went out."

"So why didn't you coast around the parking lot instead of crashing into the main gate?"

"Look," he responded with hostility. "It happened really fast. It was like half a second between the time I realized the brakes were shot and the crash."

"Sounds like you were going a little fast for the parking lot."

"*No*, it sounds like my *brakes* went out."

"Anyway, we need to get you down to Analytical to take a drug screen."

The words were icy and jarring. He had taken several piss tests for the company, but he always knew that they came around the first of the month. The first week of every month, he would come to work with a contraption in his glove box that kept liquid warm along with a vial of synthetic urine. It was called the Urinator, and it was a flat, plastic bag wrapped in a fuzzy, white cloth and connected to a heating element that ran off a nine-volt battery, all of which could fit snugly in the crotch of his underwear. Today, however, was nowhere near the first of the month, and even if it was, even if he did have the Urinator in his glove box, he obviously wouldn't be driving himself to Analytical and it would be hard to find a decent opportunity to go to his glove box and shove something underneath his balls.

He climbed into Derrick's truck, the Armor-All on the interior door handle leaving his hand as wet and greasy as he believed Derrick, himself, to be. They drove to Analytical Testing silently.

Rex's thoughts raced on ways to get out of the predicament he found himself to be in. He thought about trying to make himself throw up all over Derrick's dashboard. As satisfying as the thought was, he hadn't eaten since late yesterday afternoon and knew that he couldn't make it happen. He thought about begging for mercy, but merciful wasn't an adjective that described Derrick. He kept thinking, all the way until the plastic cup was placed in his hand.

Alone in the bathroom, he began to curse quietly to himself, still thinking that there must be a way out if he could just figure it out. He went to the sink and turned the left handle counter-clockwise. He put his fingers under the faucet, feeling for the temperature of the water. After a few minutes, he thought that maybe they reversed the hot and cold for this exact reason. With the left handle still open, he turned the right fully to the left and waited for the water to get warm.

Three knocks pounded on the door. "What are you doing in there?" shouted Derrick.

"Pissing! What do you think?"

"Sure is taking a while."

"You want to come give me a hand?"

"Why is the faucet running?"

"It helps me go. But you yelling at me is having the reverse effect."

The water never warmed. He waited and waited. He waited until it was obvious that there was no hot water, that he was doomed, and that he, in fact, was not really taking a piss behind that locked door.

He finally emerged looking sad and defeated, and

held a cup full of cold water up in front of his chest.

"Looks awfully clear," commented Derrick.

"I drink a lot of water." He grabbed the cup from Rex.

"And it's *cold.*"

"I drink a *lot* of water."

Where two hours earlier, he had an unwavering optimism rooted in the belief that he would save his band and bring himself and his friends lifestyles that they had only dreamed of, everything now had suddenly become hopeless.

14

Pretty Boy stared at his computer with his one good eye. The images on the screen appeared in two different forms: one clear, and one faded and swaying.

Sergio had blackened Pretty Boy's left eye and busted a blood vessel. The subconjunctival hemorrhage left a large, red spot to the left of his iris and forced him to wear only one contact lens. Glasses made him feel dizzy and – more importantly – ugly, so he consigned to blurry vision and a lack of depth perception.

He was looking up Prazosin, the drug that his father was prescribed. He searched for the severity of cases that were prescribed the same medication, along with the side effects and whether or not they included pissing your pants. Based on his findings, his father didn't seem to have anything too much to worry about as far as his health was concerned. And he did find cases of urinary incontinence associated with the medication, but almost entirely in females. He looked up other causes of urinary incontinence, and to his fright, the first result was cancer in the pelvic region, including colon cancer.

What was almost as debilitating as the revelation that his father may, indeed, be dying, was the fact that his thoughts went straight to more selfish motives. If his father did have colon cancer – along with his late grandfather and uncle – what did that mean for his likelihood of developing the same illness?

He wanted to think of his father. He wanted to sympathize and yearn to help him. But Frank wouldn't even disclose any of his trivial medical issues to his own son, so how could he possibly confront him about something of this magnitude? Frank loved to sit in idleness and put his hardships on full display, but worse than that, he *despised* talking about said hardships. He merely wanted everyone to know that he was suffering, but refused to engage in anything that may diminish his suffering. And being that he lacked any form of a social life, 'everyone' meant only Dale.

It was so hard to take pity on a man like that, when every condolence was shot down as being unnecessary and somewhat effeminate. And still, he would grumble in pain, he would complain of his symptoms, he would give speeches about the terrors of growing old in a godless existence, then turn away any attempt at connection.

And so Pretty Boy looked at his computer and thought little about his father and much about his own midsection and what terrors could be lurking beneath the skin.

He looked to Virgil. "And what do you think about all this?"

The parrot cocked his head to one side, then shifted his feet back and forth on his perch.

"I might be dying. Don't you have anything to say?"

"You're beautiful," he squawked.

"Ugh," he sighed. "You're no use."

He needed something to distract him. He thought about scouring the internet for more information of the Islamic religion, but that surely would add a sense of finality to things that he definitely didn't need at this point.

He really just wanted to talk to Virgil, and he knew how to summon his friend.

He went to the desk in his room and opened the empty bottom drawer before realizing what he had done.

"FUCK! No! No! No!"

He ran to the washing machine where a load was still going through the spin cycle. He flung the door open, which then bounced back down and smashed three fingers on his right hand. Not to be distracted, he threw the door back open and started hurling clothes onto the floor behind him. He came across the cargo shorts that he was wearing yesterday and rummaged through the pockets.

Foolishly, he had put his last six Lortab in his pocket without any sort of container for easy access in case he felt the need to pop a pill in a social atmosphere. He emptied the pockets of all the solid items he had also accidentally left to be washed, then turned both of the side pockets inside out. The white fabric of the left pocket was smeared with a light pink residue, somewhere between a powder and a sludge. Without contemplation, Pretty Boy began licking the residue, the taste overwhelmingly bitter and causing him to gag, but he forced himself to swallow.

He looked at Virgil and began worrying what would happen when he became just a bird again.

Terrified that this would be his last little, drug-induced holiday, he put the entire pocket in his mouth and sucked on it like a mesh feeder given to a baby.

He sat in a yoga position on the floor in front of the birdcage. He watched the bird, beckoning him to speak. Hours passed. He looked at the subtle lines dividing the barbs on his tail feathers. He watched how his movements were so quick and purposeful. He looked at his eyes and searched for some sign of recognition. His head began to bob as he struggled against drowsiness. He was jarred awake repeatedly, a common side effect with the Lortab.

Every time he was shocked back into consciousness, he hoped that it was, in fact, a result of the painkillers, and would look at the bird to confirm this thought. But still, the bird was just that. A bird.

Pretty Boy climbed into a standing position and stumbled recklessly toward the light switch.

"Whoa!" cried Virgil. "Don't knock my cage over, druggie!"

Pretty Boy gasped in shock. "Are you serious? After all this time?"

"After all this time *what?*"

"I've been waiting for you to talk for hours."

"I know. It was completely creepy. You've got to stop doing that." Virgil shifted to the edge of his perch. "How are things? Not so good, judging by your eye."

"Yeah, not so good."

"Well, no use in stewing over it. I think you – *we* – need to go outside."

"Outside? Where?"

"Is there a park nearby? I want to mingle."

"Really? You think that's a good idea?"

"Have I ever steered you wrong before?"

"Kind of."

Pretty Boy loaded up the birdcage in his car (Virgil insisted that he ride in the cage under the assumption that he wouldn't be able to keep his balance without his perch) and the two headed down toward the ocean.

Cole Park was the largest park in the city. A playground, a small amphitheater, a skate park, and a bike trail stretched alongside the ocean before the downtown skyline. Green hills rolled down to the concrete trail that traced the coastline. Waves crashed lazily in the inlet near the parking lot. The sun was gently setting behind the buildings of the financial district. Kites speckled the pink sky like gray stars, strings stretching down to children running the hilly, green patch between the theater and the skate park. Aside from the playground and the skate park – which were both crammed full of families and potheads, respectively – the park was mostly deserted. A few women in sports bras and spandex pants ran the endless sidewalks pushing jogging strollers. A couple strolled slowly and aimlessly around a picnic area. An unexpected cool breeze blew by making every tree, every wave, every blade of grass come to life. The evening sky changed colors so quickly yet so stealthily, as did the clouds that seemed to appear and disappear in a minute's time, yet always remained still.

Pretty Boy walked down to the rocks where the waves came drifting in, Virgil perched atop his right shoulder. A pretty girl hidden beneath thick-framed glasses and a gray hooded sweatshirt drawn tight around her face (despite the heat) walked past clutching a paperback book to her chest.

"Pretty girl! Pretty girl!" squawked Virgil. "He's single! Pretty girl!"

The girl turned her head back toward them and smiled guardedly. Pretty Boy noticed her coming and going out of his peripheral vision, but never turned his head to engage.

Virgil threw his voice back down an octave. "You know, you could have had that girl."

"How do you know?"

"Because she looked back at you."

"She looked back because she just got hit on by a parrot."

"Believe what you want," Virgil replied.

The two stood in silence, looking out in different directions, watching the water, the sky, the Harbor Bridge that stretched out over the water in the distance, the kids playing, the skaters springing up over the horizon of the bowl, then down again.

"Look out that way." Virgil's right foot went up, pointing its front two toes out toward the water. "If you keep going that way, way out past the water, that's my home."

"You're from the Amazon, right?"

"Yup."

"But that way is north."

"Yup."

"The Amazon is south."

"Yup."

"Ummm... okay."

"The world is spherical, so if you go in any one direction, you'll end right back where you came from. That's what you need to realize."

"What's that supposed to mean?"

"You're so worried about the future, about what's to come, but you can always end right back here." He paused dramatically. "Look out there. Think about me, and my home that you've never seen, the rainforest that you know only from nature shows. I traveled all the way here, to this point, and to get back home, I can just keep going. Look out there to the ocean. Think about all of the things that exist if I were to head in that direction. I would cross treacherous seas. I would cross deserts. I would cross mountains, and glaciers, and storms. I would see vastly different cultures, cities and villages. I would see animals that I'd never known about before. It would most certainly be dangerous. But eventually, I'd end right back where I was born."

"Alright? I don't get it."

"Now look back behind you. We can almost see your house. This is where you've been. This is the first thirty-one years of your life. That's it. A few neighborhoods, a park, a mall. Your living room. Your bedroom. Your bathroom. That's it.

"Now look back to the ocean again, and remember all of those places I would pass to get back home. Think about the *billions* of people and all the experiences just waiting for you. Doesn't your home behind you seem bland? Everything out that way is dangerous and scary and there is a *good* chance you will die. But everything that you see, good and bad, will not be the things behind you. Everything that is new is *good,* even if it is hard to swallow. And eventually, you'll be back here anyway. That's all dying is.

"You are scared of getting old, but everything that you have done to this point – playing heavy metal, banging random girls, smoking pot with the same three guys – would you really want to do that forever? Wouldn't it get old at some point? And so instead, you can venture out into uncharted waters, where things will be difficult and different, but they will all be *new.* Some of it might be bad, but a lot of it might be pretty damned awesome."

"Man," Pretty Boy scoffed, "do you always have to be so *deep?*"

"Certainly not. I hit on that girl for you, didn't I?"

Pretty Boy laughed and shook the moment off, but looking out into the ocean, something down in his belly unclenched. He still had fear and discomfort and anxiety, but a tiny, little dark spot within him gently evaporated out his pores and blew away with the wind, dissipating into the now indigo sky. He turned his head and looked at the bird perched on his shoulder and felt thankful. Whatever was out there, whether it was God or Allah or evolution, it had granted him something unique and profound. He looked back behind him, back toward his house, and remembered that he had no more painkillers and this would very likely be the last conversation he would be able to have with

Virgil.

"I really don't want you to leave."

"I'm not *really* going to fly to the North Pole and back. It was a metaphor."

"That's not what I meant."

"Oh? Why would I go anywhere?"

"You wouldn't understand."

"*I wouldn't understand why I would go anywhere?* Yes, you're probably right."

"Not that. It… it just won't be the same."

"Why not?"

"I told you. You wouldn't understand."

"Try me."

Pretty Boy took a deep breath. "You only talk to me because of the drugs. Once the drugs are gone, you'll just be a bird again."

"Well, that is highly offensive."

"I didn't mean 'just a bird.' Birds are cool, it's just---"

"I don't give a shit about *that*. I think it's offensive that you think that I'm just a hallucinatory byproduct of your little drug binge – which, by the way, I do *not* condone. I, as a matter of fact, am quite real."

"But you go away sometimes. When I'm not high. You're just… just a bird."

"My life – if you haven't noticed – is a little different from yours. I need to recharge sometimes. It's kind of like sleeping. But when nothing requiring my attention is going on, I revert to the state that you are referring to."

"I would love to believe that."

"I *still* find it offensive that you don't. No matter. You will find out. You will *have* to find out pretty soon, what with your 'painkiller in the washing machine' predicament."

As the sky got darker, the two of them climbed back

into the truck and drove home, careful not to speak for fear that one of them would mention the thought that was echoing in both of their minds.

Maybe I'm wrong.

15

Cal and Sonny's parents had just left to the ranch. The second their truck pulled out of the driveway, the two boys occupied the kitchen.

On his way home from work, Sonny had wiped out the local pharmacy of their entire supply of cornstarch. They began stacking box after box on the kitchen counter alongside two unopened boxes of aluminum foil.

"I get what we're doing, I think, but how does the steel wool fit in?" asked Cal.

"Oh, the steel wool is separate from this."

"What?"

"Well, the steel wool is going to be something I'm going to have to design. We'll have to think about a way to make that one work. But this right here, this is full-proof. Already tried and tested."

Sonny showed him what to do. He preheated the oven to four hundred degrees, took out a twelve-inch by twelve-inch square of aluminum foil, and poured a large mound of cornstarch in the center. Using a spoon, he spread the powder out evenly, making a large, yellow circle in the middle of the shining silver aluminum like a miscolored version of the Japanese flag. He put the foil directly on the middle oven rack and set the timer for thirty minutes. Cal then began making replicas of the same cornstarch and aluminum Japanese flags and spread them out over the kitchen counter.

"What do you need to figure out with the steel wool?"

"First of all, I need to find something that will contain it securely, that is still breathable, and is conductive of electricity. Then I need to find a way to spin it."

"So you need a rotating motor that you could tie it to without it getting tangled up, right?"

"Exactly."

"What about Dad's grinder?"

Sonny thought about this for a moment. "But I need something that won't short out when connected directly to an electric circuit."

"The wheel isn't metal. It would be completely isolated from the rest of the motor."

Sonny's chin shot sideways as the thought penetrated the layers of doubt. "That's actually a really good idea. We could remove – no, *cut* – the guard so nothing gets tangled."

Cal felt proud. He was the younger brother, and Sonny – with his sense of competitiveness – wasn't one to compliment his sibling. The few instances like this when he did, Cal felt elated.

"So is this done after the thirty minutes are up?"

"No, you have to mix it to make sure it cooks evenly. Three times. It has to cook for two hours. Then it's done."

Cal – unlike his brother – did notice the mess that they were making and the fact that they were more than likely going to steal their father's grinder. He did feel remorseful, but his father was so far away – emotionally and geographically – and his brother was always so close. He wanted to refrain from further disappointing his father, but pleasing his brother was a much more instantaneous reward.

16

Some time between when Rex left for work and when he got fired, Yoyo started her first day of school at the university. With the help of the internet, she found the nearest bus stop, made it to school, and even found her classrooms amid the town-sized campus with little difficulty. What she did *not* do, however, was put the pig outside before leaving.

Timmy, Rex's fire watch, had taken half the morning off to drive Rex home. He promised to return that evening to help fix the brakes on the Vanimal. Rex came home in a state of despair entirely foreign to him, only to find the house in complete disarray. The bottom corners of the couch were chewed off. His dirty laundry had been strewn about the house. The coffee table was knocked over. Brutus even managed to open the cabinet under the sink and empty a bottle of window cleaner (that Rex didn't even know he had) on the living room carpet, leaving a giant blue stain. And, of course, a pile of putrid pig shit was strategically placed just inside the front door like a landmine.

Rex was irate. He moved to strike the pig, but Brutus ran hysterically around the house, squealing loudly. Rex chased him, not to be satisfied until he could seek some physical retribution for the injustice, *all* of the injustices that had suddenly befell him. Every time Brutus would come within striking range, he would turn on a dime and bolt in the opposite direction in just enough time to make Rex swing and miss, making him look foolish and heightening his rage. After crashing clumsily into the side of the kitchen counter, Brutus made the misstep of prancing back in Rex's direction. Just the edge of an open palm caught his ear, but it was enough to add an extra jolt to his already frenetic scamper, a jolt that sent him sprinting through his own feces, tracking it all over the house. Rex stopped, panted, relaxed his shoulders, and screamed. He screamed so loud that even Brutus stopped to take notice. The whole world stopped for a moment, but as soon as his lungs ran out of air, Brutus made a few more tracks of fecal matter, and the world went back to shitting all over Rex.

He sat on the couch in defeat, feeling like he may never get back up. Being the eternal optimist had its downfall: once defeated on every front, the drop into hopelessness was so much greater than that of someone on a grayer scale. Lucky for Rex, he didn't give up quite that easily.

He went to the refrigerator and retrieved an apple from the vegetable drawer by his knees. Much like he had done in years previous to fashion a makeshift pipe when no other smoking apparatus was accessible, he carved out the center of the apple. And much like he had done before, he stuffed the cavity full of marijuana that he had stashed in the overhead cabinet on the shelf too high for Yoyo to reach. He pinched the small wedge of fruit that he had carved out of the center and did his best to shove it back into place. With a low, raspy voice, he coaxed Brutus into his vicinity and placed the apple at his feet as a peace offering. Brutus, still weary of the man that had just chased him throughout the house to give him a beating, sat cautiously from a distance, eyeing the snack. Rex left the apple on the carpet and went back to sitting on a couch, watching the spot on the wall where his television used to hang. Brutus devoured the apple.

Knowing that orally ingesting weed took much longer to take effect than smoking it, and also unknowing of the marijuana to Brutus' weight ratio, he didn't anticipate the effects. Instead, once he allowed the gravity of the problems facing him to sink in and fuse with his insides, becoming a part of him that he must hide behind thoughts of playing monumental shows and banging beautiful women, he got up and started to clean the mess.

He began with the excrement. This time didn't seem as bad as last, maybe because he was a seasoned veteran, and maybe because it was just a small part on his list of things to do. Either way, the stain and smell seemed to come out with greater ease than the last time, although two darkened circles still existed where the both piles of dung had sat after Rex thoroughly soaked and scrubbed them with Febreeze.

He picked up the coffee table. He gathered his clothes. He threw away the scattered garbage. He stared at Brutus. Brutus stared at him.

Brutus seemed to be studying Rex, waiting for a wrathful punishment, baffled when one was not issued. He bore the expression of a man being offered a meal by his psychotic ex-girlfriend – sniffing out an opportunity for sexual intercourse, but mindful of the fact that the food was more than likely poisoned.

Rex was finally understanding that his relationship with his pig was a vicious and eternal cycle. Their anger fed off of one another's. Brutus would destroy the house, so Rex would scold him, so Rex would shit in the living room, so Rex would hit him, so Brutus would dig up the backyard, and so on, and so on. The only possible outcomes would be either turning Brutus into pork chops or waiting until the house was burned down after Brutus found a way to cause a chemical reaction by spilling household cleaners in his own excrement. And so Rex looked at the mess before him and viewed it as another giant shit the world had taken on his head, then cleaned it up without assuming blame. Brutus and Yoyo were going to live there, and the longer he let the pig tearing up the house or the girl showing no signs of interest bother him, the bigger and wetter the shit on his head would become.

By the time Yoyo made it home from her first day at her American college, the house was clean (save for a new, tan-colored stain on the carpet) and both Rex and Brutus were sitting on the couch, silently watching the absence of television.

"Um, hello?" she said, curious and afraid. Rex and Brutus both cocked their heads in her direction lethargically, all four eyes droopy and bloodshot.

"Oh, hi."

"What are you doing?"

"I'm trying to enjoy this," Rex said while turning back to the blank spot on the wall and making a languid motion toward it with his right hand.

"Enjoy what?"

"Not having TV. TV makes you lazy."

"I don't understand. Are you not being lazy right now?"

"Nope. Not at all. I'm enjoying life."

She stared at the pair of them a few seconds longer, trying to decipher if *all* Americans were this weird or if she was just that unlucky to land a roommate of this caliber, then dismissed the situation and went to the refrigerator to retrieve a treat for Brutus.

"Oh, and by the way," Rex continued as she dug through the refrigerator drawer, "I hope you don't need the internet today. Brutus here ate the Ethernet cable. I'll have to pick up a new one tomorrow."

Yoyo's eyes sucked up to the ceiling as she sighed silently in aggravation. She cut the apple in four equal pieces. When she approached the pig, his eyes blinked rapidly and he looked unsure of how to respond. Yoyo paused, observing the animal. Rex watched her reaction to Brutus and recognized a small hint of the same disappointment he had during his first homecoming with the new pet. Although he knew that the drugs he gave to the animal were the cause of Brutus' muted reaction to his master's arrival, he felt content at the fact that someone was sharing an infinitesimal piece of the misfortune he was enduring.

Yoyo held the quartered apple in front of Brutus' twitching snout. His head moved toward her hand, then retracted, then back, and retracted, and once more. Her brow furrowed in confusion, then placed the apple slice on the couch cushion next to Brutus. The pig hunched over to devour the fruit, his jaw working excitedly, opening and closing, opening and closing, but his nose was still six inches above the couch surface and the apple slice. Brutus would stop and look down at the apple, perplexed at how it wasn't slithering down his esophagus yet, then continued to chew the air above the treat. After his second attempt, Brutus plopped down on the couch and conceded to go back to watching the wall with Rex.

"What's wrong with him?"

"Who?"

"Brutus!"

"He's fine. He's just... he's... well, he's *very* relaxed." Rex grinned dubiously.

"You both seem strange," she said accusingly.

"Well, maybe it's the fact that my life sucks ass."

She kept her gaze on Rex wordlessly. He wondered how much of her disposition was due to a language barrier,

and how much she was studying him like a zoo animal –
even while sitting next to a somewhat domesticated pig.
Yoyo – with no television, no homework, and no other
social circle due to the inability to communicate with the
outside world without internet access – finally succumbed
to engaging her roommate in conversation. She sat down
on the far end of the couch, gently shoving Brutus between
them to act as a physical barrier.

"What happened?"

"I got fired today."

"Oh," she said calmly, looking down as if to weigh
the impact this new event would have on *her* life and living
arrangements. "Why?"

Rex coughed out a laugh. "Politics." Brutus snorted
as if he, too, understood the joke, even when Yoyo did not.

"Are you okay?" Her words were fearful, prodding
as if he was a wild animal, unsure of what kind of reaction
she could evoke.

"Yeah. It just sucks. I know I can get another job
pretty easily, but I don't want to. I know what I want to do
with my life, and that's music, but I can't make a living
doing it. It's such bullshit."

She replied in her usual deadpan voice, "My
grandfather killed himself because he couldn't support his
family."

Rex's eyes narrowed as he chewed on this statement.
Yoyo watched him as the words sunk deep into his core,
trying to work out some sort of digestible sympathy or
explanation.

"Like… with a sword? To the stomach?"

"No. Just a rope."

Rex looked disappointed by this. He looked down at
his lap, then back at the blank spot on the wall.

"And it was the Japanese," she said, "that would stab
themselves with their swords. Not Taiwanese."

17

It was the same doctor from last time, to his dismay. She was portly and wore a little too much eye shadow. She had the same disposition as last time – sweet, concerned, and slightly unconfident – only this time she seemed to be leery of Pretty Boy's ulterior motives.

"All of your bloodwork came back fine. Your vitals are all perfect. Now, if you're still really concerned, we can do the sigmoidoscopy like we talked about."

"No, no. Not yet."

"Well," she said, looking back at the computer, her eyebrows pointed in a worrisome steeple, "everything else looks good. That's about all we can do for you at this point."

"There is one other thing." His left eye pinched at the outside corner uncomfortably like he was asking for a hefty favor – which he was. "I've got this rear molar that's killing me. My dentist won't see me for another two weeks."

"I can refer you to my dentist. He can probably get you in this afternoon."

"Oh," he muttered, caught off-guard. "Really? Well, I'm really pretty partial to my guy."

"So, what do you want?"

"It just really hurts, and two weeks is a long time, so…"

"Do you want some pain medication?" Her tone and expression suggested she was asking her son if he got in trouble at school today after already talking to the principal and knowing the answer.

"Yeah. That would be great."

Dr. Benavidez began to leave the room, but he caught her as she reached for the door handle.

"I think I would like to schedule the procedure."

"Oh," she said seeming delightedly surprised, for some reason. "It's really not much to worry about. It's very quick and painless. You don't even need anesthesia. In fact, there's a location on the east side of town that specializes in it. It's covered by your insurance and they can have you in and out in under an hour. My receptionist can help you schedule it."

"Great. I have some special requirements."

"Oh?"

"No worries. I'll talk to your secretary about it. So can I get those pain pills?" Dr. Benavidez's contentment for helping a patient in need was quickly replaced by her previous concern with aiding a drug addict get his fix. She exited without any cordiality, and left Pretty Boy to anticipate his incoming Lortab supply, and fearing the procedure that he was about to schedule.

On the way out, he picked up his prescription after scheduling an appointment for this Saturday. Trying to not look like a drug addict, he waited until he got to his car to read it.

Virgil watched as Pretty Boy paced back and forth across the living room. His breath puffed quickly and deeply, his shoulders rising and falling, as his eyes seemed to be locked intently on the spot four feet in front of his stride, like he was following an invisible mouse that was running laps beside his coffee table.

"Five pills?! Five pills! That fucking bitch knows that I am struggling with the likelihood of cancer, and she gives me five pills?!"

A dumbfounded Virgil looked at him with wide eyes.

"Do you hear me?!" he screamed at the parrot, inching his face closer to the cage. "FIVE PILLS! What are we going to do, Virgil?!"

Virgil fluttered his wings as he hopped to the backside of the cage, his feet clinging to the metal grid as he hung awkwardly, head cocked at an angle to keep an eye on him.

Pretty Boy had already gone and filled his prescription. He paced the cold aisles of the drug store and waited for them to fill it. He immediately popped two before coming home. He wanted to sit and wait for Virgil to talk to him, to console him, but he had to get to work. It was his first afternoon fishing trip, and he was less than enthusiastic. As he walked out the door, Virgil shouted from the living room, "You're beautiful!"

Music blared from the boat. From the backside of the office building, he couldn't even make out the genre as it came in muffled puffs of noise. Rounding the corner, walking through puddles as the smell of dead fish rose exponentially, it became clear that it was heavy metal, to his surprise. The squawking seagulls made it difficult to discern, but as the metal walkway connecting the boat to the dock presented itself, it became clear that the music was none other than Dead Still.

On the deck, Manny was nodding slightly in tempo with the music as he walked languidly, assessing what was left to be done to prep the boat. Tre was much less guarded in his appreciation of the music. He was wielding a mop like an electric guitar, one foot perched atop a white-painted bench that ran alongside the cabin, and forcefully banging his head while squealing out the lyrics.

Pretty Boy really wanted to be elated by this discovery. He felt a muted instinct inside him that said he should, in fact, be giddy right now. His new job was coming more and more natural to him, and now he was learning that his only two coworkers were of the same endangered species as himself. But still, this was all presented to him behind the gray curtain of Virgil's imminent departure from his life. That little slip of paper that dictated his state of mind had already been whittled down to three pills instead of five, and was going to keep counting down to zero.

"*Stone by stone I am building the walls! Palace for the flaws that the memory enthralls!*" Tre shouted along with the song. "You know this shit, Pukey?"

"Dead Still," he mumbled with a fake grin.

"Oh!" they both shouted in unison. "I knew you were a metalhead!"

"Yeah," he confessed. He kept trying to act as happy as he should have been in the situation, but he innately wore his emotions on the outside and could do little to mask them.

"So are you going to the show?"

"Actually, we're opening."

Manny and Tre both looked at each other skeptically. "Opening?"

"You know, we're the first band that's gonna play."

"What?!" Tre threw down his mop and charged. With his arms locked around Pretty Boy's waist, he hoisted him a few inches off the ground, then seemed embarrassed by his actions and set him back down and backed away, still grinning wide enough to reveal his molars. "Why didn't you tell us? I didn't even know you were in a band!"

"Listen," Pretty Boy mumbled, abandoning his attempts at waxing delightful, "I've had a pretty shitty day. I'm gonna go get my stand ready."

As he sulked back into his little cave adorned with corn chips and canned beer, Tre and Manny looked at one another, unsure of which emotion to pursue.

"What the fuck is going on with him?" Manny asked rhetorically.

"Well, he's a depressed metalhead with obvious signs of a mid-life crisis and violent mood swings, and he's studying to become a Muslim, so I can tell you one thing."

Manny widened his eyes to coax a response.

"It's gonna be one crazy concert."

Although the afternoon crowds on the boat (as per Tre's description) were usually heavier drinkers – and therefore, heavier tippers – Pretty Boy made it home with lighter pockets than usual as his morose corner of the boat didn't elicit so much gratuity. He made it home just after dusk and slid through the door like a thick loogy squeezing through a tight drain in a sink.

"Uh-oh. And what's wrong with you now?"

"Son of a bitch," he groaned. "Why do you always come *after* I need you?"

"I'm not a genie in a bottle, so you can stop treating me as such. What's the trouble?"

"I went to the doctor today."

"Oh no." Virgil's head dropped exaggeratedly, but his concern was quite sincere.

"No, no, no. It's not that. But they only gave me five pills."

The bird's head snapped back to its normal position. "Are you *fucking* serious? That's *it?*"

"Yeah, that's it. It's a big fucking deal."

"No. *Cancer* is a big deal. Your little pill addiction is quite the opposite."

"Don't you understand---"

"No!" Virgil interrupted. "Don't you understand? Don't you understand that you just made me think – if only for a split second – that you might be *dying?* I really don't think an unsatisfactory prescription is too much to fret over."

"Don't you get it? *You* might be dying. Without the pills, you won't be *you* anymore."

"I told you---"

"Stop. I'm not in the mood for this argument."

Virgil sighed. "Alright, I'll bite. So what exactly *will* five pills do for you?"

"They'll barely get me through tomorrow! Friday, at best." He plopped down to the floor, his legs bent and crossed with a force that looked like something should have broken, put his face in his palms, and pouted.

"Are you really going to be such a baby about a few pills?"

His face smeared upwards out of his palms, his chin still cradled by the heels of his hands. "I'm really going to miss you, Virgil."

"Will you stop? I told you, I'm not---"

"Stop. Not now."

The bird obliged. Pretty Boy stared at him, studying him once more, as he thought about everything that Virgil had ever said to him. He thought about the speech about moving forward instead of staying stagnant. He wondered if the speech was meant to prepare him for his life without his feathered friend. He thought about how Rex looked at him the other day after the incident at the Jam House, how *disdainful* he looked. Had he lost his best friend? If so, that meant that his friend had been replaced by a talking bird, and that bird, too, would soon be leaving. He thought about how Virgil told him to look forward to all of the changes that life presented to him, but he just couldn't find any reason to be optimistic.

Virgil hopped down from his perch and onto the newspaper bottom of his cage, covered in white and green shit. "I know you're having some really deep moment right now," he said, "but could you *please* stop staring at me? It's really creepy."

18

Fantasy Checklist #2.

It seemed that the more Rex's house was coming apart, as was the band. They all gathered in a house that smelled like a landfill, yet was all but entirely vacant, offering no clues as to where the smells were coming from. They met each other with smiles and hand slaps that were meant to mask the feeling that they were drifting apart. The band was coming undone. And Rex, in the spirit of all that he was, was desperately trying to glue the pieces back together.

Pretty Boy was the only one that wasn't even trying to feign excited. This was to be his first sober band meeting/practice in quite some time, and he was less than enthusiastic. He knew how disjointed everything was, and his blatant disregard for exactly how horrible everything would become was his only ally at this point.

"So," Rex began the meeting, "Cal was first, and whether we use 'Dale' or 'Pretty Boy,' your name still comes before mine, so here we go."

Pretty Boy tried to remember that he no longer gave a shit about anything. He thought about his best friend that would very likely be no more than an acquaintance in a month's time. He thought about his new best friend that would be no more than a *bird* in a *day's* time. He thought about his father who could very well be a corpse in a year's time. He grasped on to his hopelessness and tried not to allow the moments unfolding before him register in his brain.

Rex extracted the note from the brown paper bag.

Pretty Boy looked at the bag and chuckled under his breath. It was such a monumental occasion for Rex, and yet it was marked by a crumpled paper bag. Rex never was much for presentation. It was an idea that could be revered or derided, and given the circumstances, Pretty Boy chose the latter.

Rex opened the piece of paper, read it silently, then looked at his best friend in scorn. Three words were scribbled on the paper: *Get a colonoscopy.*

"Is this some sort of joke?"

"No."

"Yeah, it is! I'm trying to do something awesome for the band and you want to turn it into a big shit show!"

"You said *write down something embarrassing. Write down something that would make you feel young.*"

"And how the hell will this make you feel young?!"

"Look, I know this isn't what you had in mind, but I was in a really weird place that day, and…"

"Come on! Out with it! You're a Muslim pirate who likes sticking things up his ass? Is that it?"

"I'm fucking scared, alright!" Pretty Boy dropped his head and allowed a few sobs to exit. They weren't entirely genuine, but weren't entirely fake either. He tried to think back to the day that he wrote those words and what he must have been feeling. He didn't remember feeling as bad as he did now, but something most definitely was wrong and had been wrong for a long time. He could have played it off as a joke, but whatever was broken in him needed to be fixed.

Whether this was the cure or not was debatable.

"I think my dad might be dying. My grandpa died of colon cancer. My uncle died of colon cancer. Now I think he is. And I'm worried that I might be next. I've been going to the doctor for months booking and cancelling this procedure over and over again. The day that you brought up this checklist thing, I just got excited that I might be able to share this with my friends, and I could finally feel okay enough to get it done and stop worrying – well, either stop worrying or start treatment, I guess."

Sonny and Cal looked at Pretty Boy, trying to find the right facial expressions to match his emotional outburst, then looked at Rex judgmentally.

"Listen, I didn't know..." Rex backtracked.

"I know, I know. Don't worry about it. It was a stupid thing to write."

"Yeah, it kind of was."

Sonny: "Come on, you asshole."

"What? It was. We were supposed to write something that would make us feel young, mostly because *he* was afraid of getting old."

"I told you," Pretty Boy retorted, "it *will* make me feel young to know that I'm not dying just yet."

Rex sighed as he consigned to being the bad guy. He looked around the room at his bandmates. "So, are we *all* really going to fucking do this?"

"There's a clinic that does something called a *flexible sigmoidoscopy* and we'd just have to pay our copay. It's really quick and isn't a big deal. Look, I know I'm asking a lot from you guys to do this with me, but it would really help."

Rex sat in the waiting room and wondered how his

best friend had muted him. He was livid at being forced to sit through a painting class, and now here he was, waiting with his heavy metal bandmates to have a camera shoved up his ass, and he couldn't say a word.

Everything in the room was the color of ivory. Rather than offering a little bit of feeling not offered by white, it made everything seem dirty. Everything was colorless and dull. Sonny and Cal played on their respective phones. Rex and Pretty Boy sat beside one another, arms crossed, trying to look past their angers, frustrations, and depressions to talk the way they used to, but it just wasn't happening.

Pretty Boy was called back first.

After he left the room, Rex looked to the brothers of the band.

"Alright, admit it. This is a *little* fucked up."

"Oh yeah," said Sonny. Cal nodded.

"So why did you guys make me look like a dick back there?"

"Because he's our friend, and he's scared."

"We can console him without getting… you know… *entered.*"

"Whatever. We needed to be here for him. You're his best friend, after all."

Rex forfeited the conversation and stared at the poster in front of him. It was a collage of doctors and hairless children. All of them were smiling, despite the grim tone of the message, of everything in this place.

TOGETHER
WE CAN FIND A CURE

He knew his friend. He knew him better than anyone. He knew he would read that same sign and extrapolate some huge, deeper meaning, how they all need to band together to fix all of their lives, but that was just the problem with Pretty Boy. He focused so hard on the big picture that he never truly appreciated the colors. He wished he could have found a way to tell him that, to tell Sonny and Cal, to do anything other than what he was about to do, but it was too late, the nurse was calling him back.

As he put on his blue gown that the nurse gave him after a cold introduction, Rex felt like now he was not only *volunteering* to get raped, but modeling his ass in a seductive dress before the doctor could cram things into it. Even prisoners had the luxury of surprise.

The doctor entered with an even colder disposition than the nurse. This particular clinic specialized in this sort of procedure, making this duty mundane and making Rex look like nothing more than a part on an assembly line to the bored doctor. He brought the tool in with him. It seemed silly, like it should be something fastened to the wall, but that would mean that it would be used repeatedly throughout the day, so Rex thought that the doctor bringing in a new apparatus was a good thing, but still saw the doctor as a predator roaming the halls of the clinic armed with a robotic dildo. A futuristic rape machine.

"Lay on your left side," he said in a monotone voice. Was it better that he sounded *bored* rather than *excited?*

Rex accommodated. He lifted the right side of his gown to reveal his bare ass, and he was feeling more and more emasculated. He would rather put up a fight and have a group of orderlies hold him down. It still wouldn't have felt great, but he would have felt less like a girl playing shy while offering herself with little prompting.

The doctor held the black, tubular apparatus, lubricated the end, and inserted.

"So, is there a reason you're having this procedure done? Have you been having any symptoms?"

Rex inhaled in quick spurts. He grimaced in disgust. His eyebrows formed an 'M.' "I'd appreciate it if you asked the questions either before or after the penetration. Not *during*."

The doctor quickly removed the camera from Rex's anus, the snake slithering out of the hole, followed by a long, airy fart. Seemingly unfazed by the flatulence as it was surely a normal occupational hazard, the doctor repeated the question.

"No," answered a perturbed Rex. "Just checking. Could we get this over with?"

The black snake went back in and Rex clutched the paper blanket with both hands. The doctor made a series of thoughtful groans and exhalations, the kind of sounds you make when going over a checklist, every noise more haunting than the reality of what was happening behind him.

"Alright," he said while snapping the blue latex gloves from his hands and into the trash bin. "Looks good. Nothing to worry about in there."

And with that, the doctor exited, leaving Rex repeating the words 'in there' in his head, cringing at the idea that his asshole was now a place that that man could refer to using a common prepositional phrase.

When Rex came back, Cal had already been called back, and Sonny was just being summoned as well. They passed by one another, but Rex couldn't look him in the eye. And this was how they were to bond, not by being young and adventurous, not by making fond memories together, but by *shame*. He walked with long strides in hopes that the bubbles of air inside him would escape in warm whispers rather than trumpet blasts.

He sat next to his best friend, the only two people in the entire waiting room. Pretty Boy wanted to go back to when they were twelve and they didn't worry about any of this shit. He wanted to be carving their names in the wooden siding at Polly's, listening to old Pantera CDs and talking about who liked which girl at school. It was something so simple and so beautiful, and something that they could never have back again.

Rex just wanted to not be in that room anymore.

"You all clear?" Rex asked.

"Yup. You?"

"Yeah." He looked down at his lap, then back at his friend. "So, do you really think your old man has cancer?"

"Yeah, kind of. It's so hard to tell with him. You know how he is."

Rex looked up at his eyebrows trying to access a memory.

"Remember when your old man told me that Enkidu could read thoughts?"

Pretty Boy wrinkled his forehead, but was drawing a blank.

"He told me to think of a number between one and ten and write it on a sheet of paper and to make sure that the dog couldn't see it. He would always sneak a peek. Then he'd ask Enkidu what number I was thinking of, and the dog would always tap his paw on the ground however many times I had written on the paper."

"That's right!" Pretty Boy exclaimed. "What was it he did to get the dog to do that?"

"He'd tap his foot on the carpet. He was trying to teach Enkidu to wipe his paws before coming in the house, but he could only get him to swat with one foot. So instead, he used it as a joke."

"Man," Pretty Boy smiled slightly, "it's hard thinking of my dad that way. He's been so different for so long. It's like he doesn't have any joy anymore." Both of their eyes lit in a cold recognition, the fact that that was exactly what Pretty Boy was becoming.

"Either way, it took a pretty cool dude to come up with that. He was pretty creative."

Pretty Boy thought about his father, his father who canonized all of the great authors that came before him, but never had what it took to join the ranks of those very authors he revered. And suddenly he was filled with that Sunday gloom, like tomorrow was going to be the worst Monday ever.

"So what do you think happened to him?"

"He got old." Pretty Boy looked away, contemplating his own statement. "I really think it was when we first got Enkidu. He wanted this loyal companion, but the dog loved *me*. It was like all he wanted was to have these profound relationships with his son and his dog, but instead, me and the dog got close and, I guess we kind of pushed him out."

"Still, he should have been stoked that he found a best friend for his son. *Second* best friend, anyway."

Sonny and Cal came out from the back at the same time, cutting the heartfelt moment short. "Alright. You guys ready to go?"

"Well *that* was fast," commented Rex.

"Yeah. Whatever. Let's get out of here."

"You didn't do it, did you?"

"What are you talking about?"

"You didn't get it done!"

Sonny studied his face and realized that he wasn't going to let it go.

"Yeah! So! I'm here for support, aren't I?"

"No! That's not good enough! Go back there and have them shove that thing up your ass like I did!"

"Why? What's the point? I came with you guys. Whether I get it done or not doesn't matter."

"We all did it, so you do, too."

"Cal didn't."

Rex looked to Cal incredulously.

"Really, Cal?"

"It doesn't matter," continued Sonny.

"Yes it god-damn-does matter!"

"Why?"

"So we can do it together, so we can all make jokes about it in the future, and have this experience that we shared together."

"That time we all got dildoed together?"

"Exactly!"

"I can still make jokes about that."

"Like hell you can! Not until you march back there and have that doc fuck you with his camera!"

"It ain't gonna happen!"

"Motherfuck!" he yelled as he turned away from Sonny. The receptionist slid the window open and eyed them authoritatively.

"So," Sonny said to Pretty Boy sincerely, "are you all clear, or what?"

"Yeah, he is," Rex answered for him. "And I hope *you* die of ass cancer."

19

Polly lowered a brand new white backdrop for the photoshoot and began using a paintbrush and red paint to speckle it with blood spatters. Mike illuminated the undersides of the lighting umbrellas while Pretty Boy was perusing the clothing aisles to choose his outfit. Tabitha wasn't here this time, which was phenomenally good news seeing as the rest of the band was there and Pretty Boy couldn't let them see her applying his makeup.

Polly sucked the flame of a Bic lighter down the bowl of a glass pipe. While struggling to hold her breath, she strained out, "I think we're ready." Sonny, Cal, Rex, and Pretty Boy all sauntered over to the lit up backdrop that now looked like a murder scene. The four of them stood side by side, all dressed from head to toe in black, metal spikes coming out of boots, wrist cuffs, and leather collars. After Mike readied himself, the four of them all made faces either tough or grotesque. Mean pursed lips, pointed eyebrows, and extended tongues played in front of the camera.

It was Rex's idea, and the best one he had had in a while. He knew that the band was coming apart. He knew that he and Sonny weren't on the best of terms. But more than all that, he, too, wanted his best friend back. And so he gathered the troops and took them back to their Mecca, where it all began, the birthplace of their mutually shared passion.

The photo was meant to be a flyer for the show. Although the concert needed no superfluous advertisement as the entire town knew of Dead Still and their local tour date. However, their intent was to have the radio bring the crowd to Dead Still, and to have that crowd leave the show remembering only Leviathan. A quick – and free – photoshoot could only solidify that lasting image.

Polly was elated to have Pretty Boy and Rex back in the store together. She hadn't seen Pretty Boy since her last photoshoot without him. It had ended so awkwardly, and it was nice to pick up like it hadn't happened without any drawn-out explanations. And seeing the two of them together – for the first time since the new Machine Head album came out – was seeing familiarity, something youthful and old at the same time, proof that some relationships can weather age and all of the horrible changes that come with it.

After the shoot, Sonny and Cal were drawn into the back of the CD room where a wall-mounted box television set displayed a live Primus concert. Polly interrogated Rex and Pretty Boy.

"So, how is Enkidu?"

"Dead," they responded in unison.

"What? Dale, why didn't you tell me?"

"I don't know. It never came up."

Polly took another puff off her pipe. When she exhaled, her lip quivered and her eyes got a little misty. Although Pretty Boy always viewed Polly as family, he sometimes forgot that all of *his* family was her family, too.

"My dad's not taking it to great, I think."

"How so?"

"He's just really morose all the time."

"Ha, *morose*," she chuckled.

"What?"

"Nothin'. It's just a word that I'd only hear from you, Dale."

"That's not all," Rex told her excitedly. "He got a parrot, and now Pretty Boy, here, has it. He's trying to be a pirate."

"That sounds about right," she replied matter-of-factly.

"What's that supposed to mean?"

"Nothin'. I just think you'd make a good pirate. You've got kind of a Johnny Depp thing goin' on."

Rex looked at his friend and laughed. Pretty Boy knew that this remark would not be one that he would live down anytime soon. With that, the two boys marched over to the paraphernalia section and looked at the new bongs, both particularly drawn to a twenty-inch glass number in the shape of a naked woman lying on her back, the mouth piece being her left foot that extended upward, the bowl coming out of her gaping mouth.

"That one would make a nice addition to your collection," Pretty Boy commented.

"Can't afford bongs anymore."

"What about Yoyo? Shouldn't her rent money at least *dull* the hit from losing your job?"

"Yeah, but I've got to feed Brutus most of my weed now."

"Ummm... What?"

"It's the only way I can get him to calm down. He loves Yoyo, but he hates me. Fortunately for me, he loves *weed*. Well, *un*fortunately, I guess."

"I'm glad at least one of us still knows how to live young."

"Why? Because I'm broke? Because I wrecked my van into my workplace? Because I got a pig that destroys my house and eats all of my drugs? Because I've got a hot Asian roommate that is lame as fuck? Because I'm over thirty and I've still got dredlocks?"

Pretty Boy stared, unknowing of how to react to this new, depressing version of his best friend.

"Fuck yeah," Rex finally laughed. "I just heard all of that shit coming out of my mouth, and fuckin' A, I'm awesome! You *should* be glad to know me."

Pretty Boy smiled. He *was* glad to know him.

That night, Yoyo went to sleep while Rex and Brutus were still enjoying a nice high and a movie on his laptop computer. Brutus eventually passed out on the couch. Rex wanted to move him to his room, but he knew it would be a bigger ordeal than it seemed. Rex fell asleep, excited to wake the next morning and figure out his next career move and find out what life would hand him next. But Rex was once again awoken by the sounds of footsteps, only this time they were not preceded by pig squeals.

Rex tiptoed into the living room, again armed with boxer shorts and a dull machete, to find the same intruder as last time, same outfit, only with an accomplice. The intruder had the same strange disposition, but his friend looked giddy, as if waiting to witness a spectacle, but still, unfazed by being caught during a break-in.

"Are you fucking serious? Uh-uh. Not again. Get the fuck out of here."

"But I've got a friend. You couldn't take us both. No way."

"With a machete? Quite possibly."

"Yeah, but we both got guns. There's no way you could win."

"You've got guns?"

"Maybe."

"Show me."

"No."

"I don't think you've got guns."

"You want us to prove it?"

Rex sighed in defeat. "What the fuck do you want this time," he groaned.

"The couch."

"Aw, come on! Where am I going to watch TV?"

"I already took your TV."

"Yeah, but I watch movies on my laptop on that couch." He grimaced as he immediately knew he issued too much information by saying that he owned a laptop.

"Just move a chair over from the dining room."

The two of them moved into the living room, then stopped suddenly as they saw the sleeping pig on the couch they were about to steal. Brutus, as if on cue, awoke languidly, looking from face to face, then got up, and jumped down from the couch, only his left two legs crumbled beneath his body, sending him crashing sideways into the coffee table, knocking over a half-empty bottle of beer that Rex had left there a few hours ago.

"Aw, Brutus!"

The pig got up and looked at the intruders dazedly. His head swayed, sending the wavelike motions gently back to his hindquarters like he was struggling to stand on a rocking ship. Finally, he stopped, he stood completely motionless for a few fleeting moments, then vomited on the carpet.

"Damn it!"

The two intruders didn't move a muscle, like possibly they were afraid if they moved, they would wake from this freakish dream. The accomplice finally started giggling and bouncing giddily. "Aw, shit!" he yelped.

"Don't mind him," Rex said. "He's just *really* high."

The two intruders looked at one another, the accomplice giggling childishly, the intruder slightly smirking, before they went to opposite ends of the couch and began hauling it outside.

They still drove the same blue SUV, which meant that the oversized couch was to be shoved in the hatchback after folding down the back seat. Needless to say, half of the couch was not in the vehicle. Rather than tying it down, the accomplice decided to lay across the inner half of the couch to weight it down while the intruder drove. As he started up the car, the red brake lights illuminated Rex's face, and he began to feel slightly emasculated. But then he remembered the reason he allowed them to rob him again – other than the presumption that they were potentially carrying firearms.

He walked back into his house and traced circles around the perimeter of his living room with his shuffling feet. The space felt so good, just like the empty space on the wall did. No longer would he have to endure mindless programs and hear about catastrophic current events from network new stations. No longer would he have to stare at the chewed corners of his already filthy and aged couch. He could have fought them, but he just didn't care that much. And in the end, it always felt better to ride the waves and wash up on the shore wherever the currents felt he should be.

20

Pretty Boy had just ingested his last three Lortab and was sitting cross-legged on his carpet and staring at his parrot. He remembered the other times he took this approach and how long it took, and then Virgil's derogatory comments once he finally came to, and so he abandoned the waiting game.

The roads were vacated as was the sky. No clouds blocked the rays of the sun warming the airs that were finally chilled after six long months of scorching heat. White seagulls hovered overhead, so majestic in flight, yet quite the antithesis when perched atop a garbage dump and squawking coarsely. It seemed that the scenery was quite representative of his mood. When life was getting him down, the skyline always seemed cluttered with endless billboards pushing goods and services that no one needed, but on days like this, they went unnoticed. The wide lanes of the freeway seemed to belong only to him as he pushed the needle of his speedometer as far to the right as he could. The engine groaned happily and the wind whispered forcefully as it bounced off the windows. The megastores and shopping malls thinned out the further east he drove toward his father's house.

Frank was on his recliner, as usual, and watching an

old war movie, which somehow, was infinitely less depressing than daytime television programming.

"Hey, Dad." It had been a while since he addressed him as such. It caught Frank's attention, but not for long.

"What's going on?" he said with eyes still fixated on the television.

"Not much. Wanted to give you an update. Virgil's doing great. My new job is pretty cool. Everything's going pretty smoothly."

"Mmm," was all he offered back in return. Snipers were picking off a troop as they struggled to find cover.

"Rex and I were talking about the funny stuff you used to do." His eyes didn't move from the television, but his eyelids raised. "How you used to pull those pranks with Enkidu. How you'd tell Rex that he could read your thoughts."

Frank chortled thickly. "Yeah. I forgot about that."

"Me, too. That was really awesome of you."

"Aw," he dismissed it with a wave of his hand. "You were just dumb kids. It's easy to impress kids. Adults, on the other hand, are a little tougher."

"Why do you have to do that?"

"Huh?" Frank turned and faced his son for the first time during the visit.

"You always blow everything off that's good and tell me why it isn't, but you love talking about how shitty everything is. Why do you do that?"

"Well, I don't know." His voice was gravely serious and condescending. "Maybe it's because everything *is* shitty. You see, that's why you remember all of these *great* things from your childhood, because that's what a father's job is when he's got a little kid: to pretend that everything isn't completely screwed. Then you get older and you realize for yourself how shitty the world is, and you get mad because Dad isn't making goofy faces anymore, because it's all just... *pointless."*

Half of him wanted to hit his father. He wanted him to know how horrible he was, how this pessimism was infecting him like a virus, ruining him, how none of this banter was poetic or literary, it was not a beautiful tragedy, but just a *tragedy.* He wanted to talk to Frank like Frank talked to him when he was just a boy and was crying over a dead pet goldfish, and tell him to just snap the fuck out of it.

But then there was the other half, the half that listened to his father rant, and *knew* that he did, in fact, have cancer.

When Pretty Boy arrived back home, Virgil still refused to talk to him. He thought about that old story about God walking next to a man on the beach, how the footprints became one set during the hardest times because God was carrying him, and he felt like the man in the story, wondering why Virgil would never present himself when he felt like he needed him, only he didn't feel like he was being carried. He thought about Virgil's God fixation and wondered if the bird could, in fact, *be* God.

The opioids tickled his calf muscles and had him grinding his teeth, letting him know that no, the bird was no deity.

He sat and watched the bird for hours. He waited anxiously for Virgil to get after him for his creepy disposition. He wanted to tell him about his father, about what it felt like to know his own dad was going to die, and to be less concerned with losing a father than with knowing what it feels like to cross that great abyss into the afterlife. He wanted Virgil to coach him through this insurmountable fear, to act as a father to him, or possibly even a deity. Virgil turned his head upside down to suck on the water spout angled downward into his cage, then looked back at Pretty Boy as a curious pet.

It was long past the threshold of the normal amount

of time it took the Lortab to take effect. Virgil should have been talking by now, and given that this was the last of the Lortab supply, it meant that Virgil – as he knew him – was more than likely dead.

He went to bed that night knowing that everything good in his life was leaving. Every few minutes, he was jarred awake by the drugs, just long enough to remind him of the pains of reality before retreating back to sleep.

He woke up well before sunrise the next morning. The house was dark and quiet, everything so empty and morose. He walked by the birdcage, looking at Virgil with a sort of contempt, blaming him for not responding to the drugs. It was an unfair substitute for grief, but it was all he could do to cope at the time.

He drove out to the docks with a constant aching to whip the steering wheel around and go back home, go back to bed, and go back to living blissfully, ignorantly, stagnant.

Manny and Tre had the boombox blaring Dead Still again, probably more to elicit a response from their coworker than for their own enjoyment. Pretty Boy boarded the vessel and began walking straight into the cabin without a greeting.

"As-salamu alaykum!" Tre shouted gleefully. Pretty Boy ignored him and went to manning his station. Tre followed close behind.

Pretty Boy began clipping the small bags of chips to their respective columns, organized by flavor. Tre watched with an offended confusion.

"So are you too good to say hi to us, now?" asked Tre accusingly.

"Why should I? All you guys do is mock the old guy on the boat."

"Are you *serious?* How do we mock you?"

"Oh, *come on.* You guys make fun of me for being in a heavy metal band. You make jokes to the customers about me. You literally *just* finished making a Muslim comment to me."

"Yeah, to make you feel welcomed."

"Horse shit."

"Maybe I was trying to be your *friend.* But I guess that was a wasted effort." Before Pretty Boy could respond, Tre walked back to the deck, already smiling as he cranked up the volume on the boombox and went back to jamming out with Manny as the two of them prepared the boat. Pretty Boy almost felt guilty enough to go apologize, but it just wasn't pertinent. The problems in his life seemed to melt everything else away, and Tre and his feelings just didn't fit in anywhere. Pretty Boy readied the inside of the ship while Manny and Tre readied the outside.

The customers that boarded the boat weren't yuppy enough to be easily impressed by every mundane detail of the outing. They weren't rich enough to be complete assholes. And they weren't dressed like avid fishermen, either. They were nothing special, Pretty Boy thought, and by that he meant that he had nothing to go off of to catalyze his stream of bullshit that would surely translate into mirthful smiles and exaggerated tips. He didn't want to make incredulous claims about his fishing knowledge in case they were savvy enough to disprove him, and their clothing was all bland and blank, not offering any clues as how to engage them otherwise.

All twelve of them – six men and six women (six couples, presumably) – stood out on the deck as Manny fired up the engine.

"Are you guys ready to slay some fish?!" Tre shouted over the pistons that were groaning to life. Various whoops and hollers answered his question. "We've been *destroying* the snappers, the groupers, and the jacks lately, so we know where they're all hiding and we can try to target a specific group of fish. Do you guys have a preference?"

They mumbled among themselves until one man shouted out confidently, "Snapper!" He was broad-shouldered and paunchy, but quite strong. He was the only one of the groups wearing a ventilated shirt, sunhat, and polarized sunglasses that suggested he had some fishing experience. His gray goatee and pink, sunburnt skin supported this theory.

"Great choice!" Tre, in an unorthodox move with a group of customers that he had yet to gauge in terms of amiability, pulled the elastic straps of a white hockey mask behind his head and held a chainsaw with both hands. "Then prepare yourselves for the *Texas... Snapper... MASSACRE!!!*" He freed his right hand to press the play button on the boombox, which began blaring a demonic roar accompanied by a dropbeat opener from the Dead Still album, and then hoisted the chainsaw over his head and began laughing maniacally. The crowd, luckily, ate it up. The men all chuckled to themselves as the women screamed in excitement. Hands were raised to the sky. Drinks were consumed. The tip jars were all shaking in anticipation.

Pretty Boy witnessed the spectacle through the windows and open doorway. While he should have been just as enthusiastic as the customers – as their enthusiasm *always* manifested itself monetarily – he watched as Tre danced in small circles, wielding a chainsaw that had no gas and no chain, and something darkened inside of him quickly and without warning. He could feel it blooming in his stomach, something cold and black, something that was drawing everything in, imploding like a supernova collapsing in on itself. Fear constricted around all of his muscles. His breath was icy, dragging along his trachea with a serrated edge. Cold trickles of sweat ran down the backs of his legs, collecting on the backsides of the knees. His vision blurred. His mouth went dry and his esophagus pinched shut.

The trip had just started. He knew that his only job now was to maintain. He couldn't prod for tips or make vacuous conversation. He could only take orders, try to respond accordingly, and not go completely *insane*. It was going to be a difficult day on the job.

As the boat crashed through waves on its way out to sea, Pretty Boy was reviewing the past few days' drug intake. He hadn't been drunk in two days. Last night marked the end of his Lortab supply. He definitely felt the effects, yet Virgil never came to life. Could this be a delayed effect of the painkillers? Aside from the talking bird, he never had any sort of hallucinations or otherwise perception-altering effects from the drug. It didn't make sense. Nothing did.

They made it to their first fishing hole. Only one woman had come to his concession stand. She had asked for six bottles of water, and Pretty Boy accommodated. He didn't help her carry them back. Had he not been wearing his sunglasses, she would have seen how wide and white his eyes were, how he was more afraid of her than most people were afraid of the devil.

The six couples cast out their lines. Manny made his way from the captain's chamber to the deck to note their skills and help where he could. Tre sauntered around the other side of the deck behind the customers, singing jovially, *"Snapper, oh snapper, we're going to eat you all."* Pretty Boy watched from between bags of hanging corn chips. He began to pray that no one else would need any sort of refreshments for the remainder of the trip. He would have gone down to his hands and knees, forehead touching the ground in the direction of the Mecca, only the action would have only drawn more attention to him and probably would have made him vomit.

The wooden paneling on the walls of the cabin was stretching and swaying. The stains in the wood moved and reformed like clouds in fast forward. He could see the wood stretch as they mounted a wave, he could hear the cracking as the splinters separated, then the walls would bend convexly as the boat crashed back down. He felt like any second, the entire ship would be split in two, horizontally.

Laughter brought his attention out to the deck. The entire assemblage rejoiced as a brunette woman who wore her white jean shorts up too high above the waist brought aboard the first fish. The man next to her put his fishing pole in the rodholder. Pretty Boy was terrified that this was a move to go inside to his concession stand, and in response, bolted to the bathroom and locked the door.

The bathroom was smaller than most closets. He wanted to stay in there until the boat reached dry land. Maybe forever. He wanted to pace, but there was little room to do so. He felt like his feet were sinking into the floor like quicksand. The longer he stayed locked in that bathroom, the more it felt like a tomb.

The walls began to pulsate in rhythm, like they were breathing, only they were inhaling more than they were exhaling, and in turn, were constricting around him. With every breath, the room got smaller. And smaller. And smaller. Pretty Boy was weighing his fear of coming in contact with the people outside and his fear of dying in that bathroom, and the scales seemed equally balanced.

This wasn't real. It couldn't be. But what really was real? Was Virgil really talking to him? Was his father really dying? How long had he been living in a dream world? Was he already dead?

In order to balance things in his mind, he placed his palms on opposite walls. He closed his eyes and felt the smooth surface of the wood paneling. He let all of his senses flow to his fingertips and embraced the sensation of the varnish against his hands. This was real. It had to be. It was just a modified reality, where something – the Lortab from the night previous, seasickness, his fear of death – was contorting his perception into this hellish nightmare. Only the fear was fake. He wasn't dead. He had to know this. His life was real. The fear was not. He whispered these facts to himself repeatedly, until he felt his arms bending at the elbows as the walls *did* close in around him. He felt screams, like vomit, erupting out of his stomach. And much like a sudden purge, he could do little to contain it, but could merely rush to a place where they would be more easily contained.

He put his face into the bend in his arm like he was sneezing, and muffled his scream into the back of his elbow. The walls vibrated reflexively. He laughed. Something about the way the walls shook in reaction to his screams was hilarious, and it pulled him away from the situation. He saw himself locked in the bathroom on a fishing boat, having some sort of connection with moving walls. If he could back away far enough to mute the terror, it was quite comical.

He tried to hold on to that confidence, that feeling that everything wasn't out to get him, and hid behind his dark sunglasses as he exited the bathroom. Instead of walking back to his concession stand, he was drawn to the sky outside.

The clouds were moving quickly, deliberately, being painted across the sky, stretching, growing, until the blue was being absorbed by the white like it was being erased. The sun was a defined circle – no rays blinding or blurring the boundaries. The yellow circle turned to orange, then pink, then blood red. The clouds moved behind the sun, providing a white backdrop to the crimson sphere like a

Japanese flag. The splashing waters that surrounded him grew darker and darker, almost black, and somehow, the ominous color scheme was beautiful, entrancing, but still haunting.

He stood toward the stern of the ship, a good ten feet from the closest fisherman, as he admired and feared the scenery before him.

Tre stood at the pointed bow of the vessel and looked out to the seas intently, wearing his hockey mask on top of his head like an extra face. "Holy shit!" he exclaimed. "That's an African Pompano… a huge one!"

The attention of the boat was equally divided between the husky goateed man fighting with his fishing rod and the seas out in front of him. Pretty Boy looked out to the black waters and saw something emerge from the surface about fifty yards out, then submerge again. Its brief appearance was as jarring and terrifying as a Great White's dorsal fin to a surfer. Pretty Boy gasped, then quickly covered his mouth with his palm, muting any screams that were likely to follow.

Down the side of the boat, the man threw off his sunhat as he struggled with his pole that was bent in a parabola. The white sky was fading to gray and began to spin around the boat. Pretty Boy looked back to the ocean. He scanned the murky, gray surface of the waters, waiting, fearing another glimpse of the creature that was engaged in a battle for its life. When it finally peaked over the surface again, something was different. Pretty Boy's jaw dropped and he ripped the sunglasses from his face, no longer fearing anyone seeing his eyes as a greater terror presented itself. *Was that a hand?*

The now-black waves danced in rhythm, almost as if they were choreographed to a soundtrack that he couldn't hear. He felt like he was watching an unjust battle, a war built on false pretenses, a slaughter that he needed to prevent, but he just couldn't make sense of anything.

With a firm kick, a human leg, covered by blue jeans and topped with a white sneaker, protruded out of the water angrily, fearfully, then was pulled back down. Pretty Boy bit his forearm so hard that it bled.

This isn't real. This isn't real. This can't be real.

Manny and Tre both paced up and down the deck. Tre grabbed the gaff, readying himself to bring the beast onboard.

"We can't do this!" Pretty Boy shouted. Heads whipped from spectacle to spectacle. No one seemed to know where to direct his attention. "We can't bring that *thing* onboard with us!"

Everyone was ostensibly confused. Only Manny looked angry.

Pretty Boy leaned over the railing and peered down at the black water below. Everyone followed suit, but glanced occasionally in his direction, fearful to miss either the emergence of the fish or another outburst from a deckhand gone mad.

The black waters paled in a blurred spot just next to the white exterior of the boat, then faded back to a smoky gray. It was close.

"It's going under the boat!" shouted Tre.

"Bring it back this way," Manny said forcefully while directing the man's body toward the stern. He kept a watchful eye on Pretty Boy. He could feel the creature beneath them, equally scared and wrathful, fighting for his life, knowing that the battle was almost lost. Pretty Boy looked back down beside the boat and what he saw ripped the air from his lungs.

A human face, familiar in its characteristics, grazed the surface and stared dead into his eyes. Wide, downturned mouth outlined by swollen lips. Pale, flat forehead shiny with oil. Eyes wide and sagging at the bottoms. It was his father.

"NO! NO! STOP!" He charged at the man wielding the fishing pole, but was intercepted by Manny, who tackled him and pinned him to the deck.

"Hook that monster!" Manny yelled to Tre. "I got Pukey."

"NO! YOU CAN'T!"

Tre reached down over the railing of the ship and extended the gaff down toward the surface of the water ten feet below. As the beast was impaled and pulled from the water, Pretty Boy heard his father groan in agony as if they were pulling his body out from his skin.

"PLEASE! DON'T DO THIS!"

Tre pulled the fifty pound, pale and shiny, monstrous fish from the ocean. As the hooked end of the pole that speared the beast came over the railing, the fish sprung itself off the pointed end and slapped the deck just beside where Pretty Boy was being restrained. His eyes were twelve inches from his father's. Both pairs bore the realization of the horrors around them, the intense fear and certainty of doom as the blanket of death fell upon them, strangled them, entombed them.

"I'm sorry! I'm so sorry!"

His father gasped for air, twitching sporadically, his eyes wide with terror and his mouth lunging forward as he searched frantically for oxygen, or possibly, dying words to his only son. Neither of them blinked. Both were helpless and scared, watching as they faded from one another's existences. The twitching came less frequently, then stopped. With one final dip of the chin, his father ceased to be, and Manny loosened his grip.

21

"Holy shit, that's a lot of weed!" exclaimed Sonny. Rex was preparing their ritual pre-jam joint. Four, large nuggets of green and red marijuana were extracted from a plastic baggy and placed next to a grinder and a pack of papers on a wooden tray adorned with tiki gods.

"It's not all for us." Rex grabbed three of the nuggets and placed them on the carpet next to his thigh. Brutus reflexively ran to his side and scarfed down the drugs. Sonny and Cal both looked at their friend incredulously.

"What?" Rex replied. "If I don't get him fucked up, he'll never let us jam."

Black cables were strung back and forth across the living room floor like road maps. Old, hand-me-down amplifiers were positioned around the room. A pawnshop mixing board sat atop an upside-down plastic bucket in one corner.

The incident at their last jam session at Sonny and Cal's house had barred Rex and Pretty Boy from the premises. As a last minute suggestion to keep the band alive, Rex suggested that they use his house and have a 'Silent Jam,' as they called it, with the usage of headphones and keyboard drums. It was not optimum, but it would have to suffice.

Rex, Sonny, and Cal were sitting cross-legged in different corners of the room. Rex and Sonny had their guitars nestled in their crotches while a keyboard rested awkwardly on Cal's lap. As he lit up the joint, Rex began to explain how this would work.

"Sonny, I've got you and me running through our amps so we can still use our own equalizers, then from the headphone jacks on the amps to the mixing board, then everything going back to everyone else's headphones... or earbuds."

Sonny seemed pleased by this setup. Cal was oblivious, trying to find the sounds for each specific drum on the keyboard and lock them in his memory.

"You think you'll be able to handle that, Cal?"

"Maybe. Where's Pretty Boy?"

"Man," Rex sighed, "I couldn't get a hold of him at all yesterday."

"Aren't you a little worried about that guy?" asked Sonny. "He's been losin' it lately."

"Nah. I've known the guy forever. He'll snap out of it in a couple of days." But the truth was that Rex *did* know Pretty Boy forever, and he knew that his friend was capable of making *anything* a life-or-death situation, and now his problem *was* death, and Rex wasn't sure of how quickly or how far this would escalate. When no one was paying too much attention, he sent a twelfth text message to his best friend, begging him to come over.

The three of them put on their headphones and tried to acclimate themselves to this strange, new environment. Rex looked around the room nervously, praying that the Silent Jam would work. The band didn't need any other setback at this point.

In their respective headphones, they all listened to Cal play around with his synthetic drums, getting a feel for where everything was. He was surprisingly quick at picking it up. Drummers, it seemed, were already skilled in doing four different things at the same time with every appendage, and their brains were capable of dividing themselves into quadrants. Rex and Sonny both nodded along with his freestyle keyboard drum solo, amazed at his talents. Once he felt comfortable, Cal looked up at his two bandmates, smiled nervously, and issued a solemn, "Okay."

"Alright," said Rex, looking back and forth between the brothers. "Want to start with 'Wasteland'?" They both nodded in agreement.

Cal tapped the F key on the keyboard, coming out in the headphones as four rimshots, and the heavy opening blared in their ears. Cal fumbled a couple of times in the opening, hitting a floor tom when he was trying to hit the snare, but tempo-wise, he was flawless. Rex shredded a high-pitched fill that he had worked on privately to create a flow into the first chorus. Sonny looked up at him, thoroughly impressed.

Throughout the recent problems that the band was facing, Rex was obviously doing everything he could think of to glue them together, and one of those things was embellishing old riffs to keep the band enthusiastic when going through the routine of playing old songs. And it worked.

The three of them were equally shocked at how awesome they sounded when all of their eardrums weren't being destroyed by the decibels of the Jam House. They flowed together smoothly as a single unit. Even Cal was thriving on his keyboard, not afraid to throw out gratuitous drum fills.

To Rex's dismay, Yoyo had stayed out late last night at a party with the college boys that had her write their tattoos. She was just getting up to go to class, and opened her door to hear the tapping of keyboard keys, the light twang of plucking electric guitar strings, and mostly, strange, heavy, spastic breathing. She walked in the living room to find the three of them sitting on the carpet where the couch used to exist, headbanging vehemently. It was quite the spectacle as none of the music could be heard, like watching a homeless man having an argument with himself. One by one, the instruments stopped playing as they noticed Yoyo's perturbed presence in the corner of the room. They removed their headphones.

"Where's the couch?" Yoyo looked at her roommate with a slight derision. Rex looked back at her, his head and expression both darting from explanation to explanation, but coming up short.

"I thought you people liked to sit on the floor, anyway."

She closed her eyes and inhaled deeply, then headed out the front door to catch the bus. Although the Vanimal was marginally functional again, she didn't ask for a ride. And despite her abhorrence of people confusing her culture with others, she refused to tell Rex that it was the Japanese that dined on the floor.

Although Rex knew that the two of them would never get along, and much less, hook up, he always felt this emptiness when she left, like there was some missed opportunity to find that essential piece of a friendship that had to exist between them if they could just find common ground. But today, he felt no such emptiness.

By the time he turned his attention back to the jam space, Sonny was playing a familiar melody, sliding up an octave before going into a low-end arpeggio. The tune was on the tip of his tongue, but he had never heard it in this style. It was beautiful and seamless, smoothly flowing and somehow simultaneously funky with hints of slap 'n' pop. The melody was entrancing. Rex popped in his earbuds as Cal whipped out a similarly enthralling drumline. It was almost all high-hat and snare, but the rapid fire on the randomly opening high-hat cymbal was so quiet and flawless that it blended perfectly with the bassline's heartfelt tone.

Sonny, it seemed, had commandeered one of Pretty Boy's microphones, along with one of Cal's bass drum mic stands, and was using the pair of them to amplify his vocals, which no one in the band had ever heard.

As he timidly whispered out the opening line in a choir-like voice, Rex immediately recognized the song.

"Blue jean baby," he sang. "L.A. lady. Seamstress for the band."

"Are you guys seriously playing *Elton John* right now?" Rex interrupted. They played on, ignoring his disgust.

In Brutus' first act of camaraderie toward Rex, he awoke from his drug-induced slumber, trotted over to Sonny, and shoved his snout into his face, snorting vigorously and breathing out sprays of pig snot right into Sonny's mouth.

"Aw, sick!"

The song dissolved.

"Never mind that," Rex chuckled, then switched his tone to giddy. "I've got a surprise for you guys." He looked down at his watch, abandoning hope that his best friend and their lead man would make it for this monumental occasion. "But first, let's jam another song. You know, one that isn't the soundtrack for *gay porn*."

They drove the Vanimal out to the amphitheater.

They parked up front, walked through the entrance gates, and meandered up to the colossal stage that they would be standing on in nine days, all acts made extremely bizarre by the absence of people. They had been all around that stage, walked by those same ticket booths, vomited in that same parking lot, but always surrounded by thousands of other people. It felt like the opening scenes of a zombie movie. They all loved it.

A short, pale man in his early twenties walked briskly in their direction from the main office sixty yards away. He wore a sky blue button-down tucked into khaki pants. The ensemble made him look even younger than his boyish face, like a kid playing dress-up in his dad's closet. It took Sonny and Cal a minute to figure out whom he was, but Rex knew immediately, and his appearance was rather unsettling.

He had only met him once before, and that time, he was dead. It was unnerving knowing a man only as a corpse, then seeing him walk up to you and smile. Greg approached Rex, and embraced him.

Rex was taken aback, not just by the hug, but by the life flowing through the body that was holding him. He never really appreciated the gravity of the feat he performed that night. It was just another funny, drunken incident to him, but now he was seeing a living, breathing person, a person that would be rotting and lifeless in a box beneath the dirt if it weren't for him. He wanted to cry.

Sonny looked at the shocked expression on his friend's face after Greg released him. "Do you two need a minute? You know, with your romantic history and all?"

Greg pinched his left eye downward toward his upturned mouth and issued a confused chuckle.

"Didn't you two make out in an alley or something?"

"Fuck you, asshole," Rex fired back. "I saved this dude's life."

"Yes, he did," Greg answered, unfazed by the inane line of dialogue. His face was glowing with gratitude. "And I hope I can begin to payback my lifelong debt to you today."

He took them to an office behind the food stands. Nothing decorated the walls. The desks were left unstained. Papers were strewn about every bare surface. But the tone of the place was still bright and cheery, somehow. Greg sat at his desk on a cheap, swiveling desk chair, the kind with a plastic gooseneck connecting the back support to the seat of the chair that you buy from any office supply store for thirty bucks. The state of his workspace was not at all indicative of the wealth he was born into. He opened up a laptop on the desk, and on the monitor was an image of the stage that stood just outside the office door, only in this image, there was no daylight. Three copies of the same man – pixelated face and goofy smile – stood motionless and equidistant from one another on the projected image of the stage.

"Rex has asked me to help set up your lighting. For the opening bands, we normally either play with the lighting live during their set or just set them to random, but for *you* guys, we can do something much more intricate."

Rex handed him a CD that he burned from his computer. He had spent all night compiling eerie sounds – crackling electricity, pipe organs, chanting choirs, revving chainsaws, gongs, and women screaming – to provide them with a haunting entrance to the stage. Greg played the CD, and as the onslaught of sounds pulsed and climaxed, he hit various buttons that lit the stage on his computer in vibrant flashes of red strobe lights and green lightning bolts. Fogmakers spewed smoke from opposite corners. The three, stationary figures on stage were mostly displayed as black silhouettes, but as the lights flashed, their images were defined in color. As the soundtrack grew louder and more terrifying, red lights flashed from the stage floor, illuminating the goofy faces of the three men from underneath, giving their ridiculous smirks an ominous quality. Rex, Sonny, and Cal looked on in awe. This was what Rex was waiting for. He wanted them to know what it would be like to be stars, even if it was only for a half hour, if they just came together and performed the way he knew they could, for thirty minutes, they could be *gods*.

He looked down at his phone to see if Pretty Boy had called yet. He had not.

As the soundtrack came to an end, Greg entertained them with other ideas. "We will have spotlights on each one of you for when your singer introduces you, but we could set them to flash randomly throughout the fast parts of your song. It would look like you would be disappearing and reappearing. It has a really cool effect. I could show you on the computer, but it doesn't do it justice."

"Can we play with the lights?" asked Sonny. He and Cal were very intrigued by this aspect of the show.

"Sure thing," answered Greg, "but it's pretty complex. It might be easier if you just told me what you wanted to achieve."

"Actually," Rex interrupted, "the rest of that CD is our set list. Why don't you guys pick out certain effects for specific parts of our songs." Sonny and Cal were giddy. Rex went outside to have a smoke, leaving the brothers to play with the lighting scheme, a gift he had arranged for them, seeing as they were all drifting away and it was his job to bring them back to shore. He thought about the band and how quickly and easily everything seemed to be falling apart, and how he was just as quick at reassembling it. He thought about that man behind the computer in there, the man that should be dead. He breathed life into him, and he could play god with the band, as well. This was something more important than they could realize, and when he couldn't remind them of that fact, he would just have to show them.

Sonny emerged from the same door he had just exited through with a grave look on his face. He held his phone out in Rex's direction.

"I just got this message."

Rex looked down at the phone and it was a link to a video that had been posted online. The title of the video was *Singer of Leviathan: Islamic Extremist?*

Sonny held the phone out in front of them, and the two of them watched along in horror.

"How did they even know he was our singer?" asked Sonny.

"See. I told you we had fans."

22

The aspect that makes any activity dangerous is its addictive qualities, and hitting bottom was no different. Just like an addiction to drugs, sex, gambling, or watching television, hitting bottom was feeling persistent and painful problems gently melt away, and after living with the pain for so long, it was so easy to keep doing anything that could offer numbness.

Pretty Boy awoke the morning after watching his father die in the form of an African Pompano feeling particularly numb, like nothing mattered anymore. After everything was dead, there left little room for concern. It felt strangely cold and soothing. There was finally a light at the end of the tunnel, but the light was most definitely a raging fire, likely to consume him. Quite possibly, he wasn't in a tunnel at all, but crawling down the crater of a volcano.

To make matters worse, Pretty Boy also awoke to find a dozen pills in the pocket of the shorts he was wearing yesterday, pills that he believed to be a gift from Virgil, a gift that the bird magically conjured and placed in his pocket, a gift that Virgil produced to bring himself back to life, a gift that he ate – in its entirety – as his breakfast. To thank the parrot for the unusual present, he loaded up the cage and took Virgil out for a little adventure.

"Look at this shit," Pretty Boy said to his parrot as they walked past a youth male fashion store in the lower level of the mall. "They advertise a clothing store with pictures of a guy *with no clothes on*. How does that make sense?"

Virgil, perched atop his right shoulder, looked at him like he was about to whisper in his ear, then turned away, whistling at pretty girls.

"All of this. These stores selling shirts for a hundred bucks, name-brand cosmetic stores, jerseys, caps, perfumes, washing machines, and purses. Why do we need any of this crap? Everyone's so afraid of not being cool, of not getting pussy, that they spend their lives in a futile pursuit, only to get wrapped up in this disgusting cycle. It's all just sex and money, sex and money, get money for sex, sell sex for money."

"Washing machines?" Virgil finally commented in a voice just above a whisper. "Are you saying that if it weren't for women, you wouldn't wash your clothes?"

"I'm saying that people buy these thousand dollar appliances just to make sure that the other families know of their elite status, that everyone has to consume and consume and consume because these playboys and sorority girls tell them they need to. And in the end, everyone wastes their lives on things of *zero* importance, and end up all the dumber." His speech lost speed. "I guess it makes sense, though. I mean, they revere beauty for so long, killing their own brains in the process, that by the time their youth fades and beauty is no longer attainable, they're too stupid to mourn it."

"I'm sorry. Aren't you a model?"

"Fuck no. I get paid a little money from time to time for some pictures, but I am *not* a model." He thought sullenly about the fact the he probably *couldn't* get those jobs anymore, even if he wanted to.

"So if you hate all this commerce so much, then why did you drag me here?"

"I need something." Pretty Boy pointed to a store on the other side of the carousel.

"Aw, no," grumbled Virgil. The store was at too great an angle to make out the name, and they were too far away to see any of the merchandise. Pretty Boy wondered whether Virgil already knew what he was up to because of some telepathic power he had, or if a parrot's vision was just better than his own.

Although Pretty Boy had done about a dozen photoshoots with Mike, he had never visited his store at the mall.

The shop was divided symmetrically down the middle. One side looked a little like Polly's: shelves were weighted down with overpriced, stone-carved Buddhas, Jesuses, Virgin Marys, goat heads, Tutankhamuns, Stars of David, crucifixes, Islamic stars and crescents, African tribal figures, and even Medusas, all colored in ivories, jade greens, bronzes, golds, and dark mahoganies. On the other side was the apparel section. Two racks of religious garments and ceremonial robes stood in front of the display section, topped with brightly colored African dashikis, and beneath them, hidden behind the clothes racks, were the wooden bins for hats and other head garments.

Pretty Boy didn't even bother seeking out Mike, who was not behind the counter, for a greeting. He went straight to the hat bins.

"I'm not sure this is a good idea," whispered Virgil.

"You're the one who said I should be a prophet for the Islamic faith."

"I think you're going the wrong direction with all of this."

"What are you getting your feathers all ruffled about? It's just a hat."

"*That* exactly."

"What?"

"It's not a hat."

"Oh, give me a break," he scoffed as he tried on a Turkish fez. "Anyone who gets offended by the word 'hat' *deserves* to be offended.

"Well, you do have a point there."

Pretty Boy found a white, embroidered taqiyah, the Muslim-style skullcap worn on the crown of the head like a kippah, and put it on.

"I feel like you might be in danger of hypocrisy," whispered Virgil.

"What do you mean?"

"Well, why do you want to buy this hat?"

"I thought it wasn't *a hat.*"

"You know what I mean. Why do you want it?"

"For my religion."

"And do you even *know* the origin of this head garment, or why Muslims choose to cover their heads? Or are you just trying to show the rest of the world what class you belong to?"

"Eat shit, Virgil. You're the one who told me I should show people the right way to do this."

"And is *that* what you are doing? Or are you just trying to act rebellious because you aren't feeling so youthful anymore?"

"You know, we're not supposed to eat pork, but the Qur'an doesn't say anything about eating *birds.*"

Pretty Boy took his white taqiyah to the checkout counter and rang the silver bell loudly.

Mike entered through a wooden beaded curtain, dressed in a checkered button-down the color of orange sherbet topped with a dark brown bowtie and jeans the color of a ripe nectarine that didn't even crease behind the knees when he walked.

"Oh," he said as his stride suddenly went into slow-motion. "Dale. And Dale's *bird*. So nice of you *both* to visit."

"I want to buy this." He had no reason to have hostility toward Mike. In fact, Pretty Boy had always liked him. Mike, who was never afraid to openly insult people's shortcomings in their presence, quite often jabbed little one-liners at Tabitha when she started acting self-righteous, tiny jokes that – in the setting of an uncomfortable photoshoot – were like offering Pretty Boy air conditioning in Hell. Still, not only did his being replaced make everyone involved with the photoshoot his enemy, but under the influence of magically-produced drugs and two months worth of failure, heartache, and nightmarish trips, *everyone* was the enemy.

Mike rang up the taqiyah, pointed to the digital readout of the price on the backside of the cash register, and said, "I *heard* you were having a little breakdown."

"AWK!" Virgil squawked in his high-pitched bird voice. "Don't go there! Don't go there!"

"What?" an enraged Pretty Boy exclaimed. "What the fuck are you talking about?"

"I'm sorry. I must be mistaken. I thought you came in here to buy Muslim headwear while talking to a parrot."

Pretty Boy crumbled up a twenty, tossed it in his face, and left.

"Yup," Virgil whispered sarcastically. "This is *exactly* what I had in mind when I told you that you could be an ambassador for the Islamic faith."

"Damn it, Virgil!" he shouted as he exited the store, still in earshot of Mike. "What is so wrong about what I'm doing? You told me to be Muslim, and now I'm Muslim. And I'm starting to see some things that are really wrong with the way we live. Everyday, we see these pop stars that are role models for pre-teens, and they're flaunting their vaginas to gain popularity! We watch every emotion being dumbed down to an app! We see everything that we love being bottled and sold, and maybe the things that I thought were wrong before, aren't."

"That sounds like everything you've *always* ranted about. It didn't change since you put on that ridiculous hat."

"You haven't known me that long."

"I didn't have to."

"What's that supposed to mean?"

"It means---"

"Wait!" Pretty Boy interrupted. "What time is it?"

"In case you haven't noticed, I don't wear a watch. They don't really fit on account of me being *a macaw.*"

Pretty Boy looked to the clock displayed in between restaurants in the food court. "12:45! Oh shit! Which way is Mecca?"

"You've got to be kidding me."

Pretty Boy spun in circles, trying to get a feel for the cardinal directions.

"Please don't do this," whispered Virgil.

Pretty Boy got down to his knees, placed his palms on the tile floor before him, and touched his forehead to the floor between his hands.

The banter of the lunch crowd around him shifted to whispers. Some took out their phones to record the spectacle.

"Please stop," Virgil whispered. "You don't know what you're doing."

The whirlwind of conversation around them shifted up a notch, grumbling angrily as some stood to take notice, some stood to walk away, and some stood debating whether or not to intervene.

Pretty Boy picked his head off the floor, eyes closed

in thought, then bent back down, ignorant of the fact that part of the Islamic prayer ritual was cleanliness, hence the prayer rugs and the washing of the neck, hands, and feet, and the floor in a mall food court was, more often than not, completely filthy.

A young, handsome, Hispanic man approached him on his way to his table, a tray of food still held out in front of him.

"Excuse me?"

Pretty Boy looked up at him from the floor. His eyes were cold and unblinking, but he offered no verbal response.

"I think this sort of thing is better done in private. You know, *not* in the middle of the food court."

Pretty Boy wrathfully rose to a standing position. "What's it matter to you?"

"It just makes people a little uncomfortable. Look, I'm trying to help you out here."

"Who said I need help?"

"No one, it's just that – "

"What the fuck is that?!" Pretty Boy was staring down at the man's food tray. "Is that a *ham* sandwich? Don't you know that pigs are a sacred animal?"

"AWK! No they're not! No they're not!" screamed Virgil.

"Shut up!" But then Pretty Boy looked beyond the sandwich and saw something even more enraging. Underlined by the food tray was the white silhouette of a king's crown on the man's shirt that stood atop the words, 'KEEP CALM and LOVE NICKELBACK.'

Seeing either the rage or the insanity in Pretty Boy's eyes, the man turned and walked away, surprisingly calmly. Behind him, Pretty Boy yelled out, "Come to the Dead Still show. We will *destroy* you!"

By the time he made it home (after an interrogation by a police officer and mall security, who later escorted him off the premises), a video of the altercation had gone viral. Once again, the walls in his house were swaying up and down like he was aboard a giant houseboat.

"Are you serious?" Virgil yelled at him. *"Pigs are a sacred animal?"*

"What?"

"No one believes that pigs are sacred."

"Yes, they do."

"No, the Qur'an states that pigs are a filthy animal and are not to be eaten, as it *also* says in the Bible."

Pretty Boy stood silently, dumbfounded.

"You see, these are the things I wanted you to uncover: why two seemingly similar religions could have such vastly different interpretations. But instead you took the one thing that I didn't really mean and did *only* that."

"What do you mean?"

"Spreading it. Flaunting it. Acting like a prophet. Do you *really* think that you could have any bearing on how the country perceives the Islamic religion?"

"Then why the hell did you tell me to do it?!"

"I just wanted you to find something on your own, because otherwise, it wouldn't stick." His tone was suddenly drenched in sarcasm. "No, no, no. The only way you'll do *anything* is if you can find some way to show it off to the world, to tell everybody 'Hey, look at me! I'm so *totally* different from all of you!' How quickly would you have dismissed everything I said if I told you the key to becoming happy and complete again was to play golf? To wear designer jeans? To listen to Katy Perry? No, none of that is *crazy* and *edgy* and *abrasive* enough for you, is it? This was the only way I thought I could get you to stop whining about your age and your fictitious health problems and your job and *blah bl-blah bl-blah!"*

Pretty Boy had never wanted to find out what Virgil tasted like more than that moment. He fumed. His eyes darted back and forth, searching for a rebuttal that matched the intensity of his emotions. He drew in a breath, ready to let Virgil have it, then doubled over, vomited, and fainted.

23

Cal's room looked like Santa's workshop for meth-addicts. Huge bags of powders littered the spots on the floor that weren't covered in dirty laundry. Silver bags of aluminum oxide, white bags of potassium perchlorate and potassium nitrate, yellow bags of sulfur and their homemade dextrin, and black bags of ground charcoal sat beside a pack of construction paper, a roll of masking tape, a mortar and pestle, and a spool of number ten wire. Cal was rolling the construction paper into long, narrow tubes and securing them with the masking tape while Sonny was stripping the jacket off a forty-foot strand of wire. They were waiting for their parents to leave so they could open up the bags without the dominating odors of sulfur and charcoal raising suspicion.

"Make sure they're not *too* thick," said Sonny. "About the size of your index finger."

The two had been working studiously for weeks now, toying with different ideas, acquiring and producing necessary materials, enjoying the time spent away from Rex and his need to make something carefree like the band stressful, and Pretty Boy and his need to make *everything* stressful. Cal always felt loved by his brother, but loved like a puppy or a new car – something appreciated and helpful, but not particularly respected. Even as they jammed, he was merely background. Despite the fact that the genre of heavy metal yielded no room for mediocre drummers with an immutable necessity for speedy hands, machine-gun feet, and experimental fills, Cal always felt like his presence in the band was just to embellish what the rest of them had created. But now, as he and his brother worked together on something that no one else was involved in, something no one else could even know about, he finally felt integral to the process as well as the relationship.

Looking around the room, both of them felt accomplished. After the final note of a new song, they felt a similar pride. Not only had that sensation been experienced and re-experienced so many times that they had built up an immunity to the feeling, but every month they played with a half a dozen *other* metal bands. It was no longer unique. But this, this was something that belonged only to *them*.

The door knocked twice and they scrambled to cover all of the evidence with more dirty laundry. Sergio poked his head in.

"How's it going?"

"Alright," said Sonny. Sergio never even bothered waiting for a response from Cal as he knew Sonny spoke for the both of them.

"What are you guys up to in here?"

"Just watching a movie." As if on cue, an old Godzilla roared from the TV behind him.

"We're off to the ranch again." He paused as if he was deciding whether or not to say the next part. "You know, you've got one more week. Have you found an apartment yet?"

"Yeah, we found a place."

All the tightened muscles in Sergio's face relaxed. "Oh, really?"

"Yeah."

"And when are you moving out... I mean, *in?*"

"Next Saturday."

"Well, that's..." He struggled for the words to express his emotions, but it had been so long since he felt anything but wrath and shame toward his sons. "That's just great. I'm proud of you... both."

Sergio closed the door behind him and hopped in the truck next to his wife, feeling hopeful for the first time in a long, long while.

Back in the house, Sonny and Cal began ripping open bags of powder and mixing them in plastic bowls.

24

It had been a while since Pretty Boy had had an actual girlfriend, but he remembered how every one of his relationships had ended. He would lose interest. He would distance himself. He would get angry for no reason. He would avoid them. He would squint his eyes in pain and discomfort when on the phone with them and struggle to hang up after every sentence fragment. He would start to hate them for invading his life. He would do this until they would be hurt enough to dump him.

He was starting to feel the same feelings toward Rex.

Rex had been calling for days now, but Pretty Boy would grimace at the sight of his name on his caller ID. He wasn't sure if he felt that Rex represented the band or his old way of life, but both things seemed to be in the past and every phone call was dragging him backward.

Today was one of those days, just like the last day he spent with Julia, with Naomi, with Samantha, where he would have to not just answer the phone, but physically visit Rex. He knew the crossroads they were at, and he knew that a phone call would no longer suffice.

The video that was circulating online showed Pretty Boy with his parrot and a white, woven taqiyah face down on the tile floor of the food court, then getting in an altercation with a college student, and just before the video ends, the camera zooms in to catch his last statement, a threat, "We will destroy you."

The comments beneath the video were first verifying that he was, in fact, the singer of the band that was to open for Dead Still. Later comments were questioning if the statement was a legitimate threat of terrorism. People were rallying for police intervention. Some were vowing to tear up their tickets they had already bought. Some were vowing to *buy* tickets to boo the band, to throw garbage at them, and mostly, to physically assault Pretty Boy.

Pretty Boy was doing all he could to truly believe in his newfound mantra, that nothing mattered. The longer he believed this, the more he could hold onto youth. He had to be willing and ready to offend anyone and everyone, and to never fear the consequences, because that was what the Pretty Boy of ten years previous would have done. But something thick and heavy dropped inside him, like he just swallowed a paperweight, and he knew that there was no way he was going to that show.

Rex had different feelings viewing the video. Prevalently, he feared his best friend's reaction to seeing the public uprising that was forming against him. But beneath that, he enjoyed the publicity that his band was receiving, even if it wasn't in the most flattering light. With all of the talk of fighting Pretty Boy, of going to see the spectacle, of burning tickets, one theme was constant through all of them: they were selling tickets. Marilyn Manson, Gwar, Cradle of Filth, even Slayer, they all got to where they are by being ambiguously *evil*. In that sense, this was all great publicity.

Pretty Boy showed up at Rex's house just after lunchtime on Saturday. As per usual, he opened the door without knocking, but this time, was greeted by a screaming Taiwanese woman.

"Help! Help! Rex!" she screamed as she swatted the air in front of her, comically. Brutus was running laps around her in hysteria, mindful that there was an emergency, but as he knew Pretty Boy and didn't view him as an intruder, was unsure of what the emergency was. Rex ran from the back hallway, shirtless, and his confused disposition after witnessing the entire scene informed Yoyo that Pretty Boy was not a criminal, even if the internet said otherwise.

It was a strange setting for Pretty Boy to enter to. This house was a place that he had known as home, just as much as Polly's, as Frank's, as his *actual* home, but now it was inhabited by this bizarre cast, a foreigner, a pig, and absolutely *no* furniture. If he hadn't spent his week conversing with a parrot and watching his father die in the form of a fish, he would have felt like he was entering a different dimension.

These changes were almost expected from Rex. His life had been spent making strange decisions that no one else could fathom. When he was nine and his parents told him he could paint his room any color he wanted, he chose black. When he took career preparation in high school and he could shadow a person of any career, he chose beggar. When he first bought his house and had already grown tired of mowing the lawn, he tried to have a controlled burn in his front yard and almost took the house down. A pig and a Taiwanese exchange student weren't that surprising. The only difference was that when Rex painted his walls black, set his yard ablaze, and spent a day conversing with a certifiably insane hobo, Pretty Boy was *there*. He was a part of all of those decisions, and listened to Rex laugh about them immediately afterward. Hell, Pretty Boy was the one who found the fire extinguisher when the flames began climbing up the cedar risers that supported the front porch awning. But Brutus and Yoyo were strangers to him. He felt like he was being pushed out of his home. Not being an integral piece of Rex's eccentricities was every bit as lonesome as watching a spouse drift toward a new group of friends, friends that would surely become replacements. Pretty Boy resented him for it.

After Yoyo calmed down, she retreated to her room and allowed Pretty Boy and Rex to share the room alone, standing silently and awkwardly as there was only the recliner to sit on and neither wanted to take the only seat in the house.

Rex sat on the carpet, his back curved away from the wall as he looked down at the wooden tray on his lap, twisting a joint while setting aside a healthy marijuana snack for Brutus. Pretty Boy followed suit and sat on the carpet beside the opposite wall, leaving the recliner empty.

"I've got to ask," Rex announced while licking the paper tail of the joint, "who is Lori?"

"Huh?" His eyes opened suddenly. Any line of accusatory and uncomfortable dialogue was expected, but this question caught him entirely off-guard.

"Lori. From the new song. Who is she?"

"Oh. No one. Just a name."

"Don't bullshit me. You know I know you better than that. Is she the Muslim girl you're trying to impress?"

"No," he replied sternly. It was just like when Courtney accused him of cheating on her before their breakup. Chalking up his recent transformation to infatuation with a female was just as insulting.

"So she already turned you down? Is that it? I know how you get when you get dumped."

"What the fuck is that supposed to mean? How do I get?"

"You just get so... *drastic.* I worry about you, man. You act like everything is so monumental, when none of it really matters."

"Oh yeah? And what about you? Isn't that what you do with this band?"

"Are you trying to say that the band doesn't matter? I thought it was something we *both* started, something we *both* loved."

"So did I. I thought we *were* a band, that we were solid. But the second I do anything you don't like, you start accusing me of being lovesick and crazy and whatever else."

"See?" Rex shouted. "That's what I mean. We have one little talk because I'm *concerned* about you, and you act like it's the end of the band or the end of our friendship or something. Why does everything have to be so *life or death* with you?"

"Because I'm trying to *better* myself, and you're holding me back."

Rex lit the joint, exhaled the smoke in a sorrowful sigh, and looked in thought to the spot on the wall where the TV used to hang. "Look, man. I know your dad might be dying. I know you've been worried that *you* might be dying. I know you've been worried about work and life and everything else. And now you're writing songs about girls that I don't know. We used to know *everything* about each other. It scares me."

Brutus ran over to Rex's side and munched the weed off the tray. Pretty Boy wanted to comment on the occurrence, but Rex was far too deep in his soliloquy.

"And then I do this whole Fantasy Checklist thing to try and get your head back to where things are fun again, where we're not worried about our jobs and our health and we're just young and partying again, and so far – no offense – we've painted pictures and gotten penetrated by doctors. You and Frank were my family when my own family was too busy with booze. You've been there through all of my stupid bullshit. Everyone else – even Sonny and Cal – they all see me just by all of that stupid shit I do, but you were the one who looked past it all to see *why* I do these things, maybe even when *I* don't know. I just don't want to let you down when you need help."

Rex passed the joint to Pretty Boy, much like the conch shell suggesting his turn to speak.

Pretty Boy lowered his head in shame. "Maybe I do need some help," he mumbled. "Things have just been moving so fast lately. I feel like I'm trapped in this ball that is spinning too fast for me to make out anything that is happening around me, and if I stop trying to focus, I'll completely lose my concept of reality."

"Whoa!" Rex's head shot up in shock, his eyes and teeth lit up in an unexpected mirth. "It is SO weird that you should put it like that."

25

Fantasy Checklist #3

They were all piled in the Vanimal, heading northwest on Ocean Drive. They had just left Rex's house after he loaded up two fluorescent orange vests and two hardhats from work, four orange traffic cones, and two, large, black, mysterious duffel cases.

"I'm gonna have to sell the Vanimal," Rex announced as he hugged the grass median lined with palm trees. "Between getting fired and Brutus eating all my weed, I haven't been able to cover the cost of today's festivities."

"What?" an agitated Sonny yelled over the rumbling of the engine. "How are we gonna get our equipment to the show?"

"I'll come up with something."

Pretty Boy was caught up on another aspect of the conversation. "What are we doing today?"

"Zorbing."

The day Rex came up with the Fantasy Checklist idea, he ordered two zorb balls online. He would have ordered four, but as they were priced at $428 a piece (used), two would have to suffice.

Zorbing was an activity in which the participant

would crawl inside a giant, inflated, clear plastic sphere just like a pet hamster, and would then be rolled down a long hill in the grassy, rolling terrain of New Zealand. The only problem with Rex's idea was that in South Texas, there were no grand hills. The only area in the city with any significant rise in elevation was down by Emerald Cove where uptown dropped to downtown on Park Street, where the elevation dropped a quick thirty feet at a thirty-five degree incline, then rolled gently downhill for another quarter mile across the four, quickly moving lanes of traffic divided by a grass median on Shoreline Boulevard, then dropped another drastic forty feet on the grassy hill of Cole Park, and finally, hit the ocean.

This was another one of those points where Rex's line of thinking differed from the rest of humanity. Rather than the obvious risks of death and imprisonment, Rex focused on the fact that it was Sunday morning and the streets were all but completely vacated as the conservative city was all attending Sunday mass, that it was more than coincidence that he could only afford two, leaving the two others to block traffic, and that in comparison to rolling down the luscious green hills of Queenstown, New Zealand, screaming down the downtown streets of Corpus Christi, Texas was infinitely more bad ass.

Rex hung a left on Park Street and the Vanimal roared into a vicious groan in second gear as it climbed the small hill. When they reached the not-so-impressive summit, Rex turned right and parked alongside the curb outside of a Methodist church. They all got out, faced the ocean, and looked down the hill that seemed so tiny going up, but now looked like what ski-jumpers see before barreling into flight.

"No way," announced Sonny. "No way I'm doing this."

"Damn right, you're not doing it," answered Rex as

he handed him a hardhat. "You didn't get camera-fucked by Dr. Strangelove. You're blocking traffic."

Pretty Boy was terrified. He knew he wouldn't be able to back out of this. Rex simply wouldn't allow it. He tried to look down to the water, to the spot between the skate park and the ocean where Virgil told him that he could travel in any direction and get right back to that spot. As long as he was moving, it was worthwhile. He could see the exact square of sidewalk where he and Virgil had been standing when he made that speech, and couldn't help but wonder if it was an omen, that he would roll right to that exact spot, making it full-circle, and once he reached it, he would die. From this perspective, it didn't seem improbable.

Rex hooked up a battery-operated pump to the first zorb ball. It actually consisted of two spheres – one encased by the other. The outer sphere acted as a cushion, a layer of air between the participant and the ground. It stood about eight feet high. The inner sphere was about five feet in diameter and was fastened to the interior walls of the outer sphere with colorful ropes stretched tightly in every direction, resembling an army of sperm attacking an egg. One open cylinder about two feet in diameter ran from the inner sphere to the outside and acted as a passageway for the participant to enter.

As the giant bubble rose to life, so did Pretty Boy's anxiety. This was really going to happen. Rex was consistently eyeing his friend, noting his trepidation.

He craned his neck toward Pretty Boy and spoke in a voice just above a whisper. "It's gonna be awesome. Sometimes you have to let go of *everything* to forget your fear. Besides, what's the worst that could happen?"

"We could get hit by a car."

"Yeah, but we're in giant, padded balls of air. It wouldn't even hurt. It'll be like a cloud hitting another cloud."

"Or a *truck* hitting a cloud," added Sonny.

"Still, pretty gentle."

It seemed like an idiotic line of thought, but it did make sense. Pretty Boy consciously forced his shoulders to slink down from their tense position up around his ears.

"This is pretty crazy," Cal giggled as he stared down the hill.

The first ball was fully inflated. Sonny, who was already wearing his fluorescent, plastic mesh vest and hardhat, was instructed to hold it in place and not allow the wind to take it for a ride. Rex started on the second.

Verses from the Qur'an were speeding through Pretty Boy's thoughts in every direction, like he was being shot at from multiple, hidden snipers.

Those who deny God's revelations will suffer severe torment.

Some have been given the Scripture and turned away from it. They shall be sent to the Fire. When their skins have been burned away, We shall replace them with new ones so that they may continue to feel the pain.

It is not true repentance when people continue to do evil until death confronts them and then say, 'Now I repent.'

He didn't want to die. He wasn't ready. He knew he had yet to make the changes that would save him from the pits of Hell. If he died now, he would not have a chance to save his soul. He put his forehead to the ground, and prayed that he may be forgiven for every wrongdoing in his life, especially the ones that he didn't know about, the ones that he couldn't correct.

Rex looked at his friend with contempt.

"Are you serious?"

Pretty Boy ignored his friend and raised his head from the asphalt momentarily before touching it to the ground once more.

"You *do* realize what kind of shit your little religious experiment is getting the band into, right? The entire town thinks we're terrorists and we're gonna blow up the amphitheater – which I should be more pissed about, but it has worked as a great marketing gimmick."

The second ball was almost completely inflated. Rex began explaining the plan to his bandmates, one of whom was still face down on the ground praying to the Mecca, in the wrong direction.

"Cal, I want you at the first intersection. You're going to be responsible for communicating with both Sonny and us up on the hill. When both of you have cleared streets, give us the signal and we'll come down. Sonny, when we're about to start, I want you to block your intersection with the cones and stand in the middle of Park Street to stop us. I think by that time we should be almost stopped anyway. But just in case, be there to make sure we don't go flying into Cole Park. Cal, while Sonny's stopping us, you go collect the cones to get traffic flowing again – once we're safe and stopped, of course."

Cal and Sonny trotted down the hill, giddy with anticipation. Pretty Boy had finally risen from all fours, but was now a shade or two paler. Rex squeezed his shoulder endearingly.

"This is gonna be epic. It's gonna be something we'll remember forever, and that's all that matters."

"Why is that *all* that matters?"

"Because that's all that *ever* matters. You can think you need a new car or a new god or a new job," – he strategically hid 'god' sandwiched in the middle like it was random and accidental – "but when we're old and dying, all of that will be forgotten. We'll only remember times like *these."*

Pretty Boy tried to adopt this line of thinking. He tried to be like all of the others and just *choose* what he wanted to believe, but he couldn't deny the fact that he wasn't like Rex, and if he were old and dying, he would not be thinking about shows they played or rolling down a hill in a giant, inflatable ball. He would be thinking about the God he was about to meet and what fate He would have in store for him. He didn't want to be meeting God today.

Rex helped Pretty Boy climb into his zorb ball. The entrance was aimed directly toward him. He put his hands and then his head through, like he was diving parallel to the ground. He looked into the plastic sphere, everything coming through gray. The absence of color was as unsettling as the imminent claustrophobia. Pretty Boy's legs seemed to weigh triple as he hoisted them into the inner chamber behind his body. His lips were numb and his face was tingling. A cold sweat tickled the nerves all over his body. Once Pretty Boy had got himself into a sitting position inside the ball, Rex looked at him through the opening that he had just entered through, winked, and walked toward his own ball, leaving Pretty Boy alone and entombed.

Rex stood between the two balls, holding them still by the black, woven handles that existed on either side of the entrance hole. He looked down at Cal, who was posing as a road construction worker where there was no road construction, and awaited the signal. Cars zoomed by intermittently. A breeze jostled Rex's dredlocks like wind chimes. He looked out to the ocean. He was proud of himself for coming up with this idea, and proud of the fact that he could execute it with such coordination.

Cal and Sonny yelled to one another. Cal looked up the hill at Rex, and extended his right hand in his direction with a thumb extended upward.

"Alright. Here we go, Pretty Boy!"

Rex climbed into his zorb ball. Suddenly, Pretty Boy was at a loss as what to do. He was expecting Rex to give him a push, but Rex was already encapsulated in his own plastic tomb. Pretty Boy pressed his face against the plastic to watch the vague circular shape that existed outside the walls of his sphere. The ball on the other side was wobbling spastically, then started to move to the left. He realized that he was going to have to crawl like a hamster to propel the ball down the hill. Now that he was in control of the next event, his initial thought was to just climb out of the ball and watch Rex, but as Rex's ball moved away from his own, he was suddenly filled with a panic of losing his sense of direction and rolling into the traffic behind them, and so he crawled forward. It wasn't long before the momentum forced him to the back side of the sphere. He stuck to the back wall and struggled to fall back to the bottom as the ball rolled forward.

Rex's ball sped out in front. From Cal and Sonny's angle, it was immediately clear that the incline was too steep and their speed would be much greater than what they anticipated. They both, as well as Pretty Boy, were petrified. Rex was howling in excitement from inside his speeding hamster ball.

Pretty Boy reached the steepest part of the hill, and instantly felt like everything was going wrong. Rather than crawling on the floor of the ball, he was stuck to the wall with centrifugal force. He had anticipated feeling like clothes in a dryer, but he didn't expect to be in the high-speed spin cycle of a washing machine, as he was now. The speed was too great, as was the sensation, but he could do nothing to slow it down. It was like being on a roller coaster ride that was malfunctioning, but no one could shut it off. From a mixture of the spinning sensation and the intense fear, Pretty Boy puked. The vomit pulled – like himself – to the outside of the sphere, clinging to his cheeks and neck. He began hyperventilating.

Rex was passing Cal. His speed was still too great, but luckily, he veered left and hit the curb and bushes of the median, which both slowed him down. Sonny pushed the ball to a stop and looked inside anxiously, terrified of what he would find. Instead of the bloody and broken body he expected, he found a giddy Rex, laughing maniacally, his mouth gaping open in an infantile smirk. As Sonny allowed himself to release his fear and appreciate the fact that his friend had survived the ordeal unscathed, he failed to notice that Pretty Boy was coming at a much greater speed and was not in line to be slowed by the landscaped median.

"Stop him! Stop him!" Cal screamed as he chased behind the ball. Sonny and Rex both snapped to attention. Rex dove out the opening of his ball haphazardly, the weight turning the opening of the ball face-down. Rex scraped the corner of his forehead on the asphalt. Sonny stretched his arms out to both sides as he feet danced back and forth, trying to ready himself for the impact of the speeding plastic ball. The ball was not only rolling, but still bouncing twelve inches off the ground as the revolving body inside shifted the weight up and down, up and down. A car slowed to the blocked intersection and stopped ten feet short of the traffic cones that Sonny had laid out. If only they *didn't* block traffic, Pretty Boy could have hit the car that would have serendipitously blocked his path.

Sonny was off-center when the ball plowed into him, knocking him to the ground off to the left side of the speeding ball that refused to slow. Sonny and Rex were both flat on the ground as they lifted their faces to watch the ball speed over the next curb and down the hill of Cole Park, receding below the horizon of green grass, as Cal frantically chased from behind.

They hopped to their feet, Sonny's hands scraped and

bloody from stopping his fall, as was Rex's forehead. They scurried toward the park as the cars parked behind the cones watched in disbelief at the spectacle that was obstructing their drive downtown.

Inside the speeding ball, Pretty Boy was screaming in terrified whimpers as he was being bathed in his own vomit. The speed had dropped just enough so that he no longer clung to the outer walls, but instead was being tossed violently from wall to wall as the axis of gravity was spinning like an anemometer in a tornado. In his screaming mind, he was trying to discern whether it felt like it had gone on too long only because times spent in states of extreme fear seemed to stretch, or if he really had exceeded the space allotted for their zorbing runway. As the hard scraping sound of plastic against asphalt was softened and the color that appeared and disappeared and reappeared again as the ball bounced down the hill turned to green, he knew that it was not his imagination.

The ball sped down the second drop-off of Cole Park, once again sticking Pretty Boy to the wall of the sphere as the speed intensified. Rex was praying that the ball would veer into the bowl of the skate park. It might have made for a painful crash of an ending, but it would stop him from going into the water. The distance between the ball and Cal grew. The three of them gave chase, but were much too slow, and as the ball sped further and further away, all hopes of any obstruction stopping it before reaching the ocean were quickly abandoned.

Now that the grass had softened the grinding of the plastic against the ground, all other sounds had been drowned out by the plastic tomb, and it was nearly silent save for Pretty Boy's terrified gasping and moaning and the squeaking of skin against plastic. As his world spun around him, he started to lose his grip on reality. He began to forget why he was in this sphere and what was happening on the outside. He only saw it as a vehicle, a passageway to the afterlife, as he was surely dying. He panicked.

"Allahu Akbar!" he screamed. It was a phrase he had looked up before ever opening the Qur'an. It was one of the most common phrases in Muslim prayers and translated to 'God is the greatest.' It was something he could say in public to gain attention. He knew this now. Virgil was right. He was misusing the religion as a means to stay young, to attract attention from others, because that was what he identified with youth. But now, it was a desperate attempt at gaining salvation in his final moments, a wild punch thrown by a beaten boxer just before fading into unconsciousness. "Allahu Akbar! Allahu Akbar!"

And just as he muttered the words, something transformed instantaneously, like a puff of smoke after the magician yells out his abracadabra.

A splash.

One side of the ball had turned to a blue-gray, and the spinning stopped suddenly. Pretty Boy crashed into one side of the ball, just next to the blue spot that existed on the downward-facing end. Had he been of right mind, he could have now identified what was down and what was up, and been grateful at the fact that the cylindrical opening that he had crawled through was facing upward. Instead, he saw the sunlight gleaming through the hole in the roof and saw it as Heaven, and the sloshing, murky spot beneath was Hell. This was his moment, his one chance to prove himself and save his soul. He reached up toward the light, but was stuck stationary in his plastic cell. He crawled along the walls trying to reach the light of God, but as he made his first motion to do so, the hole slunk away from the sun, and the bright yellow light was blocked by the plastic, almost fading away completely, and Pretty Boy thought that he was being denied entry. He panicked. Again.

He crawled and moaned, crawled and moaned.

"Allahu akbar!" His voice was shrill with exertion. "Allahu akbar!" He felt himself being pulled downward, gravity tying him to the horrors below. He heaved rapid hummingbird breaths as all four appendages clawed frantically in every direction like a rat that was cornered. "ALLAHU AKBAR!"

The hole sunk downward, and the water poured in.

It was cold and jarring. Pretty Boy fell to his back and tried to back away, but it was pulling him so quickly and forcefully, like he was just a speck of sand being sucked down the drain of a bathtub. The water shot in with the force of a fire hose. The tomb was quickly filled.

As the water rose over his head, he was overcome by the silence. Where everything was muted moments earlier, now the outside world was entirely gone. He struggled, but every movement only led him to another barrier that existed inches away in every direction. He relaxed his body, and tried to accept his fate. This was it. He had to pay for what he had done. He had lived a godless existence, and no deathbed leap of faith could offer reparations for the years spent in wrongdoing. He wanted to cry. He wanted to argue. He wanted to fight. But he knew, his judge was too powerful. This was to be his fate. Now, he needed only to abandon all hope.

He only wished he could see his father one more time. He wished there was something there, something that he could hold onto, something that he could remember. He had no desire to hug his father, to embrace him and tell him how much he loved him. He only wanted to *warn* him. He wanted to show him what was in store if he continued on his path. He whipped his head around at the murky, gray water that surrounded him, and expected to see that dying fish, the one with his father's face, offering him a soulful goodbye. But there was nothing. Feeling more alone than he had felt in thirty-one years of life, he opened his mouth and sucked in a breath of saltwater, just as Rex's hands tore through the opening and pulled Pretty Boy from the sphere.

26

Officer Hagan was a broad-shouldered man, thick in the chest and arms, but had the smooth, rounded face of an Irishman. His hair was short and just a shade darker than red. His partner was twenty-four years old and looked sixteen. Officer Wallace compensated for this with a dark brown mustache that extended well past the outside borders of his mouth. His hair looked like he was trying to emulate Clark Kent. Both of them were waiting outside Rex's front door as the Vanimal pulled into the driveway.

After the zorbing incident, all four of them were desperately awaiting a smoke session at Rex's house, but after seeing the police cruiser parked outside, only Rex was still concerned with that.

Pretty Boy had gone all but catatonic. Rex only hoped he would stay that way through whatever was about to happen. He wasn't sure that his friend could endure any more excitement today.

"I'm Officer Hagan and this is my partner Officer Wallace. We're here for you." His arms remained crossed by his waistline, but his eyes were locked on Pretty Boy.

"What did I do?"

"Can we come in?"

They all looked at Rex. He nodded worriedly.

The six of them entered the ramshackle dump, and they were greeted by an inquisitive pig. The police officers stepped back quickly and raised their arms over their head, Officer Hagan holding a laptop with his right hand, like they were wading through waist-high water and didn't want to get their hands wet.

"Don't worry," remarked Rex. "He's an asshole, but he won't bite or nothin'."

The cops looked at one another with a look that said they should have let this one slide and been on their way. Yoyo walked by in a long nightshirt that covered her tiny shorts, making her look like she might be in her panties. She saw the policemen, froze, then put her head down and let out a disappointed sigh.

"What did you do?" she asked accusingly.

"Nothing." Rex forced a smile. "These are just some friends of ours."

"Well, your other friends visited earlier. They took your chair."

"What?!" Rex looked to the living room. Now there was only the one recliner and a coffee table. The oversized coffee table looked quite superfluous in front of the undersized recliner, like clown shoes on a dwarf. Brutus sat in the corner, eating an old tennis shoe.

"They said it was their chair and you were just borrowing it."

"What? I mean... Yeah, yeah... That's right."

All eyes were on Rex. His roommate was angry. His bandmates were confused. The policemen were worried that they were going to have to sit on the dirty floor.

"Don't you have any furniture other than a recliner?" asked Officer Hagan.

"I do... I mean, I did. But I've been getting robbed a lot lately."

"Robbed? Did you report it?"

"No."

"Why not?"

"Well, because I assisted in the robbery."

"What? You assisted in robbing *yourself?*"

"Yup."

"I'm confused."

"Never mind. It's not important. Let's have our little talk."

"And where do you suggest we should have our *little talk?*"

Yoyo walked back to her room, simultaneously escaping the situation in the living room and claiming her bedroom before they could commandeer it for the interrogation. Rex went to his room and retrieved a lime green beanbag chair. He walked it into the living room, tossed it beside the stained recliner, and looked at the police officers while gesturing with his hands toward the recliner and beanbag. The four bandmates sat cross-legged on the carpet against the wall while Brutus climbed from lap to lap, snorting playfully in all of their faces.

The two cops looked at one another again. Officer Hagan sat in the recliner. Officer Wallace looked at him incredulously before consigning to the idea of sitting in a beanbag chair during an investigation. He sunk down slowly, uncomfortably, as the chair melted around him.

"How did you know to find me here?" asked Pretty Boy.

"Your band is all over the internet." Rex smirked at this statement. "We went to all of your houses." Sonny and Cal grimaced at the thought of the cops showing up to their parents' house.

"Listen," Rex began, "Zorbing is a really common thing in New Zealand. It's becoming more popular around the world. Maybe we went the wrong way about it, but---"

"Zorbing?" asked Officer Wallace. "What the hell is

zorbing?"

"Nothing."

Between the pig in the corner and the person of interest claiming to have robbed himself, the officers didn't bother pursuing this line of questioning.

"So what is this about, officers?" asked Pretty Boy. The cops' presence seemed to have a fearful, sobering effect on his disposition.

Officer Hagan turned the screen of his laptop toward him. The video of him at the mall that they had all seen a dozen times now was playing out on his computer.

"Are you planning to commit a crime at the concert next weekend?"

"No, no, no. That video was taken *way* out of context."

"It doesn't seem like it. It looks pretty seamless. Did you know this man before the altercation?"

"No."

"So this was the only dialogue you've ever shared with this gentleman?"

"Yes."

"So if every word you've ever spoken to this man is contained on this video, how could it be taken out of context?"

Sonny and Cal looked at each other fearfully. Rex was trying to restrain Brutus, who was sitting on his lap and pushing his head anxiously toward his left pants pocket that contained the marijuana that the pig was smelling.

"Look," answered Pretty Boy, "I had a bad day. The guy got in my face. He was wearing a Nickelback shirt and I wanted to call him out. That's all."

"And how long have you been a Muslim?"

"I'm not, really."

"It sure looks like it in this video."

"I'm studying the religion, but I'm trying to take it

seriously."

"And who introduced the religion to you?"

Pretty Boy's eyes shot to the right side of the room as he thought about his British macaw and how he could explain that without being committed to an insane asylum. The officers noticed his reaction and construed it as being indicative of dishonesty.

"I just thought that it was a religion that needed some investigation."

"We actually just received another video just before we got here. Would you care to take a look?"

The screen changed to shoddy footage taken from a car window that was driving uptown. The car slowed down, and through the passenger window, Pretty Boy could see himself next to one and a half zorb balls, kneeling on the ground, right outside a Christian church.

"Why were you at the church this morning. Are you studying Methodism, too? Are you planning another crime at the church?"

"No, no. It's not that. We were just..." he struggled to find an explanation for what they were doing down there, but came up with nothing. "Zorbing."

"There it is again," interjected Officer Wallace. "What the *hell* is zorbing?"

"I think it would be easier explained if you just looked up a video."

Officer Hagan spun the laptop back toward himself and typed in the word 'zorbing' on his search page. Officer Wallace leaned awkwardly from his beanbag chair. They chuckled in quick, muted breaths as they watched the video.

"You did this downtown?"

"Yes."

"Well..." Officer Hagan looked to Officer Wallace, then shook his head in retreat. "That's a conversation for another time. We have here some lyrics from one of your songs." Officer Hagan looked down to the laptop and tapped a few buttons. He read the words off the screen. *"I'm going to blow up this entire town."* He looked up at Pretty Boy, then back to his computer before continuing. *"After this entire town blows me."*

Cal snickered. Brutus pushed harder to get at Rex's pocket, making it look like Rex was fighting off a forceful blowjob. The pig snorted angrily. Rex started to stand up.

"I'm just gonna put him outside."

Officer Wallace extended an arm toward him with his palm faced downward. "Sit, please."

"It's just a joke," said Pretty Boy.

"And what about this one," continued Officer Hagan. "In a song called 'Wasteland,' you say: *Just like Jon Savage said to Crowne, this place is going down."*

"It's a reference to *Brave New World,*" Pretty Boy said condescendingly. "You know, the book by Aldous Huxley?"

"I'm quite familiar with Huxley. What gets me is that later in the song, you say: *You will all hang like Bernard Marx.*"

"So? It's a book. It's a song about a piece of literature, alright?"

"But Bernard Marx didn't hang himself in *Brave New World.* Jon Savage did." Pretty Boy looked perplexed, then mortified. "So I'm wondering if this could be construed as a threat, if you are claiming to be Jon Savage in this scenario, and the rest of society is Bernard Marx, and you are going to change the way the story plays out, or if you just didn't really read the book."

Pretty Boy dropped his head in shame. He wanted to scold these officers. He wanted to tell them how much better he was than them, that none of this mattered, that if they could just see who he really was, they would know that they had no right to degrade him like this, but the only arena in which he could justifiably classify himself as superior was in age. He was older, and he was dumber.

Rex was still wrestling with Brutus, who had become more than intent on getting to the weed. He started to shriek, loud enough to put a grimace on all six of their faces.

"Damn it!" shouted Officer Wallace. "Put that pig outside."

Rex shot to a standing position, pulling his pocket out of reach from Brutus. "Thank you, officer."

"And what about you guys?" Officer Wallace looked back and forth between Sonny and Cal. He rested his elbows on his knees, trying to maintain dignity from the throne of a beanbag chair, but his body was being squeezed together narrowly. "Are you Muslims, too?"

"No, sir," answered Sonny. "Catholics."

"And what about this Rastafarian?" he asked as Rex came back in from putting Brutus outside.

"What's that?"

"What religion are you?"

"Rastafarian."

"Are you mocking me?" His eyes narrowed in anger.

"Alright, alright," Officer Hagan interjected. Then to the four boys, "Listen, everyone has an eye on you right now, waiting to see what you're going to do. They want to know what we're doing to stop you, and the answer is: we're going to be watching you *even closer*. We will be at that show, along with a lot of our friends, and if *any* of you try anything sneaky…" Officer Hagan squinted his eyes, puckered his lips, and sucked in air loudly. "I wouldn't want to be you."

With that, the two policemen stood to exit the house, something that they had both been waiting to do since crossing the threshold on their way in. Before reaching the door, Officer Hagan turned back to them.

"And no more zorbing."

The door shut behind them and the four boys all took a collective breath of air like they hadn't breathed since the cops showed up. Only Rex looked pleased.

"Did you hear that?" he asked the rest of the band giddily. "*All* the cops are coming to our show!"

27

Sonny had stripped one forty-foot strand of wire and two ten-foot strands and put them in his sock drawer. They had already stuffed forty paper cylinders full of their powder concoctions and had them stored in a wooden box under Cal's bed. It looked like a treasure chest and felt just the same to both of them.

It was Cal, not Sonny, that had the brilliant idea of egg whisks. They were very breathable, they would hold the steel wool firmly, and being made entirely of metal, they were conductive of electricity.

Sonny was drilling four holes in the worn grinding wheel he had just removed from the grinder. Cal had already stuffed steel wool into the heads of four separate egg whisks and was now moving all of their possessions out into the garage. It seemed that they needed very little now, or rather, couldn't keep everything other than bare essentials. Music equipment, clothes, beds, and material for the projects at hand. Everything else would have to go.

An hour earlier, Sergio had come into their room. He looked bigger, like all the time spent at the ranch had broadened his shoulders, accentuated the muscle lines in his forearms, thickened his neck. Yet, he also somehow seemed less threatening, even before he began speaking.

"It looks like you boys are finally becoming men."

"Dad, I'm thirty-one."

"Yeah, but…" he caught himself before saying anything insulting. "Maybe sometimes I forget you're not my little boys anymore."

Two things had happened on his last trip to the ranch, one the cause of the other, and both of them completely internal.

Before he left, he found out that his sons were finally leaving the house, that they were finally going to start lives of their own. Sergio had moved out of his parents' house at half his older son's age. That was when he felt he became a man. Everything was up to him. He had no one to rely on anymore. Maybe times had changed. Regardless, something warm and soft that had been closed and hardened for so long finally opened up inside him, allowing those comatose feelings that one gets for his children's milestones – the first steps, the first words, teaching him how to shave, teaching him how to drive – to finally spring back to life. Perhaps it had just been so long since there were any milestones, so long since either of his boys had done anything other than sit in their rooms and annoy the hell out of him by shaking the walls with their music. For the first time in years, he actually loved his children.

The second realization he had was that the boys were only close with their mother. This was not so much a realization as he had known this for quite some time, but now it was a cause for concern. With her growing fascination with a set of beliefs that he despised and Sonny and Cal's Muslim friend, he felt that the boys had no one to idolize with wholesome religious beliefs. Sergio had been brought up painfully Catholic, and yet he had not been to mass himself in years. How had he failed so miserably in all the things that were ingrained in him since he was an infant? He barely knew his children, and if things continued on this path, they would either become witches, warlocks, or terrorists.

He hadn't bought them a gift in years, not even for their birthdays or Christmas. He hadn't even had a real conversation with them in months. Maybe it was him, not the world around him, that needed to change.

"I got you boys something." He held out two upturned fists. Dangling from each was a slender, silver chain with a crucifix hanging from each, the tortured body of Jesus nailed to each. "My father gave me this when I was a young boy – well, one of them, anyway. He said as long as I wore it, he would always be with me. I only had the one, so I found another exactly like it and I mixed them up in the bag so I wouldn't know which one was which. That way, they sort of *both* came from your grandpa."

"Cool, Dad," said Sonny.

"Yeah," added Cal. "Thanks."

The three of them stood in the living room waiting for something more to happen, for a theme song to play while they all embraced one another, or maybe for them all just to go back to their lives. Sergio finally pursed his lips, nodded solemnly, and got in his truck to go to work.

Cal and Sonny immediately went to work on their project.

Sonny had drilled the holes in the grinding wheel and was now threading the stripped copper wire through them, leaving eighteen-inch tails at all four corners. Cal was still pulling all of the music equipment from their rooms and stowing it in the garage.

Sonny drilled a hole through the handle of all four egg whisks. The steel wool was already stuffed inside the heads of the egg whisks making them resemble 1950s era microphones. Sonny threaded the tail ends of the bare wire through the handles of each, so now the grinding wheel had four, long ponytails.

He then removed the guard from the grinder and clamped it down in the table vise in the garage. The guard was a curved triangle, like one you would see on a weedeater, but was made of metal. They needed to remove the lip on the curved end of the guard that turned down at a ninety-degree angle. Sonny found his dad's bandsaw, and as soon as he extracted it from its nook in the garage, Cal insisted that he execute this task as it reminded him of a punier version of the tool that belonged to him at work. Sonny watched as his brother used the tool methodically, effortlessly, and was amazed. For so long, Sonny had thought that his brother's only redeeming quality was how he blasted the drums – not that he was otherwise useless, just not unique. But as the two worked together, hammering out ideas and executing them however they could, Sonny learned a lot about his brother, which was good seeing as the two were going to be isolated from the world together pretty soon.

They drilled a quarter-inch hole in the guard with their father's cordless drill, then enlarged the hole to half-inch with a unibit. They inserted a plastic grommet into the hole that they bought from an electrical supply store for thirty-eight cents. As per Cal's idea, Sonny had cut the female end off of a hundred-foot extension cord and separated and stripped the two ends. After reattaching the guard and grinding wheel to the grinder, they pulled the stripped end of extension cord through the grommet so that the two copper ends were fixed to the braided ring of bare copper wire that was threaded through the holes on the grinding wheel that attached to the egg whisks.

They sacrificed a black metal guitar stand to the project and secured the grinder to the head of the guitar stand where the neck of the guitar would be supported using tie-wraps and duct tape. This way, the hanging egg whisks wouldn't reach the floor.

The contraption was finished. They stood back in the driveway and looked at it, cocked slightly downward, egg whisks drooping sadly, ready to blast off.

"Look at its hair," chuckled Cal.

"What?"

"The whisks, they look like hair." His giggle climbed up an octave. "It looks like Rex."

28

Captain Eddie called that morning to formally terminate Pretty Boy. He was nice enough about it. He never said whether he was firing him because of his online presence or because of the last fishing trip where he had to be physically restrained and spent the entire trip back to shore crying in the cabin. Pretty Boy figured that Captain Eddie would rather not have a discussion about the specifics if he didn't have to, and Pretty Boy felt the same way. It didn't really matter. There was no way he would ever look Tre and Manny in the eyes again. Even when they seemed to like him, Pretty Boy always felt like the old guy on board. He tried to distance himself from that persona with outlandish behavior, but the drug use and reading of the Qur'an only made him the *crazy* old guy.

He spent the morning reading the comments that were being posted about him online, glancing sporadically in Virgil's direction to see if he had any reaction to all that was happening. He assumed not, seeing as he had been out of pills for a long while, but it was still quite probable given the last couple of days filled with inexplicable occurrences.

Aren't most religious practices done behind closed doors? I feel like he is just trying to make everyone feel uncomfortable.

I am a Muslim, and this man is not. First of all, we don't believe that pigs are sacred animals. Secondly, we would never pray in this fashion. And lastly, any insinuation that the Islamic faith condones acts of violence is extremely misinformed and very offensive. I believe either this man just wants to hurt people and is looking for a group that supports that kind of thing (which the Muslim community DOES NOT), or he is trying to further the belief that Muslim = terrorist. Either way, he should probably expect heavy repercussions from both the Islamic community and the anti-Islamic community.

I'll tell you one thing: that guy is gonna get beat down at that show, if he makes it there before getting hospitalized.

Pretty Boy stopped reading. It was like researching health symptoms online and finding all of the potentially horrible diseases that he could have. In either scenario, he couldn't unread all the fearful phrases that were popping up on his computer screen.

He looked back at Virgil. "Is this what you've been preparing me for? You've been trying to get me to find God because I'm going to *die* this weekend, right?"

Paranoia seeped in through all of the windows. It poured in from his computer screen. His house became flooded. Every noise propped him into a standing and ready position. He kept waiting for cars to surround his house, for the door to fly open, for the assault to begin.

But if Virgil had been preparing him for death all this time, why couldn't he try to prevent it instead?

He loaded up the birdcage and drove to The Forefather's Arsenal.

The visible half of the store was the showroom. Walls, aisles, and rotating display shelves were covered with everything that a Texas redneck would ever need: snake boots, snake repellent, mosquito repellent, scent eliminators, deer attractant, duck calls, camouflage hats, camouflage vests, camouflage jackets, camouflage pants, camouflage thermoses, camouflage ice chests, gun holsters, gun cleaners, knife holders, knife sharpeners, sights, and scopes. The wall furthest from the door bore all of the larger products – mostly deer feeders and gun safes that stood almost as tall as Pretty Boy and cost more than his car. The adjacent wall was the sales counter, and behind it the wall was nearly invisible beneath the mounted rifles, shotguns, pistols, bows, and crossbows. The shelves beneath were boxes and boxes of ammunition, enough to start and end a war with Russia. The glass counters in front of the sales staff contained more pistols, more knives, and solitary rounds of ammo. The door between the displayed firearms and the corner near the gun safes led to the second half of the store that was a shooting range.

A man and a woman stood behind the counter. The woman had red hair, was heavyset, and looked like her face had been smashed in with a sledgehammer. All of her small features seemed to be caving in toward the center, like her nose was some sort of gravitational black hole. She was assisting the only other customer in the store, so Pretty Boy had to approach the man for help. He was tall and slender. His mouth was outlined by a black goatee. His thick eyebrows were hardly visible beneath his camouflaged baseball cap with some hunting name brand printed in orange cursive writing across the front. He wore a plain, black tee-shirt and had a face that looked incapable of smiling.

"I'm looking for a gun. I'm not really sure what I –"

"Wait a minute," the man interrupted. He pointed a finger aimed at Pretty Boy's chest like a six-shooter, thumb extended upward. "I know you. You're that Muslim fella from the mall, the one that's all over the internet."

"No, I've been hearing that a lot lately, but it's not

me."

"Yeah, like it's some *other* Muslim punk-rocker that carries around a parrot." In retrospect, he probably should have left the bird in the car. "I ain't sellin' nothin' to you, pal."

"What? Why not?"

"Because you and your kind are the reason that good folks like us *need* guns. And I'll tell you another thing: I've got a good mind to go to that concert myself. Even if those dumbasses don't allow guns, I could still sneak in enough weapons to stop your little uprisin' and make your faggot, little head spin."

"Are you serious?"

"You bet your ass, I'm serious. Now you better step on outta here while I allow you to."

"But…"

"Go on, now."

Pretty Boy wanted to argue, but he knew this was definitely a place where he was incapable of winning, and more importantly, a place that was constantly ready – itching, even – to attack.

He tried another gun store, but it seemed that the redneck from the first had already notified all of the other gun suppliers in town that the Punk Pirate Muslim Terrorist was looking for a firearm.

"Can you believe this shit, Virgil?" he said while driving away from the second store. "The entire town is out to get me, and I can't even protect myself." Virgil didn't respond. The silence was thick and suffocating.

"I've got to tell you something, Virgil. I think I might have been buying a gun for a different reason." He heaved a thick breath and lowered the volume of his voice. "Let's put it this way, if someone was breaking into my house to kill me, I don't think I'm the type that would shoot him. I'm more the type that would put the gun in my own mouth to avoid the suffering. I don't know, maybe I'm a coward. But with everything that's happening, it doesn't seem like an option to be dismissed. My dad is dying. I'm unemployed. My friends all hate me. I'm getting older and lonelier and less and less valuable. I feel like the world is just kind of moving on without me, like if I fell away, nothing would really change."

He looked at Virgil, begging for a response. He needed someone to talk to, but he was out of drugs. Strictly out of habit and wishful thinking, he reached in his pocket. It felt like it had been filled with gravel. When his hand reemerged, it was mysteriously filled with little pink pills. It may not have been as admirable as Muhammad splitting the moon or the loaves and fishes miracle, but it seemed miraculous, no less. Maybe more along the lines of turning water into wine.

He looked back at Virgil.

"Did you do this?"

"AWK! You're beautiful!"

He knew exactly what it meant. Virgil couldn't speak to him without the assistance of the drugs, so Virgil conjured the drugs in his pocket so that he could continue to be his personal prophet. No matter what Virgil said, this did seem like his own religion. He had often wondered what Jesus' and Muhammad's lives were *really* like, how the events actually transpired and how they felt and reacted to the dreamlike lives they were born into, and he started to wonder if they felt like he did at that very moment. It was easy to dismiss religious doctrines as fantasy, just as it was easy to dismiss everything that was happening to him as the psychotic hallucinations of a socially-imbalanced drug fiend. But could this be bigger than him, bigger than anything he had ever imagined?

He slapped his mouth with his open hand, threw his head back, and swallowed the pills.

He turned his car around, and drove to his father's house to obtain a gun.

29

Tabitha held her ballpoint pen by her ear as she repeatedly clicked the point in and out in irritation. She looked down at her blank legal pad, then back up at Rex as he situated himself in his plastic desk chair. Once Rex readied himself, Tabitha stared him down silently with the look of Barbara Walters if she was forced to interview a famous grilled cheese sandwich.

She placed her phone on the table between them. The face showed three white ovals with black triangles inside, and one, large red oval containing a white circle, the universal RECORD button. Her fingertip hovered over the circle.

"Are you ready?" she asked.

Rex didn't like this feeling, the idea of being picked apart in front of an audience. It wasn't the fear of being revealed, but the idea of being manipulated as a media puppet, even if it was all at his own request.

It began a few days ago at Polly's. Rex's mood had been shifting between enthusiasm for the show and fear for his best friend's well-being. Every new comment that would be posted online would further propel both emotions. Polly, being an entrepreneur at the center of the heavy metal community *and* a lifelong friend, seemed the perfect ear to drain his concerns unto.

"If you're really concerned, we could publish an article about you where you tell everyone that... I don't know... you drugged him or something," she suggested.

"I'm not sure that would do the trick. Plus, that would make them not want to come to the concert. If they don't have this Muslim terrorist they're all coming to see, then they won't come."

"Honey, people are *going* to come. It's *Dead Still.*"

"Yeah, but they won't come early enough for *our* set."

"Well you can't have it both ways." Her chin jerked to one side. "Unless..."

"What?"

"Unless you drew the attention *away* from Dale. If you did something even *more* offensive so they were all coming to see *you* instead."

"And how would I do that?"

"We publish our article."

"And?"

"You know this town. You know these people. You know the things they love. Bash them all."

"Do you think that'll work?"

"Everyone who is coming to this show that *doesn't* listen to Dead Still is coming because they're afraid of missing something. Whether Dale tries to shoot up the place, or there is a riot, or even if someone just *hits* Dale, they want to be there. They already have those expectations, and if you come out tearing apart everything these people care about, they know that someone will do *something*, and they'll start to forget about our little Muslim pirate friend."

As Rex stared at Tabitha's phone that was now counting up from zero in red numbers, he wasn't thinking about the negative attention he was going to receive, but just the *attention*. It seemed wrong and fake, but he knew that it was for a good cause – even if it was going to enrage everyone who read it.

"Do you really think people will even *get* to read this before the show? It's only a few days away."

"Do you not understand how media works today?" Tabitha asked condescendingly. "One person will read this and post it online. It will reach every corner of this town in *hours*."

"Alright." Rex straightened himself up in his chair, indicating that he was ready.

"I'm here with Rex, the guitarist for the band Leviathan that is to open for Dead Still this Saturday. Rex, I understand you are a man of many talents."

Dead air. Rex didn't understand that he was to answer *comments* as well as questions.

"Oh. Yeah. Well, I'm a welder by trade, but when I'm not playing or writing music, I like to paint."

Rex lifted up the canvas that he had stowed beneath his chair, the one from the painting class he took with the band, and showed it to Tabitha. She deflated with a repulsed sigh as she pinched the bridge of her nose. "We don't need that 'til the photoshoot."

Rex hit the stop button on her phone.

"Polly did tell you what I'm trying to do here, right?"

"Yes, she did. But it's *obvious* you put a lot of time into this. But I'm sure it was *just* for this interview, right?" She quickly tapped the red circle, continuing the interview. "Continue."

"Yeah… so, um…" his momentum stumbled as he chewed on Tabitha's disgust in him. "I like to work with latex, you know, just like the greats did – Pablo Picasso, Jason Pollock…" His voice elevated in volume like he was speaking directly to the instructor from Bubbly Brushes, unconcerned and unaware that his intonation would not come across in the written article. "They all used *latex* early in their careers."

"So which came first: the painting or the rocking?"

"The rocking, definitely. I like art and all, but I'm not a faggot."

"Wow, that was quite a statement."

"What are you trying to say? That I'm a fag? Hell, no. I hate fags. And I would know if I was one."

"And why is that?"

"Because I had a doctor shove a machine up my ass last week. And... I guess, I kind of made out with a dude a month ago. It did *nothing* for me... in both cases."

Tabitha's eyebrows popped up to her hairline and her mouth pinched in a delighted frown, the way one does when she wants to wordlessly scoff at someone else's stupidity. "Let's move on. The big question that everyone wants to know is: How do you feel about your lead singer being viewed as a potential terrorist?"

"That's bullshit." Rex looked genuinely angry. "You call me the guitarist, but he's the *lead* singer. Why is the singer always the frontman when the rest of the band are the ones making the music?"

"Alright, so how do you feel about your *backup vocalist* to YOUR guitar-centered band being a terrorist?"

"Pretty Boy ain't a terrorist. He's not even a Muslim. That day at the mall, I had just fed him some really *weird* fucking drugs. He was wiggin' out all day."

"And what about the footage of him praying outside of First United Methodist Church?"

"I don't even think that was him. Didn't look like him to me."

"Aren't you concerned by the hundreds of online posts of people claiming to attend your concert to assault the band before you can commit a crime?"

"Fuck those pussies. It's just a bunch of Bible-beating

jackoffs, anyway."

"Are you saying that you have a problem with Christians?"

"Not just Christians. It's all of these redneck fuckheads that hate everything that they don't belong to – if it ain't Christian, country-western, Republican, or the troops, 'Then kick it's ass! Yee-haw!'"

"So now are you saying you have a problem with *the troops?*"

"Hell yeah, I do. Everyone talks about supporting the troops like they're our guardian angels or something, but they forget that all of these army-faggots were the assholes in high school that would take your lunch money and date rape cheerleaders at keg parties. Now that they've got guns, everyone's sucking their dicks."

The printed version came to Polly that evening, and was waiting in a stack of two hundred by morning. Polly kept them behind the counter until Rex arrived just after opening time.

Some maternal instinct in her wanted to keep the papers out of her customers' sight, wanted to burn the entire stack, to keep Rex safe from all of the horrible things that he said, the horrible things that she told him to say. But she knew Rex, and she knew that he had little to no concern about other people's opinions and, more importantly, that whatever concern he did have he would sacrifice for his best friend. Perhaps that was the connection she had with Rex. There were dozens of kids that grew up in her store, but she never took to any of them the way she did with Rex and Pretty Boy. Rex, she thought, was just like a dog: loyal, fun-loving, and completely unconcerned with the world that didn't exist right in front of his face.

"Are you *sure* you want people to read these?"

"What? Do I look that bad in them?"

"Well, it does open with a picture of you holding a shitty painting of close-up pornography."

Rex looked down solemnly, seemingly weighing his options. "Really? You think it's shitty?"

30

Pretty Boy remembered fishing with his father. He had been viewing it as a skill he acquired, but had forgotten what it really meant to him. After the second trip out, he had started modifying his attire. He found three shirts in his closet that weren't black and began wearing them. His newfound love for all things metal was slowly dissolving as he envisioned his future as an adult, his father older, but still the same man, the two of them wrestling in marlins and black-tip sharks, living on the sea, sharing beers and stories and jokes, becoming best friends rather than father and son. In these fantasies, Pretty Boy wasn't wearing the black tee-shirts and ripped jeans that he was becoming accustomed to, but pleated shorts and full-brimmed fishing hats. He was drinking light beer instead of slamming whiskey and smoking pot like the teenager that he would become. He had an entire new direction that his life was heading now that he found a friend in his father.

When Frank sold the boat, something happened to Pretty Boy, something small and imperceptible, something that would grow to encompass who he was, something that he wasn't noticing until just now.

Just as they were creating their first solid bond, Pretty Boy felt like his father abandoned him. And from that point on, Pretty Boy had a growing fear of the end. The end of a friendship, the end of a relationship, the end of life, the end of youth. Sometimes he would even feel that heavy weight of despair in his gut when the credits would roll on a movie. He never wanted anything to end, but he felt that that's all everything in his life was doing. The band, his friendships, his father, his girlfriends, his life. He just couldn't appreciate anything because it was all ending, just as Frank had predicted with his 'Sunday Evening' speech. But Pretty Boy still had so much time left to endure Sunday evening that he felt he never really got a chance to appreciate Friday and Saturday.

Maybe finding a gun really was just a way out.

He walked in his father's house without knocking. He tiptoed across the tile to find his father sleeping in his recliner. His mouth was agape, his skin was pale, his arms and legs were spread away from his body. If it weren't for the snoring, he would have looked dead.

Pretty Boy snuck past his incapacitated father and entered the bedroom.

Frank's bedroom had always been explicitly off-limits. This rule was most likely due to the firearms, but Pretty Boy always presumed that there was something else in there, some hidden part of his father's personality, some other secret aspect of his life that proved that he didn't even like his son enough to share it with him. Walking into the room where the tile shifted to carpet felt like breaking into a church.

"DALE!"

Pretty Boy whipped his head around, startled and supremely frightened, but no one was there. His father was still sleeping on the couch. Everything else was still and silent.

He went straight for the closet. He slid the brass bolt on the lock to the left and pulled on the doorknob. The house had shifted and the door was stuck in the closed position as it was wedged against the threshold. He gave it a firm yank and it popped open loudly, but Frank's snoring continued.

A shotgun and a rifle were standing upright, resting their barrels against opposite corners of the shallow closet. On the floor between their inward facing shoulder stocks were red boxes of ammunition. Having no knowledge of firearms, Pretty Boy stacked up all four boxes and picked them up with his left hand and grabbed one of the two guns at random with his right.

He tiptoed back past his sleeping father. The TV was on in front of him, but muted. The picture displayed was a preacher in a gray suit and red tie, walking through the aisles of a studio audience and shouting into a microphone.

Pretty Boy reached the front door. When he went to turn the doorknob, he realized that his hands were empty. The gun and ammunition had vanished.

He walked back to the gun closet to find the boxed ammo stacked up neatly beside the bed, but now there were three guns in the closet.

"Frank, how many guns do you have?" he called out, forgetting that he was trying not to wake his father. He peaked back into the living room to see his father's body still heaving in and out in raspy breaths, and the realization of the setting shot back into his brain. He cringed as he realized what he had just done.

He grabbed the ammo and a gun, again, and walked through the living room, again. This time, the same preacher was walking around the TV, but the audience looked like it was all made up of one person, one face duplicated again and again and again, and it was his own.

The image was less haunting than he would have thought it to be, but instead, was just perplexing. It was like looking at a picture of himself at a party he didn't remember. He shook his head in a twitch and walked out the door.

"Weird shit is happening, Virgil," he said as he loaded the rifle and ammo into the back seat.

"You're telling me," the bird replied. Pretty Boy climbed into the front seat and Virgil continued. "I hope you're not hunting for macaws."

With the car still running, Pretty Boy shifted to reverse and backed out the driveway. He tried to look in the rearview mirror, but the image projected looked like it was beneath three inches of water. He put his right hand on the shoulder of the passenger seat and looked at the back windshield as he reversed out the driveway.

Driving seemed unnatural to him. The feeling of the steering wheel against his palms was oddly foreign. He kept shifting in his seat, feeling uncomfortable and uneasy. Luckily, the route he took from his father's house to his own was short and burned into his memory.

"Do you even know how to shoot a gun?" The voice came from the back seat, but it wasn't Virgil's. Pretty Boy twisted his neck to find Tre leaning comfortably against the window and wearing his hockey mask that he usually accompanied with a chainsaw.

"I think so. I mean, how hard could it be? Point the barrel and pull the trigger, right?"

"Well, there's more to it than that." His voice was bored and airy, like he was explaining a movie plot to a toddler. "There's the safety, there's reloading, there's proper posture."

"I'm not trying to become a sniper. I just need to protect myself." He looked back in the back seat, but it was only Virgil. Tre was gone.

Suddenly, he was in his bathroom at home. He couldn't remember driving home. He couldn't remember walking in the door. He had to walk to the living room to make sure he brought Virgil and his cage inside.

He had to pee. That must have been why he was in the bathroom. He went back, only this time he was diverted by the image of himself in the mirror. He looked *older*. The bags under his eyes, the smile lines outlining his mouth, all the signs of aging were suddenly much more prominent. And then he got older.

He watched as his hair started to turn white. His nose slightly enlarged. The bags under his eyes folded and filled up like water balloons. He spit out a tooth in the sink. Then another. Then another. When he looked back up in the mirror, his skin was detaching from his face like it was made of pizza dough. He pushed his fingertips to his cheekbones, trying to secure it back into place, but it oozed around his fingers and dripped down to the counter. He screamed and ran out of the bathroom, the front of his pants soaked in urine.

"What seems to be the problem?" Virgil asked as Pretty Boy ran past his cage, groaning in fear and exhaustion. He looked to the cage, but Virgil looked very different. His neck had elongated and curved like a question mark. The colors on his head were the same blues and whites and blacks as before, but there were no feathers, like the skin was bald and tattooed. He resembled a colorful, miniature vulture. A burning cigarette was pinched between two toes. He raised his claw and took a drag.

"Virgil?" Pretty Boy's face was smeared in terror.

"Don't look so shocked."

Virgil was growing. His beak curved down in a deadly point. His wings stretched out to both sides. He was getting so tall that the top of his head was hitting the ceiling of his cage.

"I think you should let me out of here before it gets uncomfortable."

"I… I don't think so."

"What do you mean, *you don't think so?* This cage is too small for me. Why can't you let me out?"

"I'm scared."

"Ha! Ha! Ha!" Virgil's cackles were loud and villainous. "What are you scared of? A teensy little bird?"

"You gave me the pills, didn't you?"

"Pills?"

"You've been putting the pills in my pocket."

"Oh, that? Yes, yes I have."

"*DALE!*"

Pretty Boy turned around, but no one was there. When he turned back, Virgil was standing on top of the cage, his neck ominously craned out toward him, cigarette still burning between his toes.

"Why are you doing this, Virgil?"

"Doing what? I have done NOTHING since I've been here. I've sat in this cage and on your shoulder and talked to you when you needed someone to confide in. But *you* on the other hand, what have you done? You have lost your job, you have become a drug addict, you have insulted an entire religion, you have become an infamous local celebrity for an ambiguous threat of terrorism, and now you're running around wielding a gun."

Pretty Boy looked down and was startled to find the rifle cradled across his upward facing palms.

"You see, the problem is that you *know* what you are, and you *know* what you're becoming. You're Pretty Boy. That's it. That's all that you are. But what happens when you're beauty fades? Then you're just a Boy. You're nothing."

"Shut up!" Pretty Boy clenched the gun tightly. "Why are you doing this?"

"Don't you see? I've been the one trying to save you from this grim fate. I've been trying to plant a distraction in your brain, but you just won't take to it."

Pretty Boy pressed the stock against his shoulder and took aim. "I don't think you're trying to save me."

"What? You're going to shoot me? And what *exactly* do you think that will do? You think I'll just go away and all of your problems will be solved? What do you think I am? If you shoot me, maybe I'll just become the neighbor's dog. Or better yet, a fly that buzzes around your room, watching, listening. Maybe... I'll become *you*."

The barrel of the gun trembled.

"Yeah, and then you'll be nothing more than the frightened, old man that talks for a few minutes while I'm taking a nap, just like your little parrot friend. Can you say, 'You're beautiful'? How about 'Pretty Boy want a cracker'?"

"This is what you wanted all along. You wanted me dead. You wanted to *become* me." He cocked the hammer.

"I couldn't possibly expect you to understand all of this. You couldn't even understand the concepts I was feeding you. Nothing beyond what's in front of your smug, little face. I try to tell you to find God, and you find a *hat*. I tell you to have faith, and you only have a means to draw attention, you pathetic, little –"

BOOM!

The door flew open, followed by a crutch. The point of the crutch lowered, planted itself, and was followed in by Frank. He entered to see his son, crying, holding *his* rifle, aimed at *his* bird, a bird that he was supposed to be taking care of.

The gun turned to Frank.

"Dale! What the hell is going on here?"

"He made me do it, Dad."

"Who? Who made you do *what?*"

"Virgil. He gave me the pills."

Frank's head sunk in shame. "Son," he said, raising his eyes to meet Dale's, "you've got to snap out of it."

A flash like a thousand cameras momentarily blinded Pretty Boy. The earth shook in a grumble. The gun fired. The ceiling fell all around him, entombing himself beside his father.

When Pretty Boy woke up, his ankles and wrists were tied to the bedposts with yellow rope. The white walls were blinding. When he tried to move, the rope rubbed against his raw skin, informing him that he had been struggling for quite some time now.

The toilet flushed from outside the room. He couldn't remember who was there. When he heard the clank of crutches being wrestled away from the tile counter, he remembered his father, and he cringed in guilt.

Frank galloped in on his crutches, looking tired and perturbed.

"How you doing? You're looking a little more right-minded."

"I feel okay. What happened? Did I kill the bird?"

"No, no. Just your ceiling."

"What?"

"You shot a hole in your ceiling. It knocked out a pretty good chunk of your sheetrock. You got lucky, too."

"How is that?"

"Well, it was right at the corner of an exterior wall, so you didn't kill anybody. Couldn't have. You had one neighbor come by. I told her there were some neighborhood kids outside playing with firecrackers."

Pretty Boy took a deep breath. It had been a long time since his father came to bail him out like this, and this was a little more than a bailout. This was a rescue, a declaration of a love that he didn't know still existed between them. He wanted to explain himself, to somehow pass the blame, but his only scapegoat was the talking bird that his father had entrusted to him. He felt like a puppy that had just been run over, dying on the side of the road, and his father was there to euthanize him. He offered nothing but shame and grief, while his father offered love and support when they hurt the most.

"I'm sorry, Dad. Things have gotten crazy lately. I don't know what to do."

"You should be fine now that the pills are out of your system. I wouldn't worry about it. You'll feel a whole hell of a lot better tomorrow."

Pretty Boy looked at him with interrogative eyes. "How did you know?"

"Your boss – Captain Jimmy or something – called me and told me you've been overdoing the Dramamine pills. I know what that's like. I guess you and I both have something in us that makes us overdo it on the medication."

Pretty Boy squinted harder in confusion.

"Well, you know," Frank continued. "When you or I get a cold, we drink the whole bottle of Nyquil. I guess we both do the same with the motion sickness pills. I don't know if you remember, but back when we used to fish together, there was an entire trip where I thought you were Fidel Castro. The next day after I had realized that I drove you home – on land *and* water – all while experiencing these drug-induced hallucinations, I gave up fishing. It scared the devil out of me. I sold the boat the next week."

Pretty Boy tried to think back to that time, to remember it the way his father was saying, but it didn't add up. It was like a bad movie twist where the hero and the villain turn out to be the same person despite all of the inconsistencies in the plotline. He couldn't shatter the memories that he had made for himself.

"I..." Pretty Boy choked on his tears. "I don't want you to die, Dad."

"What? I'm not going to die – at least, not any time soon."

"But the cancer…"

"Cancer? Is this because I got screened?"

"Huh?"

"I got screened a couple of weeks ago. I'm in the clear as far as cancer goes, but that was when they found out about my blood pressure and decided to put me on those torture pills."

Pretty Boy reached to the side of the bed where his father was sitting and grabbed his hand.

"I know what you're going through."

Frank pulled his hand away and snarled a grimace in his son's direction. "No, you don't."

And that was it. They remained silent, this awkward desire hanging in the air, this need for a resolution, but none was to follow.

Shortly after, his father left. He kept waiting for that heartfelt moment that's supposed to come at moments like these, but it never came. It seemed that rather than nursing his troubled son back to health, Frank viewed the experience more as a chore that needed to be done. He finished with no emotional investment, and went back home.

Pretty Boy thought back to the pills, how they had conjured themselves into his pocket, how it was the miracle of his own holy doctrine. He thought about the competing ideas of theology and coincidence, of history and fantasy, and how for a moment, he came to believe all of the stories of every religion, how they could all be simultaneously true, just as Virgil spoke to him and was guiding him through his own holy crusade. And suddenly, it was all gone. Jesus had reverted to being a magician. Noah was nothing more than a prehistoric Batman. Muhammad splitting the moon was just some type of eclipse. And the magical pills were forgotten Dramamine.

Pretty Boy, looking for any distraction from his thoughts, pulled his phone from his pocket. He had twelve missed calls. All Rex.

It was Saturday morning. Tonight was the Dead Still show.

31

Fantasy Checklist #4

Rex showed up at Sonny and Cal's place around 10 AM, as per their request. This spiked Rex's enthusiasm and curiosity as to what could be written on Sonny's slip of paper. He had forgotten that today marked Day Zero and Sonny and Cal were to be moving out today.

He drove over in the Vanimal. It was to be his final lap with the old beast. Timmy, his old firewatch, was coming over in a few hours to buy the van from him. It felt like watching a beloved pet die.

But more than that, he still hadn't figured out a solution to getting the equipment to the show. While Sonny and Pretty Boy both own cars, neither of them could get the guitar and bass cabs to fit through the door. The opening between the backseat and the opening of the doorway was just large enough to keep them attempting different angles, different sides, and different cars for loading up the cabs, but eventually equated to the need for another transport vehicle. When they were in high school, they had a dozen different friends with trucks that were willing to donate their services. Now in their thirties, they couldn't come up with one.

Pretty Boy wasn't to attend this meeting. Rex had gotten a hold of him earlier after fifty hours of incessant calling. Pretty Boy claimed to be sick, but was coming out of it. He vowed to make it to Rex's house some time before the show. While Rex was utterly disappointed about his best friend missing the final Fantasy Checklist, he had to remain upbeat to assuage Sonny and Cal's fear that Pretty Boy wouldn't make it to the show tonight. Rex assured them on the phone that he would make it, and in his heart he knew this to be true. He knew that his best friend was going through some cataclysmic shifts and their friendship would more than likely be permanently altered – if not completely dissolved – but more than all of that, he knew that Pretty Boy wouldn't desert him tonight. He knew this in his heart, but his head was starting to argue with the logic.

Sonny and Cal's parents' house sat on the corner of two residential streets. On one street was the front of the house, white brick with dark grout, uninvitingly dark front door, porch surrounded by brick planters full of cacti and aloe vera plants, and two overgrown mesquite trees on either side of the yard, looking down on the sidewalk that curved up to the front door. On the other street was a fence divided by a rolling chain-link gate that led up the driveway to their garage.

Rex was requested to enter through the back.

As he pulled the Vanimal up beside the house where the front yard met the back, he caught a glimpse through the chain-link gate and what he saw made way for some uneasy realizations.

The garage door was open. Whatever was inside the garage was hidden in darkness and unimportant as two orange extension cords trailed out from within like umbilical cords leading to a tan pop up camper with pull-out bunks extending from both ends. The whole thing was surrounded by matching tan vinyl coverings and black screen windows. Before he opened the gate he could already smell the marijuana. A smoke signal barreled out one of the screen windows. This was where they had moved.

Rex knocked on the door of the camper, feeling ironic and uncomfortable. When they opened the door, both brothers looked elated and completely high.

"Come on in!" Sonny shouted gleefully.

The two of them went back to their seats, which were places on a cushioned bench that was attached to the wall behind the table. There was one other wooden chair that they had obviously stolen from the dining room on the other side of the table. The chair took up the entirety of open space that wasn't taken by a bed. Rex sat.

"So," he muttered uncomfortably. "You finally moved out, huh?"

"Yeah," Sonny replied while blowing out a bong hit. "It feels so good to get out of the house. So much freedom, you know?"

It was his first remark, and already Rex had all that he could stand.

"Out of the house? You're nine *feet* from the house! Technically, you're still electrically connected *to* the house!"

"We're paying for electricity."

"Oh my God," Rex grumbled from beneath the palm of his hand, rubbing his face in agitation. "Aren't you the guy that told me that the *band* was childish?"

"What's your point?"

"My point?! My point is that your thirty-one years old and you can't even make it out of your mom's driveway!"

From his right side, Cal softly blew a bong hit in his face as if he was hoping the smoke would wash over him like a wave and calm him down. "Are you ready for the

Fantasy Checklist?" He was exhibiting a strange sense of confidence previously unknown to Cal.

The hand quickly dropped from Rex's face. His voice lost a bit of its irritation. "Yes! Thank you, Cal."

Rex removed the brown bag from his pocket. The paper was rolled up like a cigar. Once it flattened out, it appeared to have been crumbled and opened forty different times. The paper was fuzzy and worn. He extracted the note and opened it up with a subdued smile. Judging by his excitement, Rex hadn't peaked in the past month.

Scribbled on the paper in horrible handwriting read the words: *Play Soft Rock Show.*

"No! No, this is bullshit!" Rex exclaimed furiously. "I'm changing this one to 'play the best show ever,' which we *will* do tonight."

"But we did all the others," Sonny whined.

"Yeah, yeah we did. I painted like Frida fucking Kahlo and got a camera stuck up my ass. Yeah, we did all the others, and we're not doing *this* one. I worked my ass off to get us this show and we're not going to ruin it by playing some Neil Diamond horse shit!"

"You worked your ass off?" Sonny repeated sarcastically. "You made out with a dude in an alley, *that's* how you got us this show."

"I saved his life, you dick!"

"Still, we don't even have to do mine for this show, we can do it at the next."

"So help me God, we're not playing any easy listening crap. Not now, not ever. This has been the biggest fucking waste of time. I'm changing it to 'play best show ever,' and you can save the Billy Joel for your bubble baths."

"Maybe we should change it to 'play *last* show ever,'" Sonny responded.

"GOD DAMN IT! We're a motherfucking *metal* band, and you wanna quit because we won't play The fucking

Eagles? Can't you just do this as a solo side project or something?"

"I thought the point of this was so we could all do them together, so we wouldn't feel scared or unconfident or something?"

"The *point* of this was to reconnect with our wild and spontaneous roots, to... you know... regain that youthful vigor we had. Not to paint pictures and stick shit up our asses and change our fucking metal band to a Don Henley tribute band!"

"Alright!" Cal interjected, playing the referee. "Let's focus on the show tonight and agree to leave the soft rock conversation open for after the show, cool?"

"Cool," agreed Sonny.

"Agreed, but not cool. Definitely *not* fucking cool, man."

Sonny's phone rang playing the tune of an old Buried in Bile song. He looked at the caller information, then silenced it and buried it back in his pocket.

"I know you're pissed right now," said Sonny, "but I think we have something that you'll like." Sonny and Cal shared a mischievous smile. "Something you'll *really* like."

The brothers escorted him outside. It was propped up in the middle of the driveway. Rex would have been surprised to have passed it over had it not been for the giant camper drawing his attention away from it.

"It looks like me."

"That's what I said!" Cal's phone vibrated loudly. He checked and silenced it.

"So what the hell is it?"

"Let me show you," said Sonny excitedly. He grabbed the heads of two extension cords that were coiled beneath the contraption like cobras, one black and one orange, and strung them out toward the open garage door. In the outside corner of the garage was a power strip plugged into a wall outlet. Sonny plugged the two extension cords in.

"Alright." His voice was fearful and anxious. "I hope this works."

"Should I be seeking some shelter right now?"

"No." He crouched down to flip the red switch on the power strip. "I don't think so."

The grinder wailed into gear, spinning the egg whisks around like fan blades. Even in daylight, Rex could see an orange circle marking the perimeter of the vertical egg whisk orbit. And a second later, it was like the sun exploded in their backyard. Sparks shot out from the revolving steel wool encapsulated by the egg whisks. The copper wire had ignited them and they were flaring up like electrical fires, which essentially is what they were. The embers crackled as they burnt out on the concrete driveway.

"Holy shit!" shouted Rex. "That was *awesome!* Can we do it again?"

"Not now. We've only got enough steel wool for the concert."

Rex looked at Sonny and realized that they had been working on this project for a long time, something they were preparing for the show, and he wanted to hug him. For the first time since he locked in their spot in this concert, it seemed like someone other than himself was ensuring that it went smoothly.

Sonny and Cal knew their friend. He was abrasive, moody, careless, reckless, and unhygienic, but when they saw his eyes, they knew that his previous anger toward them, like all of his grievances, was quickly forgotten.

"That's not all," chimed Cal. "I know about your little pre-show breakfast ritual, so I stole a shit-ton of steaks from work. Want to have a barbecue at your house?"

The three of them piled in the Vanimal. It felt so right that they all be there for her farewell ride, but it felt blasphemous to do it without Pretty Boy. As disappointed as Rex was that Pretty Boy couldn't be there to watch the light show and to see what the brothers had done for the band, he was glad that he would be surprised by it on stage.

But all of these thoughts were just masking what he was really feeling. While they were still eight hours away, every minute was an excruciating countdown to the point where his best friend would fail him during their most crucial hour.

He pulled into his driveway past two sports cars parked curbside. His initial reaction was fear. The visitors could have been undercover cops, his serial intruder and accomplice, or environmental protection agents coming to save his drug-addict pig. He couldn't think of any potential visitor that could have a positive bearing on the day's events.

He was quickly proven wrong when he opened the door to find five college girls in his living room, all standing awkwardly around the perimeter of the room as there was no furniture. Yoyo stood at the corner where the living room met the kitchen, as if observing it from the perimeter, presenting the girls to Rex with magician-like waves of the hands.

"Well, hello," Rex announced with a childlike smirk. "What's all this about?"

"You said we're having a party today, right?"

It was amazing the effect that pretty girls could have on a man like Rex. Everything in his life was so gruff and agressive: his tattoos, his hair, his music, his hygiene. But a woman's soft whisper, her subtle smiles, the way she would look up at him from under her eyebrows like she was trying to hide her attraction, they all melted the sludgy exterior right off of Rex. Even after Timmy came and picked up the Vanimal for a skinny stack of cash and left them with no means to transport their equipment to tonight's show, Rex still wore a boyish grin as his eyes moved from chest to chest.

32

His beak was large and smoothly curved, but came down to a lethal point. His feathers were long and sleek. His eyes were colorless, white and black, put together in a fashion that was simultaneously simple and endless, blank windows to another dimension. While the eyes of most any mammal could be analyzed to being representative of a slew of emotions, Virgil's eyes were vacant, yet keenly observant, like the eye of a shark, or a camera, offering nothing, but taking in everything.

But what was more noticeable were the physical adaptations not acquired for survival, but for aesthetics. The lines composed of black feathers lined up single-file curved around his eyes like trails of army ants moving around an obstruction. His head was topped with a vibrant green the shade of lime-flavored hard candy and melted into the glowing azure that cascaded down his backside. The yellow of his belly was bright enough to flag down traffic at night. The ocean skyline colors blended together like the layers of an expensive island cocktail. The bird's appearance was a flow that dragged one's vision downward, tracing the interwoven colors, passing by the exquisite blues, greens, and yellows until attention was finally drawn to the feet, the only part of the parrot left strictly for utility - sharp, coarse, and ugly. The rough claws were like little reminders that evolution was at work here, that even the colors were determined over eons of scrupulous modification. One tended to relate evolution to survival of the fittest, but would often forget that almost as important as fitness was beauty, because an asymmetrical specimen with brown and gray feathers could never procreate. After evolution did its best in creating impeccable killing, eating, and fleeing machines, it needed only to work on beauty. And while Pretty Boy tended to scoff at inventions that had already reached their pinnacle of usefulness, yet reinvented themselves semiannually to deem the last version aesthetically archaic, as he laughed at the world seeking progress to eternity, forgetting that they were already comfortably alive, as he sneered at his peers crying and cheating and dying to become fashionably elite in everything they were and everything they owned, he could look at Virgil's undeniable magnificence and remember that even superficial beauty had its merit.

Then he would remember that he was a model.

This is something that the Virgil he knew would be sure to remind him of, that voice that kept him honest, that kept him from straying too far into his allegorical way of thinking. Then again, given the recent events, maybe Virgil didn't do too great a job.

Pretty Boy circled the cage like another animal examining this intruder to his environment. He scrutinized every feather. He tried to discern where the green turned to blue, where the blue turned to yellow, but could find no visible point as it glided across tones so seamlessly. But it wasn't the colors or the claws that he was really looking for. He was looking for his friend.

The past month of his life all revolved around a beloved companion that he was just now realizing was completely imagined. The blow was so severe that he felt like he could never again take anything at face value, that every relationship and event and setting in his life would have to be examined thoroughly before he could accept it as reality. His entire world was a maze of mirrors. But again, he wasn't concerned with the future, but only with his lost friend. No matter what was real and what was not, no matter what triumphs and what catastrophes had come from the past month, he just wanted to say goodbye. He supposed he could do just that, but it would be undeniably fake.

There were two undying forces in Pretty Boy: the desire to give up, and the hatred of the other part. They had battled inside him for as long as he could remember. Every heartache and hardship urged him to quit, while another part of him despised his pitifulness and weakness. But today, for the first time, the two were in agreement.

Everything was gone, it seemed. Even the one approaching light that was the concert now only promised to be a physical assault against him and possible imprisonment.

Perhaps the most flooring pain was the thought of the father of his memory, teaching him how to fish, creating this kinship that he had been consistently trying to bring back ever since, and the disillusionment of knowing that it was all the result of a drug trip. The only real father-son moment that the two ever shared was as real as the bird before him.

The only thing that brought him out of the house was a promise made to a friend.

He would make it to Rex's. He would make it to the concert. There was a good chance that it would be the last thing he would do. Rex was right when he told him that he had always taken every setback as the end of the world, but there was something intrinsically climactic about the concert, something that penetrated all ideas that everything was going to be okay.

He made the drive to Rex's. The roads were blindly navigable to him. Every stop sign was like an old friend whispering goodbye.

The sight of Rex's house would have probably turned him around, but the fact that he had to park in front of the neighbor's house because of an overflow of company had him greatly intrigued. He had known Rex for more than two decades and had only seen one party at his house that consisted of more than a dozen people.

Rex greeted him at the door like he was holding a giant check. He screamed. He hugged him. He lifted him off the ground. Sonny and Cal whooped from behind him. Pretty Boy smiled, but his friends' enthusiasm only seemed to magnify his lack thereof.

But then something – or someone – caught his eye. In the living room, puffing on a joint, surrounded by smoke and an air of superiority, glancing around the room with eyes utilizing every facial muscle to look aloof, was Tabitha. Rex noticed him noticing.

"Yeah, I know. Can you believe it?" Rex asked as they made their way into the living room. "I keep trying to get Yoyo to bring some college babes home, and when she finally does, she brings *this* one."

"Hey asshole," Tabitha snarled. "I can totally hear you."

Pretty Boy leaned in close to his friend. He dropped the volume of his voice. "What's going on?"

"I don't know, man!" Rex cackled. "Apparently all parties in Thailand happen in the morning."

The remark caught Yoyo's attention amidst the crossfire conversation, and replied, "TaiWAN, asshole." The other girls cheered. They had been trying to teach her when and how to use curse words, and although she mis-accentuated the word, making it sound like a reverse playback of normal conversation, she nailed the timing and placement.

Pretty Boy stood awkwardly in the corner. He didn't want to see Tabitha, especially not in the state he was in right now. She would feed off of his weakness and exploit it to make herself look better. But more than that, he didn't want to have to explain to the rest of the band what was going on with him. He felt the question floating around the room like a ghost, waiting for the crowd to dwindle so it could present itself, and he didn't know how to answer it. The pills, the job, the parrot. It was a chapter that he wanted to seal in a chest and bury. And he wanted to be buried with it.

As Cal went out back to check on the cooking steaks, a dirty, blue SUV crept by the window. Rex sprang from the couch, trying to catch a glimpse. The rest of the crowd was alerted and looked on as well, but quickly dismissed it without question and went back to normal party banter. Rex tried to go back to the party, but kept one suspicious eye on the window looking out to the front porch.

The girls all screamed in laughter. Rex and Pretty Boy both flinched wildly at the sound, as spastic as cartoon characters. Brutus was excited by the change in scenery. He snorted playfully as he scrambled from girl to girl, whiffing at their toes through their sandals. Each girl would scream excitedly and quickly high step as if someone was firing a gun at the floor beneath them. Brutus would move on to the next.

Rex sighed. It was the second time he had seen his roommate acting girlishly – she routinely acted childishly, most certainly, but not girlishly. But now, her words and looks were drenched in flirtatiousness, just as the others, only hers were twisted with an Oriental accent. It was almost like beneath her disgust for him, she actually was the girl he had fantasized about prior to her arrival. Rex himself was the antidote to her sexuality.

"I forgot," she said to Rex, "I invited your friends."

"What?" He tried to contain his confusion as every one of his friends was already present, besides Timmy. "Who?"

She pointed to the window beside the front door. "Him."

Everyone in the room looked toward the front window, then flinched back in shock.

His palms pressed against the glass on either side of his head like an unseen cop was frisking him from behind. His nosed flattened at the tip where it touched the glass. His purple baseball cap was worn backwards. It was the intruder who had now robbed him thrice. Rex couldn't even fathom what he wanted this time. There was almost nothing left to take.

Before he could react, Yoyo was already opening the door to let him in.

He walked in just as confidently as when no one was opening the door for him. His sauntered casually over to the kitchen and made himself a drink, nodding with a silly grin in the direction of the ladies. Everyone's eyes were on him, partially because of his eerie confidence, and partially because of how Rex locked his eyes on him in trepidation. Fear was not a normal emotion for Rex, but something was most definitely askew.

The ladies all went back to passing around a glass pipe and giggling about insipid events and relationships within their group of acquaintances, but all made random glances in the direction of the nameless newcomer who had crashed the party without an introduction and the alerted host. Everyone was waiting for a brawl to ensue.

The man sat down on the floor beside where Rex was standing, swirling the ice in his drink, the transparent cubes turning the amber liquor orange.

"I'm sorry about taking your stuff," the intruder told Rex without looking at him. "I'm really not a thief."

"Could've fooled me."

"No, seriously. I've never done anything like this."

"So what made you start?"

"My son dying." There was a long pause, but the intruder didn't look sad or wistful. "I didn't know what to do with myself. I was gonna check myself out, but I didn't. I don't think I had the balls. And then I just decided that I was gonna take anything I wanted. I was gonna live my life however I decided, and if someone else had something that I didn't, I'd take it, 'cause even if I wound up in jail, it didn't matter. Nothin' did. Nothin' 'cept my little boy, and he wasn't around anymore. So I came here. I took your TV. And you *helped* me take your TV. You see, you taught me something."

"And what's that?"

"Life's fuckin' *weird*."

Rex looked around the party to see if anyone had been listening, if anyone heard of the pathetic crime that he had committed against himself. Only Pretty Boy was listening, and his face was tight in attentiveness.

"You confused the fuck out of me. I *had* to come back. Maybe I should've just knocked on the door or somethin', but instead I just came back and robbed you again. I don't know why. Call it an addiction. And when I saw you the next time, you *let* me rob you again – not to mention the fact that you had a pig that was ripped on ganja. I couldn't fuckin' believe it. And that's when I realized: life is fuckin' *weird*. You keep hittin' these walls, and every time your head plows into wood, you want to give up, you want to just sit there and do nothin'. But all it means is that there's a wall there. You just gotta turn. That's all bad shit is. It's just a place to *turn*. And the more you turn, the more weird motherfuckers you meet like you.

I don't know. It kept me movin'."

Rex started to scoff at this little speech, but as he rolled his eyes and head away from the intruder, he caught sight of his best friend who looked moved to the point of weeping. His lower lip quivered. His eyes glassed over. He reached out and shook the intruder's hand.

Rex whipped his head back and forth between his best friend and the intruder that had robbed him of his dignity and most of his furniture, feeling like some profound moment had just entirely eluded him.

"Come on," he said, shaking the moment off. "It's time to load up for the show."

Sonny's attention was caught by this comment. "And where exactly are we loading the equipment *into?*"

Rex pointed a stern index finger straight at the intruder's forehead. "In his SUV."

33

Sergio and Maria were driving home from the ranch. Sergio was so excited about his boys finally growing up that he didn't notice how uncomfortable his wife was. He tried calling both of his sons, but neither would answer. He had a vision of the two of them carrying a new couch across the threshold of their apartment, which would explain why they couldn't get to their phones.

Maria switched the station to Tejano. It hadn't become an everyday occurrence, but it had become mundane enough for Sergio to pass it over. She studied his face fearfully, but he didn't seem to notice.

Approaching their neighborhood, Sergio looked down at the face of his phone, awaiting his sons to call him and tell them about their new home. He used his thumb to tap on the screen, about to dial them back, when he received a message from his work buddy, Rob.

Sergio didn't know how to text and barely knew how to receive a text, so he waited to arrive at his house before opening the message. He pulled in the back driveway alongside his popup camper. His eyebrows lowered at the spectacle, understanding why the boys might have needed to move it out of the garage to move their furniture, but trying to find a logical need for them to set it up.

Temporarily dismissing the conundrum, he looked back to his phone.

The message only read, "Isn't this your boys' friend?" atop a hyperlink. Sergio tapped the link and immediately recognized the boy that he had coldcocked a couple of weeks ago. Maria watched as the expression on her husband's face wrinkled more and more, like watching time-lapsed footage of a pumpkin aging and caving in on itself.

Sergio jumped out of the truck and ripped open the door of the camper. His head jerked from one side to the other as he took in the contents and their implications. He looked back at his wife. "The bastards are living here!!"

She looked down in shame. She didn't even bother making him one of her teas for relaxation. She knew that this time he was beyond any remedy.

Sergio tore apart the contents of the camper, flipping over mattresses, tossing clothes out the open door, groaning in a wrathful, physical exertion. He lifted a small bass amplifier, muscles pulsing as he prepared to hurl it to the concrete, but found something that caught his attention. On the floor were three, meticulously rolled, red cylinders of paper. They looked like long cigars, wrinkled and packed tight. He lifted one to his face for closer inspection, thinking it was some sort of drug. A distinctly familiar scent passed by, and he brought the end to his nose. He thought about that self-righteous little Muslim asshole that played in his sons' band. He thought about the video he had just watched. He though about his own shithead children and how they refused to see the imminent consequence of not leaving the house today. And then he thought that maybe the paper he held in his hand didn't resemble a cigar at all, but a stick of dynamite.

He jumped in his pickup truck, and sped out the driveway toward the concert.

34

Sonny and Cal rode with Pretty Boy to the concert. Rex rode with the intruder and all of the equipment. Both vehicles were ostensibly silent.

Sonny and Cal were yearning to ask what was going on with Pretty Boy. He gripped the wheel with white knuckles. His jaw was clenched shut. It seemed that he was living in a world that they couldn't see. They didn't dare ask.

Rex only wanted to be out of that car. He didn't know whether he needed to punch the intruder, thank him, or apologize for the tragedies in his life. So naturally, his instinct was to pull on the door handle and dive out of the speeding vehicle.

They were instructed by Greg to arrive at the back entrance and call when they got there. He met them outside and opened the gate. While Sonny, Cal, and Pretty Boy all knew why they needed to come in through the back entrance, Rex believed that this was just where the bands entered. For the headliner, this was true, but for them, it was something much less impressive.

"Good to see you guys," Greg exclaimed as they inched through the gate with windows open. He was genuinely excited to see them as he seemed like the kind of guy that was aching for new friends and amused by the rock star bad boy persona, but there was definitely a worrisome fear in his eyes. It was obvious the risk of letting this concert go on as scheduled. His father, Geoff, saw what Rex saw, that all of this publicity ultimately meant greater sales, but he still wouldn't have allowed the risk to continue if Greg didn't plead for it. It was his first real gig, even if it was for his father. But the more that Greg rallied against his father's wishes, the more it felt like *his* gig, and not something that was merely handed to him.

The band emerged from their cars, plus a tall, husky thief wearing the same clothing that he always wore that seemed to accumulate stains with every meeting between him and Rex. Handshakes and smiles were all genuine for everyone except Pretty Boy. Rex knew that Greg was instrumental in allowing the show to continue, and Sonny and Cal knew him from working so accommodatingly with them on the lighting. Pretty Boy had only met him once from across a parking lot when he was clinically dead.

Greg escorted them back to their section of the backstage area after instructing the sound crew to unload the equipment from the SUV. Rex felt like the rock star he had always dreamed of becoming, even if all of the roadies were eyeing him with looks as sharp and caustic as samurai swords dripping in hydrofluoric acid.

As they climbed up the concrete stairs of the loading dock for the equipment, Pretty Boy caught the eyes of one of the many men dressed in yellow shirts that were in charge of the sound equipment. He approached with a dubious smile.

"Kick ass today, Pukey." Tre's voice matched with his sinister eyes made it difficult to tell if the statement was meant as sarcastic, a threat, or genuine.

"What are you doing here?"

His voice dropped and he held the side of his hand to

the side of his mouth in secrecy. "Got the job last week. Wanted to meet the band." He winked at him and went back to his business.

Initially, it seemed just like something Tre would do. He loved Dead Still and was the type of guy that would get a job just for a day. He and Rex would be great friends, Pretty Boy thought.

But as he walked on, the words echoed in his head. *Wanted to meet the band.* He didn't specify *which* band. The words could have just as easily been an ambiguous threat against him, something he was growing quite accustomed to. And of all of the fears that went with coming to this show and playing in front of a crowd that had been continuously threatening him online, being assaulted by his friend was by far the most difficult idea to digest.

Greg walked them through the corridors to the rehearsal area. He spoke timorously, finally addressing the concerns that were on all of their minds but too delicate to just put out on the table.

"We have hired extra security for this show. And I've been informed that the police are going to be stationed at most corners of the audience... *just in case.*"

They all did their best to not look at Pretty Boy, but the more they looked away, the more obvious it was that he had put all of them in the most awkward of positions. He had turned the greatest show that they had ever been offered into a suicide mission.

Their room backstage was the size of a small bedroom. It had three foldout metal chairs and a ratty old couch lined with a fuzzy blue fabric, discolored from cigarette burns and spilled bong water, making Rex feel right at home. And to make them all feel welcomed, on one end of the couch sat a familiar face.

Polly took a drag of her cigarette, confidently, flirtatiously. "I was wondering when you boys were going to get here."

They had expected to see her at some point as her store was one of the main promoters of the show, which earned her VIP passes to the entire event, but they hadn't expected her so early and in their personal preparation area.

"Are you sure you boys want to do this?" she asked. "Those people out there are *livid.*"

35

Colossal steel rafters emerged from the black stage like the vertebrae of some giant, robot carcass. The gathered masses herded toward it with the haunting calmness of hangmen approaching the gallows. It was the first Saturday since the end of daylight savings, and the evening sky was already black. Clouds of smoke grazed calmly overhead and carried with them the scents of cigarettes, marijuana, beer, and body odor.

The crowd was strangely mixed, as was expected. The diehard metalheads gawked angrily at the college kids in polo shirts and the middle-aged radio listeners. Visually, it looked like a high school cafeteria divided by cliques, but it felt more like the recreational area of a prison divided by rival gangs. They all felt a war bubbling inches beneath the concrete they were standing on, but they didn't know from which direction the assaults would begin.

The bass drum pounded in a slow tempo as a stage technician checked the sound levels. A few people screamed and applauded. With every strike of the kick pedal against the drumhead, the lungs of everyone in the crowd compressed from the force like beating hearts. Some of the more energetic audience members up front began jumping up and down, breathing heavily, and stretching in preparation for whatever was about to follow. The collective banter of the crowd was growing to a whispering roar.

Pretty Boy stood backstage behind Rex, Sonny, and Cal as he was to enter last. He kept thinking about what that strange man had said about life being weird, and how all of the bizarre events in life were what kept him going. He tried to look at the stage entrance as just another opportunity to experience something unordinary that would add merit to his existence, but as he listened to the crowd grumbling to life, he was terrified.

The bass drum checks made way for the snare drum, which pounded along in a slow march. It was an anthem for war – not upbeat like the rolling drumlines of colonial soldiers, but slow and steady like a heart monitor that would soon flatline. Eight-dollar beers were hurled into the air, sacrificed to the night, then rained down on unsuspecting victims like napalm.

Roadies rushed back and forth across the fire blankets that lined the stage. Sonny and Cal, being the only two members of the band that weren't easily recognizable due to recent horrible publicity, were able to set up their areas on stage without being assaulted. They did so with old, orange fire blankets and homemade pyrotechnics. They had worked clandestinely, hoping that the homemade fashion of their fireworks would disguise their purpose from anyone that mattered.

The levels on the high toms had been adjusted and the sound tech was now pounding the floor tom, the monotonous boom low and heavy with reverb. The crowd's anticipation was slowly turning to irritation as they awaited the impending battle.

The drum tech stood from his stool and emerged from behind the drum kit, only to slink away stage-left. The head roadie peaked in from the right side of the stage and clicked his flashlight on and off like Morse Code in the direction of the sound booth, letting them know that everything was ready and all Hell was about to break loose.

The lights turned to black, and the crowd erupted.

The distorted church bell that Rex had mixed rang out of the speakers in a harrowing clang. Fogmakers spewed smoke onto the floor of the stage. Strobe lights flashed at random like a lightning storm as electricity crackled and pipe organs howled. The shrieks of a terrified woman that bellowed out of the speakers were barely audible over the screaming crowd. A deep, ominous voice grumbled, *"You are in the mouth of the whale."*

Rex looked back at Pretty Boy. "This is gonna be *awesome*." Pretty Boy couldn't even feign excited. He only tried to mask his terror. Rex crept forward, leaving Pretty Boy horribly alone.

Cal walked out onto the stage like a serial killer, slowly, confidently, and stood behind his drum set, staring out to the crowd, sizing them up. Beneath the flashing lights and smoke, he was only a shadow.

You are in the mouth of the whale.

A choir sang out one high-pitched tone in an eerie harmony, long and drawn out, soaring over the crowd and soaking them in a creepy ambiance. Lights beamed through the low-lying smoke, illuminating it in red like steam rising from Hell. Rex sprinted across the stage through the glowing smoke, then stopped abruptly, bent over his waist, hanging over his black, sharp-angled guitar, peering through his dredlocks at the bellowing crowd in front of him, eyes sharp and focused like a lion peaking through the thicket at its prey. He leaned over the floor monitors, inches from the reach of the hands stretching out toward him from the front row.

You are in the mouth of the whale.

Sonny was on the opposite end of the stage, standing

tall and strong with his right arm outstretched toward the crowd before him, pointing a finger of warning and slowly sweeping it across the entire assemblage. Next to his right foot was an overdrive pedal. Next to his left was the power strip that was connected to his egg whisk pyrotechnic contraption that stood center-stage.

Chainsaws revved through the speakers. More terrified screaming. The voice of the choir amplified. The whirlwind of noises was reaching a pinnacle and was matched by more frequently flashing lights in different colors.

Pretty Boy inhaled deeply, summoning all of his strength, but as he exhaled, his chest and arms were clammy and tingling, feeling as they would during the onset of a bad case of the flu.

You are in the mouth of the whale.

The smoke from the fogmakers was now waist-high and dyed slime green by the beaming lights. Pretty Boy walked out onto stage as if he was wading through the mist, and the crowd exploded once again. At this point, it wasn't discernable whether they were screaming in anger or excitement, but it was deafening.

And all at once, the audio track went to silence, and the lights blackened.

The crowd roared.

Beneath the blanket of darkness, Sonny fumbled with the fuse connected to a long string of Quickmatch.

In a long, pain-stricken scream in the voice of a man being disemboweled, Pretty Boy shrieked, "HOW DOES IT FEEL TO BE IN THE BELLY OF THE WHALE?!!"

Just as Cal beat the high hat in four quick taps, the Quickmatch that connected to the cylindrical pyrotechnics strung overhead end-to-end flared up in a white smoke. Three, low-pitched, growling power chords under heavy distortion accompanied by three crashes of the overhead cymbals and three pounding kicks of the bass drum echoed out over the crowd. The rolled-up cylinders of construction paper packed full of potassium perchlorate, mesh aluminum, and homemade dextrin hanging eight feet from the floor stretched from one side of the stage to the other just between where Cal's drum set resided and the other three members of the band. Waterfalls of sparks cascaded down, spewing from each hand-rolled firework, separating Cal from the rest of the band. The wall of sparks was thick and solid and presented Sonny, Rex, and Pretty Boy as stationary, black silhouettes. The last chord was still ringing out as was the reverberation of the crash cymbal. The note grumbled for almost a minute as the band stood like demonic statues at the entrance gates to the Underworld. Cal, invisible behind the wall of fire, was laughing giddily as their untested pyrotechnic display worked flawlessly. As he saw the first link in the strand burn out, he hit the snare drum twice and the song began.

Pounding triplets shook the concrete floor of the amphitheater. A mosh pit the size of a large house's floor plan opened up in the front center of the crowd. Bodies were hurled back and forth across the circle, occasionally slapping the cement. Crowdsurfers glided in from both corners, their faces smeared with a violent enthusiasm like warriors that had just conquered their enemies. The entire place was a riot in an insane asylum.

On stage, Rex was jumping off the floor monitor and banging his head in wild thrashes that could have fractured the vertebrae in his neck, his dredlocks snapping down like bullwhips. Sonny was running back and forth in short sprints, screaming at the crowd in battle cries over his bass guitar. Pretty Boy raised the blue flames painted on his forearms. He brought the microphone to his lips and began screaming out his lyrics with all of the pain and anger he had felt over the past month.

Lori, Lori, what happened to the glory?
You've left me struggling to breathe on my own
You kept me young, but now I'm inching toward forty
And death will surely come now that I'm alone
I never knew that it was derogatory
When you called me baby, 'cause I'm helpless and weak
Losing you was expurgatory
But I still lie awake waiting for you to speak

As the drop beat of the verse made way for the machine gun, grindcore prechorus, Sonny tapped the orange switch on the power strip with the toe of his shoe. The grinder spun into action, spewing out more sparks like a flame-throwing windmill.

The mosh pit spawned two smaller circles on either side as more and more bodies dove into the pandemonium. Some stopped to witness the visual insanity that was taking place on stage. Some continued to bash the others.

Rex shook his head spastically back and forth while his right hand vibrated across the low string of his guitar. He looked like a rabid, shaggy dog shaking off water. Pretty Boy shrieked into the microphone while an orange flower of sparks sprayed out behind him in the form of a glowing halo.

Just before the steel wool in the egg whisks burnt out, the grinder wobbled quickly and fell to the floor of the stage. The copper wire had loosened and slipped out of the holes on the handle of one of the egg whisks, sending it flying in a line drive out into the audience. A hole in the crowd opened up where the recipient of the flaming projectile had gone down. The song went on, pounding into the chorus as all four members banged their heads in unison, but as the hole around the victim widened and onsite paramedics rushed in, the instruments faded out one at a time.

It was the second show in a row that they didn't make it through their opening song.

After all four of them had stopped the song short – Cal plowing through the drumbeats as he couldn't see what was happening, and finally ending his drumline as no other instruments were accompanying him – they all watched on with a building concern. That concern spiked as the crowd opened up further to reveal two legs stretched out motionlessly from the floored body, legs wrapped in a long, pink skirt and quirky black sandals that strapped around her ankles and wound around her legs all the way up to her calves, the eccentric attire of a Taiwanese woman new to this country.

Pretty Boy glanced over at Rex, who was glaring out into the crowd with a look that unmistakably recognized the victim.

The crowd around Yoyo slowly began shifting their concern from the wounded victim to the assailants on stage. Faces began looking back to the band with all of the anger and violence that they exhibited in the mosh pit now directed solely at Pretty Boy. It started with a few, then spread like a puddle under a water spout.

None of the boys moved. With all of their eyes locked on Rex's roommate, the faces turning in their direction went unnoticed. And as her legs kicked back to life, the angry members of the audience shifted their attention back to Yoyo. A few men helped her to her feet. Her hand still clutched to her forehead where the whisk struck her, she looked to the men on both sides and nodded that she was okay.

All four band members exhaled in relief.

When on stage or in the Jam Room, it became second nature for Pretty Boy to bring the microphone to his lips before saying anything. And as most people in similar moments of relief, Pretty Boy spouted out an exclamation of gratitude. However, the past few weeks had changed his natural dialogue by means of constant repetition.

Pretty looked down in a relieved sigh, brought the microphone to his mouth, and said, "Praise Allah."

The moment he uttered the words, he realized what he had done. All of those faces that were looking at him in anger had suddenly multiplied. Some of the crowd made their way to the exit in fear that the launched, flaming egg whisk was only the beginning of the terrorist act, but most stayed to seek retribution. The shouts that echoed up to the stage no longer bore any hint of enthusiasm as beers and half-eaten slices of pizza were hurled on stage. Rex looked at Pretty Boy with disappointment and shock. The muscular security guards in tight black tee-shirts that lined the gap between the stage and the audience all had their arms up as they were all frantically fending off men crowdsurfing their way toward the stage to get at the singer of the band. The police officers at both corners of the stage shined their flashlights out to the crowd to identify the instigators to try and soften the backlash of the accident.

Cal rushed out from behind his drum set to stand next to his brother. It was a much more vulnerable position, but he felt safer in Sonny's proximity. The four of them stood silently watching as the crowd rose up in anger against them. Had this not been the highlighting achievement of their band, they undoubtedly would have already fled. Instead, they kept waiting for something to pacify the crowd or for the wrath to burn itself out so they could move on to their next song, but that moment never came. More and more crowdsurfers lunged toward the front. The security guards worked tirelessly to keep them back, but if they continued at this rate, a few of them would inevitably barrel past them and open up the proverbial floodgates.

Rex looked out to the crowd that he had waited to stand in front of for so many years, a crowd that was rallying against him, then looked to his best friend standing ten feet to his left, looking helpless and afraid. He rushed to his side, threw an arm around his neck, and hurried him offstage.

Two men, one in flannel and the other in a sleeveless, white tee-shirt, climbed up on stage as the security guards wrestled with the growing pile of crowdsurfers that had come over the railing, trying to escort them off to the sides where the police officers were making arrests. The two men confusedly approached Sonny and Cal, who were cowering in the corner of the stage. Both of them presented their crucifix necklaces that their father had given them, extending them out from under their chins as far as the silver chains would allow. The crucifixes seemed to act as effective deterrents as the assailants walked away, looking for the backstage entrance to the stage where the singer and guitarist had just exited.

But out of that backstage entrance emerged Polly. She approached the microphone that Pretty Boy had graciously returned to its stand. Her crazy-aunt intonation carried out through the crowd.

"Listen up." The microphone squealed in feedback, gaining everyone's attention like a clinking glass at a wedding reception. "I've known these boys since they were shittin' in their diapers, and they're not bad kids. This was just a freak accident. Dale's no terrorist. He's just *stupid.*"

From backstage, Pretty Boy could hear Polly's words. Initially, he was offended, but he then realized that she *must* be talking more about Rex. Then again, she did specifically call him out.

Polly looked like she wanted to continue, but was already short of words to say in their defense. A white, plastic cup launched up to the stage in her direction. It went overhead and slightly right, but succeeded in soaking her hair and shoulder in draft beer.

The crowd was not pleased with her line of reasoning. The shouts died down only long enough to hear her four-sentence speech, then peaked again. As a police officer chased off the two men that made it on stage to one side, another made it up on the opposite end of the stage.

More and more police pushed in on the crowd from all sides, but it only seemed to agitate them rather than disperse them. Being violently compressed with nowhere to go, they all pressed forward toward the stage. Those in the front row were slammed into the steel bar that divided them from the security team. Some piled over on top. The ogre-like security guards that were trained to never show facial expressions were looking quite fearful as they provided the last line of defense before complete chaos.

And then it happened.

It began with a clear, crisp note that rang out like a solitary drop of water falling into a pool, amplified times a million. It shifted up a full step then hit the same note an octave up. And as the notes seamlessly flowed together, they multiplied and shifted in the most entrancingly beautiful and strangely familiar melody.

Sonny took center stage as he tapped the higher frets with his right hand and slid his left up and down the fretboard. All at once, the anarchic crowd was subdued, at first out of sheer confusion, then enthralled by the sound.

Cal rolled his drumsticks over his high hat and ride cymbals, the high hat opening and closing, providing a beat that sounded almost computer-generated in its quickness and precision. No one in the crowd had ever heard two predominantly background instruments accompany one another with such a full and moving sound. Some still pushed forward, but at a much slower, distracted pace.

Sonny approached the microphone, still effortlessly

pouring out notes from his bass guitar. His voice carried like a Wandering Albatross taking flight.

"Blue jean baby. L.A. lady."

Some of those that were previously ready for battle were looking at one another and smiling in a humorous recognition. No one could decide whether the spectacle was funny or just plain magnificent. They kept trying to laugh, but it quickly turned into smirks and more gawking in awe at the two boys.

As the house and stage lights went out, a spotlight illuminated Sonny as if he was the only person in the universe. He tapped out a short solo, eyes still looking out to the crowd as his fingers worked without thought. He glanced over to the left side of the crowd, right in front of where the police were making their arrests, and saw his father.

Sergio's face was still hard and emotionless, smeared with years of consistent anger and disappointment. Sonny's fingers almost stopped moving, but luckily played on from rote memory. Sergio held a hand straight up in the air, purposefully, with eyes still locked on his performing son. And with a quick flash, a small orange flame appeared where his hand was, and he began to sway his arm back and forth like seaweed waving with the current.

The vocals continued. *"Looking on, she sings the songs. The words she knows, the tune she hums."*

The cymbals finally turned to a solid, building rhythm on the two high toms, sprinkled with unusual cymbal fills that blended smoothly. A high-pitched note squealed from somewhere else, mutedly, as Rex emerged from backstage and bent up on a high string to accompany Sonny's melody. As he walked out and the song continued, they all waited for his presence to kill the moment, but it refused to die. Instead, the left half of the crowd followed Sergio's example and began extracting lighters from pockets and swaying small orange dots like choreographed fireflies.

The music escalated, and from backstage, Pretty Boy knew exactly what he was expected to do, but wasn't sure that he could do it.

"But oh how it feels so real, lying here with no one near..."

Even those in the crowd that didn't know the words were humming along and swaying with the slow beat. The feeling washed over the crowd, a certain calmness, an awareness that they were all here together, that maybe they all came looking to give a face to all of their internal enemies, to give them a tangible face to punch, but perhaps it was better to appreciate the beauty than to attack the ugliness. It was something like what Pretty Boy felt when the Lortab would first take effect, slithering down the backs of his calves, softening his muscles like a gentle massage, and melting away all of the unnecessary thoughts that swarmed around his brain like bumblebees.

"Only you, and you can hear me..."

Pretty Boy emerged from backstage, toting the microphone for the backup vocals.

"When I say softly..."

His voice began quietly harmonizing with Sonny's.

"Slowly..."

And in that moment, everything didn't just fade away, but it vanished with the quickness of a trap door opening up and swallowing them all in one healthy bite.

It was the one part of the song to which everyone knew the words, and all seven thousand of them sang in a deafening, celestial harmony.

> *"Hold me closer, tiny dancer*
> *Count the headlights on the highway*
> *Lay me down in sheets of linen*
> *You had a busy day today."*

Amidst the spectacle, Yoyo made her way on stage

and stood between Rex and Pretty Boy. She didn't know the song or any of the words – or even how to dance – but she still swayed back and forth in a statement to the crowd to retain this emotion and to not allow it to die so quickly the way everything in this world tends to do.

Another, stronger arm curled around Pretty Boy's neck as they all repeated the chorus in unison. Tre's other arm was reaching up to the night sky and topped with an orange flame as he bellowed out the lyrics.

"Hold me closer, tiny dancer…"

Rex looked out to his bandmates playing their hearts out, just in a way that he had never imagined them playing, and realized that *this* was it, this was the Fantasy Checklist, it was their moment doing something together, something meaningful, something that they would all take to their deathbeds.

The song played out and never allowed that feeling that encompassed the entire assemblage to leave or let up. Perhaps it was just the one song that could transcend generation, religion, and all of the other things that were dividing them.

36

Rex and Pretty Boy were driving to Frank's house to return the parrot. Both of them were still feeling lingering traces of elation from last night's concert, but neither could be vocal about their feelings. After previous concerts, they would yell and high-five and compare bruises from the mosh pits, but this one was different. High-fiving to playing Elton John didn't seem suiting. Initially, the concert didn't seem worthy of such virile acts of congratulations, but truthfully, a high-five was much too ingenuous for what happened last night.

Frank had requested that Virgil be returned. He called Pretty Boy and said that he was feeling better, but in a voice that was tarnished with the need to convey the pain and discomfort that he was in.

Pretty Boy asked Rex to come along. He had finally felt some reprieve from the relentless beating he seemed to be enduring, and he knew that seeing his father could quickly end that moment of relief. He needed his best friend there for comfort.

"Are you gonna miss being a pirate?" Rex reclined the seat back as far as it would go and put his hands behind his head. He wore a dark pair of aviator sunglasses and an elated grin that refused to be repressed.

"I guess."

Pretty Boy put his left hand at the twelve o'clock position of the steering wheel and twisted around to glance at Virgil. He looked back to the road.

"He is a pretty bird," mumbled Rex.

"That's bullshit."

Rex turned toward his friend and lifted the sunglasses up to his forehead. "What's that?"

"Everything. My parrot. Your pig. Everything we strive for is completely arbitrary and backward. We like parrots because they are beautiful, but beauty fades. We like pigs because they are smart, but intelligence brings suffering, it brings awareness of things we shouldn't know. We should like birds for being stupid and pigs for being sloppy and carefree, but no, we value the very things that bring us pain."

"Whatever."

"You wouldn't understand."

"Don't fucking do that!" Rex snapped. Pretty Boy's eyes widened as he looked back at his livid friend. "You think I don't see what you see? You think just because you've read some books that I haven't, you understand the world in ways that I can't? Everyday, less and less people listen to metal. We get older. We get more obsolete. Just because I'm happy and reckless doesn't make me stupid. I see this shit. But I still enjoy playing. I enjoy meeting people, even if they're younger than me and different than me. And I know death exists and it's coming for all of us. I know that beauty fades. Everything dies. But I still like to look at your parrot for it's colored feathers and I like to watch Brutus look at me like a human being. That pig and I, we... well, we hate each other. But we have a *real* connection, an actual relationship that transcends *species*. That's fucking amazing. I can't deny it just because he eats my furniture and shits in my living room and we both know that we're going to die."

Pretty Boy pulled into his father's driveway. The silence begged him to say something, but nothing came to mind.

As he stood up out of the car and went to the back seat to retrieve the birdcage, Rex continued to lie in his reclined seat.

"Aren't you coming?"

"You got this. You and your old man don't need me."

Pretty Boy wrestled Virgil out of the door that was barely wider than the birdcage, a job that should have been for two.

He didn't bother knocking as he didn't want his father to have to get up to answer the door. With the cage perched upon his knee and clutched tightly with his left hand, he freed his right just enough to twist the doorknob and throw the door open.

"Dad! It's me!"

Frank grumbled inaudibly from the living room – his usual response to any question that didn't deserve an answer.

Pretty Boy returned the cage to its place atop the wooden table in the entryway. He began to go check on his father, but got caught up looking at the bird. He tried to see the beauty and forget the Virgil that he knew, to appreciate the wild blues and yellows and greens, the way God or evolution or whatever made this vibrantly beautiful creature, but he couldn't. He missed his friend. He pulled a tube of Dramamine from his pocket, wanting to bring him back to life, but no, that would be cheating. He would already know. It was a truth that couldn't be unlearned, a black cloud never to dissipate.

In the living room, Frank was stretched diagonally across his recliner, vacantly watching television.

"How you doing, Dad?"

His glassy eyes finally peeled off the television and looked back at his son.

"These pills are death."

It was an overly dramatic answer, Pretty Boy knew, but it still came from a genuine struggle. He looked at his father, his skin paling, his eyes yellowing, his wrinkles enhancing. He looked at his eyes and saw the endless storage of bullshit that had accumulated over the past sixty-five years, the thoughts and ideas that we should never have to know, the parasites that were eating away at him until he would finally become nothing.

Pretty Boy looked through the doorless threshold to see Virgil, sitting comfortably in solitude, without any distraction, and he envied him for his tiny brain that couldn't possibly fathom all of the things that we are doomed to learn.

"Mind if I use your restroom before I leave?" Frank languidly raised his right hand a few inches from the armrest, then plopped it back down to show how little he cared.

In the bathroom, Pretty Boy looked for piss-stained pants, but thankfully found none. The bathroom, in fact, had been cleaned recently. There was no razor on the sink. There were no dirty clothes littering the floor. It was almost like the same restroom that he remembered before his father broke his ankle, except for one, small addition.

Beside the sink on the cream-tiled counter was one of those pill holders that had separate containers for each day of the week. He popped open tomorrow's little plastic square labeled 'M' to find six, white, circular pills. His head dropped, thinking about the father that he remembered from his fishing trips, young and healthy, reeling in fish and tying up the boat at the dock. He chose not to remember him as being drugged out from too much motion sickness medication, and really, he *couldn't* remember him like that, because the memory had been cemented in the way he had recalled it for so many years. He cringed at the thought of his father being an old man, taking multiple pills at every meal, pills that may or may not have been bringing his father severe anguish.

He popped open the tube of Dramamine he had in his pocket, and noted that they looked remarkably similar to the plain white pills in his father's pill case. With only the container marked 'M' open and the other six still firmly sealed, he dumped Monday's contents in the toilet and replaced them with his own.

He walked back into the living room and sat in the recliner beside his father's.

"Played a show last night." He started to wait for his father's reaction, but quickly realized that there wouldn't be one. Instead of succumbing to his father's indifference, he went on to tell him all about it. Frank never responded, but something softened in his eyes, some appreciation for the moment that he couldn't bare to speak of.

Within a few minutes, Frank fell asleep. Pretty Boy got up and walked out of the living room. As he passed by his father, he whispered, "Keep your chin up, Dad. And take good care of that bird. I've really grown to like him."

Pretty Boy passed by Virgil's cage one last time. He stared deep into his face, the snow white, wrinkled skin, the thick, short black feathers that emerged in a zebra-like pattern, his eyes, always wide, always studying, always seeming to look beyond him. Pretty Boy searched for some sign of recognition, but the bird turned away and shifted down the wooden perch to the opposite end of the cage. In a high-pitched squawk – the antithesis to the voice of the Virgil that Pretty Boy had come to know – he shouted, "You're beautiful."

Pretty Boy swallowed back his tears and whispered

back to the bird, "Thanks, buddy. See you later." But before he could turn to exit the house, Virgil spoke back, but this time, an octave lower.

"Don't worry about your dad. We'll have a little talk later."

He knew that he was trying too hard, that he wanted to hear Virgil speak so bad that maybe he was just imagining the things he wanted to happen, but it didn't seem to matter. He closed his eyes and thanked God, whomever He might be.

www.ingramcontent.com/pod-product-compliance
Lightning Source LLC
Chambersburg PA
CBHW070919260626
47162CB00007B/2733